model
UNDERCOVER

Carina Axelsson

Copyright © 2016 by Carina Axelsson
Cover and internal design © 2016 by Sourcebooks, Inc.
Cover design by Rose Audette
Cover illustration © Yasuko

Sourcebooks and the colophon are registered trademarks of Sourcebooks, Inc.

All rights reserved. No part of this book may be reproduced in any form or by any electronic or mechanical means including information storage and retrieval systems—except in the case of brief quotations embodied in critical articles or reviews—without permission in writing from its publisher, Sourcebooks, Inc.

Originally published as *Model Under Cover—Deadly by Design*, © Carina Axelsson, 2015.

The characters and events portrayed in this book are fictitious or are used fictitiously. Any similarity to real persons, living or dead, is purely coincidental and not intended by the author.

Published by Sourcebooks Jabberwocky, an imprint of Sourcebooks, Inc.
P.O. Box 4410, Naperville, Illinois 60567-4410
(630) 961-3900
Fax: (630) 961-2168
www.sourcebooks.com

Originally published in 2015 in the United Kingdom by Usborne Publishing Ltd., an imprint of Usborne House.

Library of Congress Cataloging-in-Publication data is on file with the publisher.

Source of Production: Versa Press, East Peoria, Illinios, USA
Date of Production: November 2015
Run Number: 5005177

Printed and bound in the United States of America.
VP 10 9 8 7 6 5 4 3 2 1

For Annie and Mary, with love and thanks.

MONDAY NIGHT
Message from Miami

I'm sending someone to you. Trust her. No time. Boarding. See you in London. Ellie x

TUESDAY MORNING

London Calling

I was at home in Notting Hill, standing in front of my closet, looking at my shoes. And while anyone watching me could be forgiven for thinking that I was eyeing my heels, dreaming of walking down the fashion runway sometime soon…well, *not*.

I was actually wondering if I'd ever have another case to solve.

Despite my mom's well-laid plans to turn me into the next Karlie Kloss, all I wanted to do was solve mysteries—and I'd always felt that way. Well, ever since my granny started spoon-feeding me detective stories: Nancy Drew before I could read and Agatha Christie's *Miss Marple* reruns instead of after-school cartoons. By the time I was old enough to play Clue, I think it's fair to say that I was obsessed with the idea of becoming a detective.

Besides, as my granny liked to remind my parents, "It's in her blood, you know." Eye rolls would follow, but the fact was, Granny was right. My grandfather—Granny's husband—had been a detective with Scotland Yard. My fate was, as Granny and I saw it, sealed by destiny's kiss.

So despite what my BFF and neighbor, Jenny Watanabe, liked to say—"You read up on Scotland Yard forensic techniques more often than you crack open *Miss Vogue*, Axelle. You do realize that's not normal?"—how could I resist the path I felt destined to follow?

Then, a few months ago, my parents, in a shrewd attempt to derail my sleuthing efforts, sent me to Paris for Fashion Week. However, the detective gods intervened, and fortunately for me, the biggest, juiciest mystery Paris fashion had ever seen landed in my lap. Okay, maybe not in my lap, but close enough. My Aunt Venetia, fashion editor supremo, became a suspect in the case of missing fashion designer Belle La Lune. I mean, what was I supposed to do—ignore the chance of a lifetime and make my granny spin in her grave? Do fashionistas wear socks with Birkenstocks?

No way.

So I did what I had to do and found Belle La Lune before the police did. Not that I talked about it afterward. Going undercover as a model to find Belle taught me: (A) that a real case was, like, a gazillion times better than Clue, and (B) that if I wanted to figure out more fashion crimes, I'd have to be discreet about my intentions.

That plan paid off when I was asked to hunt down a diamond thief in New York City during the fashion shows there.

Both the Paris and Big Apple cases had given me a dream start to my detective career…or so I'd thought.

But, maddeningly, since returning from New York City three months earlier, I hadn't had a single case present itself. Nothing. Nada. Right now, I was feeling about as wanted as last season's trends.

Which was why I was staring at my heels, asking myself if another fashion mystery would ever come my way, when my mom rapped on my door and walked in, catching me by surprise.

"Ah! There you are!" she chirped. I could feel her eyes on my back. "Can't wait to get back on the runway, can you, darling?"

"Actually, Mom—" I said.

But I was interrupted before I could say anything more. "Well, I wouldn't worry, Axelle. The agency has kept you busy since you finished your GCSEs, and, with the resort shows starting this week, you'll be back in the thick of it before you know it. Speaking of which, didn't the agency say you had a fitting for the La Lunes tomorrow? And something about doing Jorge Cruz this week too?"

Argh! My mom—all she could think about was my modeling career!

She was right, though. My London modeling agency, Thunder, had kept me busy the last couple of weeks. After I first returned from New York City, I'd concentrated on studying for my GCSEs—these are the standardized tests all British high school students have to take—and I liked to think that I'd done well. But rather than fret while I waited for the results, I thought I'd accept some of the options my agency had run past me. If I put myself in the thick of things, so to speak, a juicy mystery might come my way. Not that this strategy seemed to be working.

I sighed and was just about to turn and face my mom when she stopped me in my tracks.

"And now the fashion world is even beating a track to our door," she said enthusiastically. "There is a fashion blogger downstairs and she's asked to see you. Her name is Tallulah Tempest, and from the little she's told me, it sounds as if she'd like to interview you. So there you go—no need for any of those detective dreams you used to harbor—your fashion career is here to stay! Can I tell her you'll be down?"

I shut the doors to my closet, leaned down, and scooped up Halley (my West Highland white terrier) from the floor, planting kisses on her head as I thought about it.

As far as I was concerned, there was only one reason a fashion blogger would have taken the trouble to find me at my home, and it didn't have anything to do with fashion—at least not right away. Because no matter who is looking for information—blogger, magazine journalist, interviewer (and often all they want to know is what a particular supermodel eats for breakfast)—anyone in the business always contacts a model's agency first, unless they know the model well. So for a fashion blogger to search me out at home…

Ellie's text from late last night came to mind—the one she'd sent just as she was about to board her flight from Miami to London. Surely Tallulah was the "someone" she'd been referring to. I looked at my watch quickly and saw it was still too early to call Ellie. She wouldn't be landing for another hour at least.

"Axelle? Should I tell her you'll be down?"

The name Tallulah Tempest rang a bell. Hmmm… I felt a ripple of excitement. If my suspicions about her visit were correct, then I didn't want to waste another second. I set Halley down on the floor.

"Axelle?"

"Don't worry, Mom," I said as I pecked her on the cheek and walked past her. "I'll go and see her now."

Tallulah was standing looking out over our garden from the window of our living room. As I shut the door behind me, I quickly ran my eyes over her. I liked her at first glance.

Tall and whippet-thin, with raven-black hair that was shaved on one side of her head, she wore a short, tight, black leather skirt under a slouchy patterned pullover. This was accented with a loose, black snood around her neck, black tights, and ankle boots decorated with studs. The latter looked like something I'd seen on the Valentino runway when I'd done Paris Fashion Week. From the gold chain across her chest hung a tiny, bright-turquoise, quilted-leather Chanel handbag. Tallulah looked both fierce and exotic in that fashion-y way London has become known for: edgy, unstudied, and mysteriously cool. Furthermore, her self-possession and quiet confidence were tangible.

I caught a quick glance of myself in the large mirror across the room as I approached her. My big, geeky glasses and unbrushed hair definitely brought my score down in the style stakes. On the other hand, all the better to blend in as a detective, I told myself.

She turned and extended her hand, keeping her blue, kohl-rimmed eyes on me.

I saw her eyes dart rapidly over my shoulder to the door as we shook hands. The action took less than a second, but it was enough to make me understand that, whatever she had to tell me, she'd prefer to do it without being overheard.

Without a word, I led Tallulah out through the back door, Halley at my heels, and down to the bottom of our somewhat wild but romantic garden. There I searched for a key under a stone and opened the garden-shed-cum-teahouse that didn't get as much use as it should.

Although it was a cool, sharp morning for the end of June, we'd had a couple of warm weeks, and the roses and peonies were in full bloom, their fragrance heavy in the moist air. The last of the morning mist had burned off, and overhead, the clouds scuttled by at a rapid pace. Halley chose to do a reconnaissance tour through the garden rather than join Tallulah and me in the shed.

"Ellie sent me," she said before we sat down. "She told me you could help…"

I nodded. So Tallulah *was* the mystery person Ellie had messaged me about. That was good, I thought, because knowing I could trust her made things much easier. We'd be able to move along more quickly—if this was indeed a case.

"She says you're a…a Sherlock Holmes in the making…"

I raised my eyebrows at Tallulah. "She did?" I asked. Coming from my modeling BFF, Ellie B (non-modeling name: Elizabeth Billingsley), that was high praise indeed. Ellie always teased me for being too single-minded about my detective pursuits, so the compliment was nice to hear—especially as I doubted I'd ever hear it directly from Ellie's lips!

"I…I was surprised she sent me to you. I know you as a model, but I didn't know…"

I watched her struggle to describe what I do. To help her, I said, "That I help out with…tricky situations?"

She nodded. "It's not something you advertise, exactly, is it?"

"Not at all. I keep this interest of mine quiet—I have to. I wouldn't be able to gather half the information I do if everyone knew I was a detective."

"Of course," Tallulah said. "And just to reassure you, nobody, apart from Ellie, knows I'm here."

"Thank you."

"No problem." Tallulah took a breath before continuing. "I'm not sure where to begin…"

I said nothing, waiting for Tallulah to start without my prompting. This was one of my grandfather's interviewing techniques, and I knew from experience that it worked. The rule is, when someone is nervous yet wants to spill a secret, do not—under any condition—interrupt him or her. Sit quietly and let them unwind their story at their own pace. Pushing for information will only scare them off.

"My brother, Gavin, is a fashion photographer—or, rather, he's working in fashion to make ends meet. He's studying photojournalism. That's what he'd like to concentrate on eventually. But he's very talented with the camera, and the fashion world loves his work—his portraits especially. Anyway"—Tallulah fidgeted for a moment before finally sitting still and looking me in the eyes—"Gavin's in the hospital." She let out a big sigh before continuing. "He was found unconscious on the Thames Embankment near Westminster Bridge on Sunday. The police told us he'd had a vicious blow to his head."

I was shocked. "Will he be all right?" I asked.

Tallulah nodded slowly. "Eventually, yes, the doctors think so. But right now it is a bit touch-and-go. He's in an induced coma."

"For how long?"

"If he continues to respond as he has been doing, then they'll bring him out of it by the end of the week."

Tallulah turned away quickly, but her clenched jaw and fists told me how hard it was for her to talk about the situation. It took her a moment before she turned back to face me.

"So what happened to him on Sunday?" I asked.

"We think he was attacked…"

I thought for a moment. "Was he missing anything?"

"His camera."

"Nothing else?"

Tallulah shook her head.

"Was he going to meet somebody?"

She shrugged her shoulders. "I don't know. He told me that he had to 'check something'—those were his precise words—near Westminster, but he didn't tell me what. And he didn't mention that he was planning to meet anyone, although I've got a strange feeling that he was. It's odd though. He doesn't usually keep secrets from me. Normally we each know exactly what the other is up to. Gavin and I have always been close," she explained when she saw my eyes widen, "and since we both moved to London at the same time, we've only gotten closer—especially with both of us working in fashion. Anyway, to answer your question, no, he hadn't noted anything in his agenda about a meeting on Sunday morning." Tallulah paused and then, looking me straight in the eyes, she said, "The police are convinced it was just a random mugging."

"Because of the missing camera?"

"Yes. And because of the images from the CCTV surveillance cameras at that location—there was nothing unusual on the footage they have, just a couple of elderly people, a blind lady, and a few joggers. Also, they say that stretch of the Embankment is a target area for muggers because of the tourists, even so early on a Sunday. The police estimate that Gavin was attacked shortly after eight o'clock because that's the last time he was seen unharmed on CCTV. He was found at eight fifteen." She hesitated for a moment before continuing. "But I don't think it was a random mugging. I think someone was looking for something—something my brother has."

"What makes you say that?"

"After I visited Gavin in the hospital, I went back to our flat in Camden. Someone had broken in and searched it while I was away." For the first time I saw a tiny chink in her cool facade. She suddenly started picking at the dark-purple polish on her nails.

"Searched? Like, everything turned upside down, every drawer emptied, kind of searched?"

Tallulah nodded. "I've never experienced anything like it—and I don't want to ever again. It's been horrible staying there, but I feel I have to do it for Gavin."

Apparently I'd been right about her self-possession and confidence. Not many people could stay alone in a flat that had just been ransacked. I listened as she continued. "I've cleaned the flat up as well as I can, but I didn't want to tell my parents. You see…they're worried enough as it is. I did call the police though."

"And?"

"Well, because nothing was taken, they didn't seem to think there was much they could do. They filed a report, and that was that."

"Could it have been a burglary that went wrong? Perhaps whoever broke in was disturbed before they managed to take anything. Maybe a neighbor's dog barked, or someone went up the stairs. Is there a stairwell in your building?"

Tallulah nodded. "Yes, but our neighbor on the floor above us was away for the weekend, and the store below us—it's a secondhand bookshop—is closed on Sundays. So I doubt the intruder was caught by surprise."

"Hmmm…so they went through everything in the flat?"

She nodded. "They were methodical, rifling through every book. They even cut into our mattresses, but neatly along the seams, so I didn't notice right away."

"Yet they took nothing?"

"Not even a Q-tip."

"So you think the attack and the break-in are connected?"

Tallulah nodded slowly. "I do, yeah… That's what I feel, even if the police don't. And like I said, it's why I've come to see you. I want to get to the bottom of this—with or without the police."

I was quiet for a moment before asking, "So what do you think they were searching for? What do you think they attacked your brother for?"

She clicked open her little turquoise Chanel handbag and carefully pulled something out of it.

"This," she said as she placed a small object in my hand.

It was a flash drive.

"So why do *you* have it?" I asked as I plugged the flash drive into my laptop.

I'd quickly gone into the house and fetched the laptop from my bedroom. Now, back in the garden house, I was sitting at the round table, while Tallulah stood behind me.

"Gavin gave it to me on Sunday morning before he left the flat. He said, 'Make sure you hold on to this. Don't let it out of your hands. It's valuable.' I tried asking him about it, but he was in a rush to leave. Thinking about it now, maybe he was just trying to evade my questions. Anyway, he told me again that he had to check something near Westminster, and that he'd see me later.

"I didn't really give the stick much thought at the time because I figured he'd be back soon and could explain everything. Besides, Gavin has masses of flash drives that he uses on a daily basis. So I slipped it into this handbag," she said as she lifted her tiny Chanel crossover, "and it hasn't left my side since."

"Did he seem nervous or scared about what he was going to do, or whoever he was going to meet?"

"No. But then again, Gavin isn't the type who gets nervous…although…"

"Although?" I prompted after a moment's silence.

"He was excited. I mean, you'd have to know him to have noticed, but *I* saw that he was excited about whatever he was going to do. And then, like I said, he seemed evasive. Normally, he confides in me about everything. I remember thinking it was like he knew something he shouldn't. What's that expression, 'like the cat that got the cream'?"

"Uh-huh." I nodded.

"Well, that was Gavin on Sunday morning."

"You said the attack must have happened at around, or just after, eight a.m.?"

Tallulah nodded.

"Did your brother often go out so early on a Sunday morning? He must have left your flat by seven."

She shrugged her shoulders. "He actually left the flat at six forty-five. Like all photographers, Gavin loves the morning light. Yes, it was early, but not unusual for him—not if there was something he was keen to photograph or investigate."

I nodded and made a note of the time. "And when your apartment was ransacked, did they take Gavin's computer? Surely he'd downloaded whatever is on the flash drive onto his computer too."

Tallulah nodded. "He did. I checked as soon as I got his computer back. But you see, at the time of the break-in, his laptop wasn't in our flat. He'd taken it to a friend's the day before for safekeeping. When I called the friend to tell him about Gavin, he told me he had the computer."

Tallulah and I both fell silent as I mulled everything over in my mind.

"Is there anything else you can tell me? About Sunday, I mean," I asked eventually.

I saw Tallulah hesitate for a moment, as if deciding whether or not to say what was on her mind.

"Any little thing?"

"Well, there is one slightly odd thing I noticed…but only later on, at the hospital."

I waited.

"This may have nothing to do with anything—I mean, the police didn't even notice, but…"

"Tell me anyway," I said. "Details—even ones that seem insignificant—can sometimes say a lot."

After a moment she said, "I picked up my brother's clothes at the hospital to take them home."

"And?"

"And his shoes, socks, and the bottom half of his jeans were wet—not soaking wet, they'd had some time to dry. But my point is, it wasn't raining on Sunday morning. His jacket, for example, was bone dry. So why were his jeans and shoes so damp?"

Good question, I thought—and one I had no immediate answer for. In my notes, I labeled the detail "TBLI"—To Be Looked Into.

The contents of the flash drive had finally downloaded. I clicked open the only folder on the stick—Gavin had named it *Close-up*—and Tallulah pulled a chair up next to mine as I started scrolling through the images.

"I don't understand," I said. "There doesn't seem to be anything suspicious or even odd about these images. In fact, they're really beautiful photographs; Gavin's good."

The images were of fashion designer Johnny Vane. He was one of a small handful of Brits—like Vivienne Westwood, Alexander McQueen, and Christopher Kane—who had started very small in London and managed, through sheer creative talent, to build strongly individualistic and highly identifiable brands, putting London back on the fashion map as they did so.

The photos were all of Johnny and seemed to be "day in the life" reportage. By the look of it, Gavin must have taken the photos just before the Vane fashion show a couple of months earlier. Many of the pictures showed Johnny at work in what I presumed to be the Vane design studio—sketching, pinning fabric, and so forth. There were also photos of Johnny and his team doing fittings with various models, and even some interior shots of his streamlined, stylish home. (At least I presumed it was his home.)

A large number of sleek portraits of Johnny rounded out the contents of the stick. In all of them, he wore what seemed to be his trademark look: spiky hair, perfectly clipped salt-and-pepper stubble, black leather biker jacket (the knock-off versions of his famous Vane biker jacket were cult favorites at my school), black skinny jeans, black shirt, biker boots, studded fingerless gloves (he seemed to wear these all the time—even in the photos of the fittings!), and an assortment of silver rings. The lighting was beautiful, and even the candid shots had a strong sense of composition. Gavin clearly knew what he was doing.

Of all the photos on the flash drive, however, it was the last one that really caught my eye, precisely because it was not beautiful and slick. In fact, it seemed to be a photo of a photo—and an old one at that. Furthermore, the careless way the old picture had been photographed, lying on a nondescript brown envelope and with little attention paid to cropping or lighting, suggested that the shot was a candid one.

Otherwise the original photo in the picture was charming. It was of two young boys—they looked to be about five or six, and possibly twins. They stood knee-deep in water, smiling and happy, with one boy holding the other in a big bear hug.

Presumably, I thought as I looked at it carefully, *one of those boys is the young Johnny.* All the other photos on the stick were of him, so it seemed likely that this one must be too…although I'd have to find a way of verifying that.

"What are these photos for?" I asked Tallulah. "Why did Gavin take them?"

"They were for an interview with Johnny Vane, something one of the fashion magazines—*Harper's Bazaar*—hired my brother to do. I think Gavin said something about the story running next month, in time for Johnny's anniversary—twenty years since he first established himself as a designer. Incidentally, this is an edited selection of the photos he took. Gavin sent the same choice of images, minus the old one, to *Harper's Bazaar*.

"I know because I checked his emails when I got his computer back from his friend. Anyway, photographing Johnny Vane for *Harper's Bazaar* was a real coup for Gavin because this is the sort of reportage work he'd like to do more of. He was super excited when his agent called him about it, although I suppose now he'll regret ever having taken it on."

I shrugged my shoulders. "Maybe the attack had nothing to do with these pictures. We just don't know yet. Then again, maybe Gavin was on the trail of something important. And if we can uncover what that was, maybe he'll feel it was all worth it, once he recovers." I paused for a moment as thoughts crowded my mind. "Speaking of which, you said that the doctors hope to wake him up at the end of the week, right?"

Tallulah nodded. She'd gone quiet again, and her

face was tight with agony and fear. "Like I said earlier, it's a bit touch-and-go right now, but, yeah, the plan is to wake him on Friday evening—hopefully. Why?"

"Just wondering…"

I scrolled through the photos again and again, Tallulah by my side. But apart from that last slightly odd picture, nothing obvious jumped out.

When I mentioned this to Tallulah, she said, "Yeah, that's the problem, isn't it? Nobody looking at these images could possibly believe that there was anything strange or sinister about them, but my brother would never ever have said, 'Don't let it out of your hands,' if he didn't have a good reason. And he wouldn't have taken his laptop to his friend's unless he was worried someone might want to steal it. I've never known him to do that, not even after his first shoot for Italian *Vogue*, when he was so worried he might lose his photos that he made copies on ten different sticks, just in case."

Tallulah was flustered, and color had risen to her cheeks. I watched as she stood up suddenly. A look of frustration flashed across her face, and her eyes narrowed in anger as she crossed and uncrossed her arms. "I'm sure the images on this flash drive, our flat being searched, and what's happened to my brother are related—I'm sure of it! I want to find who has done this! I want to find the person responsible for hurting my brother!" She stopped and breathed deeply, then fiddled with her fingernails in silence.

I turned back to my laptop and flicked through the images. "Have you any idea why your brother named the file 'Close-up'? I haven't seen any close-ups on the stick at all."

"I hadn't thought about that, but it's typical Gavin," Tallulah said as she bent over my shoulder to look at the screen. "He tends to give his files slightly coded names. They always have something to do with the content of the file, but usually the connection is only obvious to him. I remember once looking at a bunch of photos he was editing. They were all on a file labeled 'Elle,' so I thought they were something he'd shot for *Elle* magazine. But, no, they were photos he'd taken for some Japanese magazine editorial inspired by the actor Elle Fanning."

After a few moments, I heard Tallulah move behind me again. It sounded as if she was looking through her handbag. I turned around just as she pulled out a phone and offered it to me. "It's Gavin's," she explained. "Surprisingly enough, the attacker didn't take it. Gavin had it zipped up in an inside pocket of his jacket, so I guess they didn't notice it. Anyway, I thought you might find it useful. I've had a look and couldn't see anything suspicious, but maybe you'll have a better idea of what to look for."

I took the phone and asked Tallulah for the code.

"Oh yeah." Her mouth broke into the first semblance of a smile I'd seen since we'd shaken hands. "That might help… I have it written down somewhere. Hang on."

She rummaged in her tiny bag again. "Oh, I don't have it on me right now, but I'll look it up as soon as I'm back home and send it to you. Luckily I know where he keeps his passwords."

"Fine," I said.

"So, Axelle," she said as she watched me, "you will take on this case, won't you?"

I nodded slowly. "Yes. Yes, I will…but we won't have much time."

Tallulah raised her eyebrows.

"Remember I asked you when your brother is expected to regain consciousness?"

She nodded.

"Well, I imagine whoever put him in the hospital will still want to get their hands on this stick. Unless they found what they wanted on the memory card in Gavin's camera."

Tallulah shook her head. "He changed memory cards for every job. I even saw him put a new one in on Sunday morning. Whoever has the camera won't have found much—if anything."

"And they didn't find anything in your flat, so I reckon the only option they have now is to threaten Gavin into handing the stick over the first chance they get."

"I hadn't thought of that." Tallulah's voice sounded distressed, and she started picking at her nails again.

I watched her for a moment before saying, "There's another scenario we have to consider too…"

"Yes?"

"Gavin probably got a good look at his attacker, right?"

Tallulah nodded.

"Well, it might not just be the stick the attacker's looking for now."

Tallulah didn't say anything, but she stopped picking her nails and stared at me.

"They'll also want to stop Gavin from identifying them…"

"But how?"

"By silencing him for good."

TUESDAY AFTERNOON
Castings and Clues

After Tallulah left, I ate a quick lunch at home, then changed for my *Teen Chic* casting at Chic House on Cavendish Square in Mayfair. Annoyingly, though there was nothing I would have loved more than to concentrate on the new case, I knew I'd better go to the casting or risk ticking off my agency—and my mom. And the last thing I needed right now was to draw any of *that* kind of attention to myself.

I didn't have to wear anything superspecial for the casting—you don't necessarily need to see magazine editors in high heels or anything—but still…dressing to see *Teen Chic* was not like dressing to hang out at home. Ratty old pullovers and unbrushed hair wouldn't cut it. And my large glasses would definitely have to stay behind—or at least in my shoulder bag. I went upstairs and changed into a pair of dark skinny jeans, covering the sweater with my favorite Burberry trench coat (both detective-y and trendy!). Then I took the blue leopard-print scarf I'd found in Topshop out of its drawer and chose a pair of Converse.

My last and by far my best "accessory" for the day was Halley. I figured it would be more fun for both of us if she came along, and if her excited barks and wiggles were anything to go by, she totally agreed. I snapped on her leash and left the house before Mom could interrogate me about Tallulah's visit.

Halley and I walked to Notting Hill Gate and caught the 94 bus. Thirty minutes later we arrived at Oxford Circus, and from there it was a ten-minute walk to Chic House.

As I pushed the heavy revolving door of the building, I told Halley, "This casting better be good because it's seriously eating up sleuthing time."

With a sweet look from her bright, little button eyes and a wag of her short, white tail, Halley made it clear that she understood exactly what I meant.

Chic House is the headquarters for the London-based magazines owned and published by Sid Clifton. *Teen Chic* shares the large office building with *Chic*, *Chic Bride*, and *Chic Rogue*, among others.

The casting I was going to—as my booker, Jazz Bhatnagar, had excitedly explained to me the previous Friday—was for a "special" booking. This is fashion industry speak for a booking involving someone famous and talented—an actor, musician, or sports star, for instance.

"Now I can't tell you who you'll be working with yet, but—fingers crossed you get the job—you'll find out as soon as you sign the confidentiality contract." Jazz had practically squealed with excitement as she'd given me my casting details.

A casting basically involves meeting a client—in this case, *Teen Chic*—or a photographer for a potential job. And while that may sound pretty banal and stress-free, the fact is, it's anything but.

A model can easily have a day filled with at least a dozen castings and go-sees—and each casting is like a full-on job interview. Not only do you have to make an impression with the way you look—clear skin, clean hair, groomed nails, cool-ish outfit—but you have to show a lot of personality too. If, in the ten minutes the average casting lasts, you can convince the people you're seeing that you'd be professional, amusing, upbeat, energetic, and fun to have around all day, then you're halfway to getting the job—or at least you're likely to be remembered for another one.

The zed cards (a kind of business card for models) of girls who don't sparkle sufficiently are immediately relegated to the bottom of the bottom drawer…if not the wastepaper basket. And keep in mind that it's all subjective, so sometimes you can sparkle all you like, but you still won't be that client's cup of tea.

There were a lot of girls at the casting; Jazz had mentioned that a few models were needed for the editorial. Half of them were on their phones or tablets, while the other half were chatting. Models are normally quite friendly—at least that's my experience. Yes, it can be intimidating to walk into a room of super cool and pretty-looking girls...but actually, because most models travel so much or may have just arrived in a country, they are usually happy to have someone to talk to.

I said hi to the girls that I'd met on other jobs or castings, and then I found an empty seat and sat down with Halley at my feet. Needless to say, Halley drew a lot of attention—especially from a tiny, cream-colored, long-haired Chihuahua that belonged to a Brazilian model.

While Halley played with the Chihuahua, I managed to get my head in the right space to do the casting, pushing all thoughts of the case out of my mind. But then, just as my turn came, my phone vibrated with a new message that made me feel nervous and excited—even if I had been expecting it:

> **On my way to Gare du Nord now. Can't wait to see you tonight. xxx**

My eyes quickly swept over the short text and I felt my stomach flip-flop. *No time to think about him right now, Axelle. It's time to do your casting, then get cracking on your new case.*

I put my phone away, ran my hands through my hair, quickly applied a touch of lip gloss and, taking Halley with me, walked into the editor's office.

"Hi," said the editor, Jacky Sykes, when we walked in. Then, before I even had a chance to say hi back, she told me that she'd seen me walk at a couple of the shows in New York and knew exactly who I was. I was just about to ask her which shows, but she cut me off by answering her desk phone. She spoke in a series of rapid-fire queries and comments, punctuated by short girlie giggles at odds with her crisp body language.

With a wave of her other hand, she motioned that I should hand her my "model book." I gave the portfolio of photos to her and watched as she rifled through the pages while continuing to speak on the phone. I knew she must have been studying my pictures, because her eyes were glued to them, but like most editors, she didn't give anything away.

After a minute, she handed my book back to me. I didn't know if I was supposed to say anything or not. *Surely there has to be more to our appointment than just this?* I thought. Apparently not. Phone still glued to her ear, Jacky caught my eye and looked pointedly at the door as she creased her lips into a tight little smile. It looked like something a hungry tiger might do. I was about to tell her that it might help if she'd actually speak to me, when she abruptly finished her call and pushed a bright-red button on the large telephone on her desk. She spoke loudly into the phone.

"I have a model in my office who doesn't seem to speak. Could you please show her out?"

I'd had some bad castings but this was ridiculous—so much for my chance to sparkle. Before I could tell her what I thought of her, the door swung open and her secretary came in. "There you are!" she said loudly, as if I were deaf. "Why don't you come with me?"

Why, I asked myself with mounting anger, were fashionistas so often incapable of giving you the chance to speak for yourself?

As if to prove my point, the secretary kept up a nonstop monologue as she ushered me and Halley out of the editor's office and back into the foyer. I was so angry that I was now willing myself to keep quiet so I wouldn't snap her head off. "Will you be okay?" she asked finally after calling us a lift.

I stepped into the lift, moving back to allow Halley in, then turned and said, "Actually, the sooner I get out of here, the better I'll be. Thanks." I watched as the doors shut on her surprised face.

Argh! Fashion! What a waste of my time! I took a deep breath and told myself to calm down, and then, with Halley moving at a brisk trot beside me, I strode out of the lift and into the lobby. I was desperate to get out into the fresh air and, more importantly, get working on the case. I bounded to the revolving door and pushed my way in. As I shuffled toward the open air, I looked down to make sure that Halley was right next to me and not about to get squashed.

I was still looking down as I prepared to step out into the street—so I barely saw a tall, fast-moving figure speed toward me, aiming to enter the revolving door as I walked out. But instead—*bang*—I was sent flying and landed on the ground with a thump, right on my bottom. As I sat sprawled on the pavement in front of the Chic House entrance, I heard the gentle swish of the automated door as it continued to rotate slowly behind me.

Could this day possibly get any more dramatic? I thought as I checked for injuries.

"I am so, so sorry. Really. Really. Sorry," said a deep, concerned voice from above.

Please let that be the voice of a friendly, normal person, like a fireman or shop assistant, I told myself as I sat on my sore bottom, with Halley licking my right ear. *I really can't take another fashionista right now.*

I looked up and saw exactly that. With annoyance I took in the tall figure with long, untamed dark-brown hair and super cool clothes: brown leather pointy-toed boots, skinny blue jeans, and an old white T-shirt under a checked flannel shirt. Two long chains—one with a cross pendant, the other with a key—dangled from around his neck. I could just make out the top of a tattoo peeking out from underneath the collar of his T-shirt. He didn't seem to be that much older than me.

He was peering at me through mirrored aviator sunglasses, his hands held out to help me up.

I debated refusing his offer, but considering I'd already made enough of a fool of myself, the last thing I needed was to fall over again while I was trying to get back on my feet.

"Next time, you might want to slow down a bit," he said, pulling me up with a smile.

I couldn't believe the guy's arrogance. I spoke out before I was even standing on my own two legs. "Before you start lecturing me on my conduct, why don't you stop trying to pretend you're a famous rock star and take those ridiculous bug eyes off your face. It might help you to see better so you don't go barging into anyone else."

I watched as his smile flattened into a straight line. "Are you always this friendly?"

"Are you always this arrogant?"

"Look, I'm sorry. Why don't we start over, okay?"

"I don't think so. Unfortunately, I don't have the time, and I'm not even sure it would be worth it."

Mr. Cool didn't say anything but simply stood there, openmouthed. Even though he had his sunglasses on, I could see the shock on his face. Clearly he felt I'd been in the wrong, and clearly he wasn't too pleased with the turn our conversation had taken. Well, I'd had my say, and I'd had my fill of fashionistas for the day. I didn't wait to hear or say more. Halley and I headed off. I heard him call after me a few seconds later, but ignoring him, I turned the corner and disappeared.

I took a few deep breaths as we walked briskly back toward Oxford Circus. Maybe on another day, it would have taken me longer to calm down after the casting I'd just had, but honestly, I was so intrigued and anxious to get working on my new case that my anger was rapidly evaporating with each stride I took. I pulled my phone out of my trench coat pocket and called Ellie. *She should be back from Miami*, I thought with a glance at the time. I hadn't seen her since I'd started studying for my GCSEs, and I was eager to discuss the case with her. Fortunately she answered and was ready to meet me whenever. She had the day free.

"Where?" Ellie asked.

What I wanted to do more than anything else was to check out the scene of the crime. I wanted to see where Gavin was attacked. It was, I felt, the logical place to begin my investigation. Not that I told Ellie any of this—yet.

"How about down on the Embankment?" I said. "I need to walk Halley. I'll be somewhere between the entrances to the Westminster and Embankment Tube stations. On the Big Ben side of the river."

"Perfect—I can go for my run down there… But don't you usually walk Halley in Hyde Park? Why the change?" I could hear the curiosity in Ellie's voice. She knew something was up, and I could practically feel her smile through the phone as she teased me.

"That, Nancy Drew, is on a need-to-know basis."

"And I don't need to know?"

"Not yet. But don't worry; you'll soon be in the picture."

We made plans to meet an hour later and hung up. Then, as I slipped my phone into my trench coat pocket, I realized with horror that Gavin's phone was no longer in my other pocket! I'd been carrying both phones, one in each of the two large front pockets of my coat...but now I had only mine. The other pocket was empty. *Argh!*

I started to panic and quickly moved to the side of the pavement to search through my shoulder bag—but Gavin's phone wasn't in it. Panic really set in as I realized it might have slipped out of my pocket when I'd fallen. If that was the case, then I'd have to go back to Chic House. *Double argh!*

I stomped back the way I'd come—scanning the pavement all the way, just in case—and into the lobby. I asked at reception whether a phone had been handed in within the last fifteen minutes. The answer was no. Hmm...then had it somehow slipped out of my pocket while I'd been on the casting? I was fuming with myself—why had I kept Gavin's phone in an unzipped pocket? I wanted to get going. I should have been meeting Ellie down at the crime scene, but instead I was stuck back in Chic House retracing my steps.

I took a deep breath as the lift doors opened and Halley and I stepped back out onto the *Teen Chic* floor. I searched all over the waiting area and asked the models present if they'd seen my (Gavin's) phone, but no one had. Not that anyone was paying much attention to me; since I'd left, the atmosphere at *Teen Chic* had suddenly become charged with an air of excitement. Furthermore, all the models were preening (even more than usual), checking their reflections in their powder compacts and arranging their hair.

What is going on? I wondered, as I headed toward Jacky's office, hoping to find the phone under her desk or something. I turned the corner, and the scene outside Jacky's closed door stopped me in my tracks. About a dozen people—junior editors, stylists, even a bike messenger—were pushed up against the door, obviously trying to listen in on Jacky's conversation. *How odd*, I thought—and more to the point, how would I be able to get past them and into her office?

Surprisingly, it wasn't difficult. They were all too intent on listening in. I just kept saying, *Sorry, sorry, excuse me*, until I was within reach of the doorknob, then turned it, ready to walk straight in. Jacky's PA suddenly realized what I was doing and tried to stop me, but I brushed her off. It wasn't as if the casting with Jacky had gone so well that I was going to get a booking. Clearly, with the amount of time she'd spent "talking" to me, my zed card had gone straight to the bottom of her pile. At this point I was willing to risk coming off as rude to save myself some time.

I opened the door and saw Jacky, giggling, eyes sparkling as she leaned on her elbows and gazed adoringly into the eyes of Mr. Pretend Rock Star. She was an entirely different creature from the abrasive editor I'd seen twenty minutes earlier. He, on the other hand, once he bothered to look up and see who'd walked in, began to smile at me, as if my unannounced visit amused him. Pointing to his sunglasses on the desk, he said, "Do I still look like a pretend rock star?"

As I looked into his eyes (brown, with flecks of green-gold, in case you're wondering), I felt like a bucket of cold water had been thrown over me. Mr. Pretend Rock Star wasn't a pretender at all—he was the real deal!

He was none other than Josh Locke, the lead singer, guitarist, and songwriter of a very, very popular boy band. And I suppose it was no big surprise that he was at Chic House. After all, he was on every fashion designer's wish list of personalities they'd like to dress. Jenny and Ellie were huge fans—like ninety-nine percent of the teen female population of Great Britain. Or probably the world by now.

No wonder the models had been preening, I thought. *What is it about fame that turns people's heads?*

Jacky stopped batting her eyelashes at Josh Locke long enough to look at me. "Axelle!" she cried, her voice suspiciously friendly, as she waved her PA away (although I noticed that the PA didn't shut the door completely, and through the one-inch crack she left, I could make out about six pairs of eyes). "We were just talking about you."

Was she pretending to be almost human for Josh's sake? So that he wouldn't think she was a model-eating editor? And why were *they* just talking about *me*? "Have you found your voice yet, Axelle? And, by the way, I hear you've met Josh already."

"Actually, Jacky, I never lost my voice. And as for Josh, I think I know enough," I said tightly.

"I told Jacky that we met downstairs. I recognized you from your zed card." He pointed to the card on Jacky's desk.

"Yes, Josh said you bumped into him in the lobby," Jacky said in a honeyed voice.

I glared at him. "Actually *Josh* bumped into me."

"Well, anyway, seeing as you're here, we can discuss the booking—"

I interrupted Jacky before she could go any further. There was no time to talk. I had to get out of her office and down to the crime scene as fast as possible, so I gave her the best excuse I could think of. "Jacky, I'm very sorry, but I have another casting across town that I'm running late for. I really have to go. I just wanted to ask if I'd left a phone here."

"No, I'm sorry, Axelle, I haven't seen anything. But have a look around, if you like."

"There's no need to do that," Josh broke in.

"Oh? Why's that?" I asked.

"I think I've found it." He reached into his jacket pocket and pulled out a phone. He held it across the desk for me on his open palm. "Is this what you're looking for? It flew out of your coat pocket when you bumped into me by the revolving door."

I glared at him again. "Thank you," I said as I reached for Gavin's phone. "Although if you hadn't knocked me over in the first place, none of this would have happened."

"Absolutely," said Josh with a wry smile. "So it's a good thing I was wearing my sunglasses."

I ignored his comment, and after thanking Jacky and saying good-bye, Halley and I left. Josh had insisted on opening and shutting the door for us, and it was quite funny to see how everyone scattered from behind the door as he opened it.

As we retraced our steps to the Oxford Circus Tube station, I took deep breaths and pushed all thoughts of pop-star arrogance and fawning fans out of my mind.

At least I had Gavin's phone again, thank goodness, and now nothing else was going to stop me from getting on with the case. A sense of renewed energy surged through me as I realized that I could forget about fashion for the day and my time was now my own. Halley and I got on a southbound Bakerloo line train to the Embankment station. Then I found a quiet corner and sat down with Halley snoozing at my feet. Next to my TBLI list I started writing another list—of the things I needed to do *now*…

First, I needed to check out the scene of the crime.

But I also needed to dig into Gavin's background. What if the mugging was totally unrelated to the flash drive? It could all be an incredible coincidence.

Fleetingly, my granny's mantra—*Remember, Axelle, there is no such thing as a coincidence. Keep that in mind once you start solving cases...*—intruded upon my thoughts. I ignored it and chose to take the thorough route. Unlike my grandfather, I didn't have hundreds of cases under my belt. Jumping to conclusions was something I couldn't afford to do.

Simultaneously, however, it was important to dig into Johnny Vane's background. Thorough route aside, my gut (and Tallulah's conviction) told me this was the line of inquiry that would eventually lead me to Gavin's attacker. The question was, how?

If Tallulah was right, an important clue was buried somewhere in the images she had brought me on the stick. But *what*? What was so suspicious about those pictures that someone was willing to do anything to get hold of them?

I looked at the top of my list:

Go to the scene of the crime.

While I'd been at the casting, Tallulah had emailed me twice: once with Gavin's phone code, and a second time with the details of the exact location where Gavin had been found, so I knew where I was headed. With a bit of luck I might stumble upon something interesting. It was definitely worth a look.

I looked at Tallulah's first email again and jotted Gavin's phone code in my notebook for safekeeping. Then I accessed his phone and started looking through it. His photo album was the first place I checked. Needless to say there were thousands of images on there. And although I wasn't as thorough as I could have been, nothing popped out at me. I did see a few shots from the Johnny Vane shoot, but nothing I hadn't already seen on the flash drive. There were also quite a few of Gavin and Tallulah goofing around, and many of the London cityscape.

Like Tallulah had said, Gavin's calendar and agenda gave absolutely no information about a meeting on the Embankment on Sunday morning. Everything else noted in his agenda had to do with work, and each entry was clearly marked as such. I searched his contacts list, but nothing there struck me as unusual either. (Although, how could I really judge?) I sent Tallulah a message asking her to verify that she'd been through her brother's list of contacts. Her answer was unambiguous:

I know everyone on there.

Hmm…I sent Tallulah another question:

Can you think of anyone who might have a grudge against Gavin? Or a score to settle?

A message came back:

No. Everyone likes Gavin. No enemies that I know of. Although obviously there's one now…

Another quickly followed:

> **BTW the police are still looking into these possibilities. But so far, nothing. Why am I not surprised? Zzzzzzzz...**

I had to laugh. Tallulah certainly didn't rate the police highly for their efforts. I wrote back, asking her to notify me of any updates. Then, pulling my tablet out, I turned to my next line of inquiry and started scrolling through the images from Gavin's flash drive that I'd downloaded earlier. But again, apart from the last shot—the one of the old photo—nothing struck me as especially strange. After a few minutes I put my tablet away and pulled out my notebook.

Inside was a paper copy of the old photo from Gavin's flash drive, which I'd quickly printed at home before leaving for the casting. As the train came to an unexpected halt, I carefully examined the image of the smiling boys under the stark fluorescent lighting of the train car. If I was hoping to find the fragment of an address written on the brown envelope in the background, I was disappointed. It was clean. And whatever marks I could see on the picture itself appeared to be scratches on the surface of the original.

The more I thought about it, the more I questioned why Gavin even had this image on the stick. I mean, the photo itself seemed banal enough: two young boys having fun on a sunny day. I could only guess that it was included because one of the boys was Johnny Vane, but if so, why this particular old picture—especially when all of the other photos were of Johnny now, today?

I wondered whether Gavin's job brief from *Harper's Bazaar* magazine had included getting images from Johnny's childhood. I quickly opened his phone again and searched in his agenda. Nothing. Then I searched his emails, and while I found several relating to the booking, I didn't find anything that gave specific details. I quickly sent Tallulah a message asking about it. Her answer came back immediately:

> Yes, looked into that, but found nothing on G's laptop and nothing printed—though he must have had an email with the details. I tried his agent but he wouldn't release any details. That's standard procedure for any kind of agency BTW.

Grrr!

I scribbled a reminder to myself on my TBLI (To Be Looked Into) list.

I picked up the photo again and noted another interesting thing about it: in the background, across the river in the right-hand corner of the picture, I could just make out the edge of a tall, turreted building that felt somehow familiar, like it was somewhere in the city. If it was, that meant the boys had been snapped at some point along the Thames. I needed to find out where that photo had been taken. Maybe it was near where Gavin had been attacked. And if so, was that a coincidence—or not?

While those thoughts ran through my mind, I grabbed my tablet again and started researching Johnny Vane online. (For once the Tube's Wi-Fi signal was strong.) If I assumed that the photos of Johnny were a factor in Gavin's attack, then perhaps the closer I was able to get to Johnny, the closer I would also get to Gavin's attacker. It was a lead worth following, I thought.

I knew who Johnny Vane was, of course, but I had no idea about his background. After a few minutes of delving into his personal history though, I was more convinced than ever that I should follow my gut concerning the old photo.

According to various online sources I checked out, Johnny had a twin brother—so he was probably one of the boys in the old photo, though I'd still have to confirm this.

Also, according to his Wiki page, tragedy was a strong feature of Johnny's childhood:

Johnny Vane's father, James Vane (from a junior branch of the Somerset Vane family), died of a heart attack in 1973, while having supper at his London club. Johnny's twin brother, Julian, drowned in 1977, and his mother, Clarissa Vane, the famous fashion model and muse, died in an accident at their home a few months later.

Apart from these two sentences, no other details were given about the deaths. Even so, my head was buzzing just from reading the word "drowned." My mind jumped back to Gavin's photo of the two boys standing knee-deep in water. Could Julian have drowned in the Thames? I saved my questions for later as I finished reading the article, which went on to tell me:

Johnny Vane's younger sister, Georgiana Vane (born 1973), works in PR for Johnny Vane Ltd.

I clicked on the link to Georgiana Vane's page, but it was notably brief. Apart from confirming that she worked for the publicity department of her brother's fashion company, no other information was given.

I learned more about Johnny's mother on her Wiki page:

A renowned beauty and model, Clarissa Vane (née Ryder) was, and still is, often cited as a muse to many of the most influential London fashion designers and fashion photographers from the 1970s to the present… Entire fashion collections have been dedicated to her beauty and style.

I wasn't sure what a muse was exactly, not in the fashion sense, at least—although I'd heard the word used, especially in connection with Kate Moss. But presumably a modern muse was to fashion designers and stylists what a classical muse was to poets and artists: someone who inspired creative types to, well…create.

Wiki confirmed that Clarissa Vane had appeared at the most glittering jet-set parties of the late 1960s and early 1970s, not to mention in front-row seats at all the

Paris fashion shows. She had certainly traveled—from Marrakesh to Gstaad to Jamaica. No destination seemed too far away for a party.

And: *Two portraits of Clarissa Vane, dating from 1975, are on view at the National Portrait Gallery in Trafalgar Square, London…*

Hmm…muse and sometime model…how tragic to have died so young, I thought as I looked at various images of her beautiful, symmetrical face and lithe figure. Ironically, her face was serene and classical, with a halo of thick, shoulder-length, dark-blond hair and large, long-lashed blue eyes. It gave no indication of the nomadic and bohemian existence she'd lived. She seemed otherworldly, almost like a beautiful statue.

Fleetingly, I wondered when—or if—she'd seen much of her children. My mom was hands-on. (I had the impression she was also feet-, arms-, and legs-on.) What would it have been like to have a mother who was always on a plane, jetting off to a party or photo shoot? And then to be orphaned so young?

According to the dates given, Johnny must have been about five years of age and Georgie three, nearly four, when they'd lost Clarissa. I wondered who'd cared for them after that. Had there been anyone else in the family to look after them?

I went back to Johnny's page to take a look at one other fact that had leaped out at me: *Johnny Vane grew up in Notting Hill.*

Considering that I'd spent my entire life in Notting Hill, this intrigued me.

The train had started moving at some point in my research and was now pulling into Embankment Tube station. I quickly put my tablet and notebook back in my shoulder bag, and Halley and I jumped off the train. My mind was still on Johnny Vane as I climbed the stairs out of the underground station and onto the pavement. Who, I wondered, could introduce me to Johnny? It would certainly help with my investigation if I could meet him…

One name came immediately to mind: Charlotte Gilford, the flame-haired, London-bred, outspoken and glamorous owner of my London agency, Thunder. If anyone could do it, Charlotte could. I walked to the river's edge and called the agency.

Charlotte came on the line, and I jumped straight to the point. Could she organize a go-see for me with Johnny Vane? She put me on hold for a few moments before picking up my call again. There was a pause before her deep voice vibrated through the phone. "I'm in my office now, Axelle. Tell me, you've never asked for a go-see before… Is there more to this request than pure fashion?"

"Yes," I answered after a moment's hesitation. There was, after all, no point in *not* being honest with Charlotte. She might have to cover for me at some point, and besides, she knew all about my detective work. Miriam

Fontaine, my Paris and New York City agent, had told her I was a magnet for mysteries, so she must have been expecting something to happen at some point.

"I thought so... Well, I'll try my best to get you a go-see with Johnny. I can definitely get you into Johnny Vane Ltd., but I can't guarantee he'll be there. I'll send you over for their resort collection casting. You fit the bill perfectly for that anyway, so no one will be suspicious." She paused again, then asked, "Does whatever you're working on have to do with Johnny Vane himself? Directly?"

"Maybe..."

"Well," Charlotte continued, "he's an important part of the British fashion establishment..."

"And?"

"And if anything you find out could possibly paint Johnny in a less-than-flattering light, you'll have to tread carefully. He's very aware of the position he holds, and I have no doubt he'll fight tooth and nail to keep it. I've known him many years, and while he has lovely manners and is funny and charming, I have seen him snap with people who work for him. And I mean *really* snap. Not that it's unusual in the fashion business. I can reel off a list of big names like that. A famous Italian designer springs to mind... But anyway, just be careful. And for heaven's sake, call me if you need any help whatsoever, okay? Is that it?"

One more thing occurred to me: the job brief for

Gavin's *Harper's Bazaar* magazine spread. Charlotte could be just the person to help me with that too. There must have been a detailed brief for the booking, and at least two people would have known exactly what that job brief entailed: the magazine editor and Gavin, the photographer. I'd tried—with no luck—looking for information at Gavin's end of things. Surely the editor would still have a copy of the brief or remember the important details. And surely Charlotte had the right contacts and enough pull to get it for me.

"Actually," I answered, "I've just thought of something else. Do you think you could find out for me what the exact job details were for a booking the photographer Gavin Tempest shot for *Harper's Bazaar* magazine? It was for a profile piece on Johnny Vane. I need to know if he was asked to include background shots, like old family photos, images from Johnny Vane's childhood, that kind of thing."

"Gavin? For *Harper's Bazaar*?" She seemed surprised.

Briefly, without going into too much detail, I told Charlotte about the attack.

"I'm very sorry to hear that. Gavin isn't just super talented; he's an all-round lovely person. Anyway, yes, I'll ask for you. I'll get back to you as soon as I hear something—although it may take a day or two. Editors aren't always the easiest people to get hold of."

I thanked Charlotte, said good-bye, and looked out over the Thames. After a moment, I picked up my phone again. There was one more message I had to write—this time to my mom. (Dad was away on a business trip.) I let her know that I was down at the Embankment with Ellie, and that although I'd be home later, I had dinner plans.

I looked at my watch. Only a few more hours until we met. We hadn't seen each other in months...although we'd been Skyping a lot. But Skype was...Skype. What would it be like to see him in the flesh? And smell him and hear his voice whisper in my ear? I was really excited about spending time with him...but I was nervous too. We'd had our ups and downs lately because of the distance between us. Would we be able to put everything behind us when we stood face-to-face? Tonight...

Halley barked suddenly, pulling me out of my daydream. Her little tail wagged furiously.

I shook my head—I needed to focus. "You're right, Halley, it's time to get cracking. Come on," I said. I turned and started walking in the direction of the Houses of Parliament, close to where Gavin had been found last Sunday morning.

It may have been late June, but you wouldn't have known it from the weather. The early sun that had burned through the morning mist while I was sitting with Tallulah in our little garden house had disappeared by the time she'd left, replaced by dark-gray clouds that still hadn't lifted. I tightened my leopard-print scarf around my throat and turned up the collar of my trench coat as a strong summer breeze blew up from the Thames.

The wide river swirled beside Halley and me, carrying a varied assortment of boats, large and small, on its undulating currents. However, I tried to concentrate on my footing. I looked carefully for any large holes in the paved and cobbled surfaces, but there was nothing deep enough to have made Gavin's shoes wet, let alone the bottom half of his trousers. So how had that happened? Where had he been before or during the attack?

I stopped to examine the view, pulling the photo out of my notebook to compare it to what I could see. The photo really did seem to have been taken somewhere very nearby. Perhaps farther down the river? I slipped it back into my notebook.

I continued to stand—with Halley at the end of her leash sniffing something on the ground—and watched as, across the river, the London Eye slowly turned. A pair of slim hands suddenly closed over my eyes. At the same time, a voice I knew well said, "You're easy to sneak up on! Guess who?"

It was Ellie, and she was laughing. "You get more zoned out than Benedict Cumberbatch in *Sherlock*!"

"Very funny," I said, smiling as I turned to hug her.

I hadn't seen Ellie in weeks—she'd been traveling the globe, going from one modeling job to the next while I'd been studying for my GCSEs.

"It feels so good to be back home!" Her long,

honey-blond hair was tied in a knot on top of her head, and her skin was glowing from the run she'd just finished. Even sweaty and without makeup, she was stunning. Her long limbs were sheathed in navy and gray Gore-Tex. I couldn't tell you why or how, but Ellie even made running gear look like something we should all be wearing. *And that's why she's a supermodel*, I thought.

I quickly looked down at my scruffy Converse and thought of the fair number of Halley's white hairs that had woven their way into the fibers of my well-worn (okay, maybe "tattered" would be a more accurate description) pink pullover. I wasn't going to win any awards from the British Fashion Council, but even I had to admit that the model "off-duty, civilian" look had rubbed off on me a tiny bit. The jeans and leopard-print scarf I was wearing were more fashionable than anything I'd ever worn in my preceding sixteen years of life.

After a month of traveling nonstop, Ellie was finally in London for a couple of weeks' work and rest before her next slew of bookings took her around the world again. I'd met her in Paris, while solving the mystery of missing French fashion designer Belle La Lune.

After Paris, our friendship had continued to grow. While I'd been in New York City to find a famous black diamond during Fashion Week, Ellie's understanding of the fashion business and nearly encyclopedic knowledge of vintage clothing had been a huge help. Plus, what I loved about Ellie was that she was as excited helping me track down clues as she was shooting magazine covers. We'd become good friends, and she had proved to me that I could trust her with anything to do with my detective work.

"By the way, why are we meeting here? What are you up to?"

I laughed. "I'll explain once we're across the river."

She untied the running jacket from around her waist and pulled it on as we walked up the stairs from the Embankment to Westminster Bridge. My idea was to see this bank from across the river, in the hope that I might notice something I'd missed from up close.

Up close. *Close-up.*

The name of the folder on the flash drive echoed through my mind. What had Gavin meant by it?

As we walked across Westminster Bridge, Ellie and I stuck close together so we could hear each other above the sounds of the wind and the busy late-afternoon traffic. Apart from a short break midway over the bridge to take a selfie for her Instagram account, Ellie brought me up to date on what had been going on in her life. I heard all about her latest advertising campaign—one that would soon grace the pages of *Marie Claire*, *Love*, and *Chic* magazines, among others—and about some of the more unpredictable aspects of modeling, including a shoot she'd done the previous week before flying to Miami.

Ellie had been booked by French *Elle* magazine for an editorial spread that was to be shot on the Italian island of Pantelleria. But somehow the many suitcases packed with the clothes the magazine's stylist had pulled for the story had gotten lost in transit.

"So what did you do?"

"We ate lots of pasta and relaxed by the pool for two days and then ended up shooting the whole story in twenty hours straight—no break. At least I slept well on the plane back." She laughed. "So how about you? Has Charlotte been keeping you busy?"

"Umm-hmm." I nodded as I tugged Halley away from the attention of a very large male boxer. Charlotte represents me and about five hundred other models, covering women, men, and new faces, not to mention a slew of famous personalities including various supermodels, actors, bloggers, television celebrities, and musicians.

She and her brother Charlie started their agency about twenty years ago. Driven, savvy, and fiercely protective of their talent, they'd built Thunder into a well-respected and prestigious modeling and talent force. They also worked a lot with Miriam Fontaine, my Paris and New York City agent—which was why Miriam had recommended them to me. She'd set up my first meeting with Thunder so that I could see if I clicked with Charlotte and vice versa.

Of course, with my mom along, there wasn't going to

be much chance of us *not* clicking. My mom was shaping up to be a typical stage mom—or whatever the modeling equivalent was (runway mom or photo studio mom?).

Ellie was also represented by Thunder in London (and, like me, by Miriam in Paris and New York City), so she knew how much work Charlotte and Charlie could find me.

"So who's been keeping you busy since you finished your exams?" Ellie asked, as a red double-decker bus roared past us. "What jobs have you done?"

I told her about the *Teen Chic* casting I'd had earlier, and the various fittings and options I had for the week. I also told her about the two lookbooks I'd shot, one for designer Alice Temperley and the second for Topshop, and the editorial I'd done for edgy and cool *Dazed* magazine. Although I'd been one of a group of five for the magazine editorial, my agency seemed to think that each girl in the shoot would get a solo shot out of it—which was good.

Unless you're a supermodel, and you're going to be photographed surrounded by other supermodels, agencies can be hesitant to book you in for a group shot. From their perspective, a tear sheet (a page torn from a fashion magazine to use in a model's portfolio) makes a much stronger image when only one girl is on the page.

Charlotte had also sent me on quite a few castings—including a fair number at Vogue House, the Condé Nast headquarters in Mayfair. By now I was fairly certain I could make my way around their labyrinthine offices blindfolded. "But it's paid off, hasn't it, Axelle?" I remembered my booker, Jazz, saying as she showed me the options I had with Condé Nast magazines *Allure* and *Miss Vogue*. She'd been beaming with excitement. "At this rate, you'll end up like Lily Cole—modeling now, then catching up with university later."

I'd crinkled my nose. What I really wanted to do was concentrate on my studies *now*, especially criminal justice and languages. Speaking multiple languages gave a detective an added edge (when, for instance, interviewing witnesses whose first language might not be English).

"You'll see," Jazz had continued, her enthusiasm undimmed by my silence, "modeling can be fab. It can lead to all sorts of other things."

As long as it leads me to more mysteries, I'd said to myself.

"And does Charlotte know about what you do?" Ellie meant my detective work.

"Yes, Miriam told her and Charlie. The arrangement is the same one I have with Miriam. They'll be discreet, help cover for me, and in between my cases, push me like they do any other model. Jazz doesn't know though—and neither do any of the other bookers at Thunder."

"So what about Tallulah?" Ellie asked. "Is she the reason we're here? She called me, you know, on Sunday, saying she needed help with an unusual and possibly dangerous situation—which is when I told her about you. You said you met her, but what did she want, exactly? I haven't heard from her since I sent you that message yesterday—except for a brief thanks—so I'm assuming you got along okay."

"We did…and I've agreed to take on her case."

"She wouldn't give anything away to me. She said that she'd prefer you to explain…"

I nodded. "She has her reasons." As we turned left at the end of the bridge and walked past the Aquarium (where my dad works!) and toward the London Eye, I told Ellie all about my meeting with Tallulah.

"I know how close Tallulah and Gavin are," Ellie said when I'd finished. "And I can well imagine she wouldn't be happy with the police calling the attack a 'random mugging' after Gavin's and her flat had been ransacked. It sounds…*complex*."

Clue suddenly sprang to mind. *It was Colonel Mustard with the candlestick in the library.* Despite the random factors at the start of a game of Clue, it always ended with a clean and tidy solution. And while my mom liked to tell me: "Life isn't a game of Clue, you know, Axelle" (normally when I was spying on the neighbors), that didn't stop me from wanting a tidy solution for my real-life cases. Not that I was anywhere near a Clue-like unveiling for this one.

"Hmm…I guess it is complex," I said as I pointed back across the Thames to the riverbank opposite. "Gavin was found more or less where you found me.

And going on the information—official information from the police report—that Tallulah emailed me earlier, the police believe he probably fell where he was found—or a few feet in either direction at most."

It was difficult to imagine the violent scene as I stood with Ellie and Halley, observing the Embankment and Westminster Bridge from this distance. I couldn't help but think that London looked amazing even in gray weather. Beyond the tugboats and tourist launches puttering up and down the river, the city's iconic, bright-red double-decker buses stood out against the busy background, and the large, ornate streetlights decorating Westminster Bridge looked like something straight out of a Sherlock Holmes film.

To my left, buses, black cabs, cars, and bicycles of all shapes and sizes zoomed over the bridge, while dozens of people crossed it on foot.

From the northern end of the bridge, the London traffic followed the contours of the river along the road running above the Embankment. I couldn't help but feel the irony of what lay behind the large trees and impressive stone buildings overlooking that part of the river: the original Scotland Yard.

"So you said his shoes were wet?" Ellie asked, bringing me back to the task in hand. "What do you make of that?"

I shrugged. "I don't know... Perhaps he got wet in the river somehow? But standing here, I don't see anywhere nearby where he could have easily dipped his feet in. The water is too far below the bank. And why would he have wanted to do that anyway?"

I had to admit that Gavin's wet shoes had me stumped. *Where had he been? And why?* It made no sense to me yet—but I had a feeling it was connected with the attack.

My eyes scanned the riverbank in both directions, but I didn't notice anything that led right down into the water. I'd been hoping to find something like the old stone ramps and steps I'd seen on the Île Saint Louis in Paris that descended directly into the Seine. I'd never noticed any along this part of the Thames, but then again, I'd never really looked.

As Ellie and I made our way back across the bridge, however, a small pavilion in the far left corner of the Palace of Westminster caught my eye. I hadn't seen it before—it was small and whimsical, like a miniature turret. Because of its dainty size, it was completely overshadowed by the Palace of Westminster itself (otherwise known as the Houses of Parliament).

But what interested me about the tiny pavilion was that leading down from it, directly into the Thames, was a narrow stone staircase. And while it probably had nothing to do with Gavin's actions on Sunday, now I knew that there was at least this one point of direct access into the river near where Gavin had been hit. Something else occurred to me: the tides. I wondered how high the tide had been that morning…

"What are you looking at?" Ellie asked.

I pointed out the staircase to her.

"Do you think that's where he went in?"

I shrugged again. "It has to have been somewhere pretty close to where he was found. He wouldn't have had time to move very far before the attack. Gavin left home on Sunday morning at about six forty-five a.m. He wanted to 'check something'—his words. He didn't say *see* someone or *meet* someone, but who knows. Maybe he did. In any case, it seems Gavin came straight here from his flat on Sunday morning. His agenda notes for the day didn't suggest he did anything else, and Tallulah emailed me a while ago to say the police had checked the CCTV images for the train he'd taken—in case he'd been followed by his attacker—but everything looked normal."

"Hmm, nothing seems suspicious so far," said Ellie.

"Gavin came out of Westminster Tube station at just after seven thirty a.m.," I continued, pointing toward the Tube exit at the far end of the bridge. "The police estimate that he was attacked around eight a.m., and he was found unconscious just after eight fifteen. That means he had about thirty minutes of time to himself before the attack. So what was he checking on?"

"Or who was he talking to?" Ellie interjected.

"You're getting good, Nancy Drew." I smiled and went on. "So whatever or whoever he was checking on, it couldn't have been that far away, and he must have wet his shoes and jeans in that time too."

As Ellie and I walked the rest of the way north over Westminster Bridge I asked her about Johnny Vane. I was itching to find out more about him after the little bit of online research I'd done on the Tube.

"Do you really think he might have something to do with Gavin?" Ellie asked, eyes wide.

"Well, my gut says there must be some kind of link to him—even if it's tenuous—because all the images on Gavin's flash drive are of Johnny, his design studio, or his home." We stopped at the base of one of the Sherlock Holmes–style lampposts for Halley to have a sniff. "Is he nice?" I continued.

"Yes," Ellie said, "he is. He's funny, never says anything boring, and is a brilliant designer. He has a bulldog called Roger who follows him everywhere. He's quite intense, though…but then many designers are. I have an amazing peacock dress he made. The colors are unbelievable."

"Any gossip?"

"No…" She hesitated.

"But?"

"Well, it's not really gossip, but I've heard he had a tragic childhood. I think he lost his parents or a twin or something."

"Try all three," I said before filling her in on what I'd gleaned from my brief online search. I pulled the photo out of my notebook and showed it to Ellie.

"Is that him? As a boy? With his twin?" she asked.

"It might be. I have to have the identities confirmed,

but they look like twins, don't they? This is one of the images Gavin had on his flash drive."

Ellie handed me back the photo and said, "I know his mom was a model—or more of a muse, I guess—and quite a famous one, among fashion people at least. I've learned most of what I know about her through my love of vintage. There are photos of her in many of the old fashion books I collect. When she modeled, it was only with the best editors, photographers, and magazines. She did it for fun, really, or for the artistic buzz, I guess. She didn't need the money—at least not from what I've heard."

"So the family had money?" I asked.

"Well, they say that both Johnny's parents had wealthy families. But Clarissa was a muse in the true sense. She really inspired a lot of designers with the way she dressed and looked. And even now I'll sometimes see a photo of her pinned up on a designer's mood board. I think it's the combination of how she looked so perfect and cool, and yet wasn't precious with her style or clothes. She really wore what she liked, and because she traveled so much, she had her own take on how to put an outfit together. Like, she would pair the most amazing Yves Saint Laurent gypsy dress with a pair of flat, strappy sandals that she'd had handmade by a Corsican shepherd. Anyway, the designers all still love her."

"So a muse, in the fashion sense, is someone who inspires a fashion designer to create their best designs?"

Ellie nodded. "Yes, I think that's a pretty accurate definition. Lots of today's designers and photographers cite Kate Moss as their muse. And again, not just because of the way she looks, but because of the way she puts an outfit together and injects her personality into the clothes. By the way, do you know Johnny has a sister—Georgie? And that she works with him?"

I nodded.

"And, believe it or not," Ellie continued, "I've even met his old nanny! I mean a *real* nanny—not his granny. He's very devoted to her."

"His nanny? She must be ancient!" If Johnny was still so close to his nanny, maybe she had looked after him and Georgie after their parents had died. But what about a guardian? Someone legally responsible for their well-being. Surely that would have been a relative rather than a family employee?

Ellie nodded. "She is pretty old and quite…quite unassuming. Like, you don't really notice her. I was totally surprised when I found out she used to be a model for Biba and Ossie Clark…or was it Mary Quant? Anyway, she modeled, but I think she was a fit model—not a fashion model."

"What's the difference?" Despite the fact that I'd been working undercover as a model for a few months, I'd never heard of *fit models*. "I mean, we do fittings too."

"Yes, we do—but when we do a fitting it's because we've been booked for a job and the client wants to be sure the clothes will fit us properly on the day of the booking, right?"

I nodded.

"Well, for a fit model," Ellie explained, "it's different. They don't work for the magazines or do advertising for fashion designers or for the shows. They stay behind the scenes, trying samples, standing still while a designer drapes the fabric on them to see how an outfit will look."

"Like a living, breathing mannequin?"

Ellie nodded. "Exactly. But my point is, even back in the 1960s, there was already a big difference between the two. Fashion modeling was the glamorous, jet-set big sister to anonymous, behind-the-scenes fit modeling. And if anything, the gulf between the two is even bigger today. So while Clarissa was a big star—for her style, glamour, and modeling work—Johnny's nanny would have been standing in a showroom or atelier all day, never leaving London. Honestly, fit models and fashion models never did, and still don't, have anything to do with each other."

Sometimes, when Ellie gets into her "fashion expert" mode, she might just as well be speaking Chinese or Russian. I was always amazed by how much she knew, not just about vintage clothing, but about the business in general. Even its history.

She laughed when she saw my face. "Welcome to the world of fashion, Axelle!"

"Thanks. By the way, you don't happen to know her name, do you?"

"The nanny's name? Hmm...Jane. But I don't remember her surname. I didn't speak to her much—just hi and bye—but she's often hovering in the background during the shows."

"And you're sure she never modeled for any of the magazines?" Although many of the magazines that Ellie and I worked for didn't exist back then, a few—like *Vogue* and *Harper's Bazaar*—did. I could possibly track the nanny down through the magazines' vast archives.

Ellie shrugged her shoulders. "I can try to figure out more information about her if you'd like."

"Yes, please."

"No problem. But why the interest in Johnny's childhood, Axelle? Do you really think it has something to do with what's happened to Gavin?"

"To be honest, at this point there are a couple of leads I'm looking into..."

"But...?"

I turned and looked at Ellie. "But my instincts tell me Johnny Vane is the key to cracking this case." I fingered the photo in my pocket. "I just don't know how—yet."

I wanted to see if I could walk to the pavilion I'd seen from across the river, so Ellie and I turned left at Parliament Square, then walked until we reached a small park, the Victoria Tower Gardens, attached to the western end of the Palace of Westminster. I'd hoped to be able to cross the park and reach the pavilion, but it was impossible. Because of its proximity to the Houses of Parliament, it was closed off to all public access. So Ellie and I walked back to Big Ben and stood among the tourists to admire it.

I'd seen a photo in the newspaper a few days back that had shown four cleaners washing the face of the enormous clock. As I gazed upward, I couldn't help remarking that there was no way I'd ever dangle from a rope like that.

"Not unless you were after a clue," Ellie said as she turned to look at me, a smile in her eyes. "Under those circumstances I bet you wouldn't even bother with a rope before climbing out there."

I laughed. "You might have a point."

TUESDAY EVENING
Burgers and More

Ellie and I had parted ways under Big Ben. We both had early fittings with Belle La Lune the following day, plus Ellie was jet-lagged. But before going home to Notting Hill, I thought I'd drop by my agency. It was on the way, and with a bit of luck, I might have Charlotte's undivided attention for a few minutes to ask her more questions before she left for the day.

Halley and I rushed to the Tube and caught a Circle line train to Sloane Square. From there we walked down King's Road until I reached the small, leafy lane just off it that housed Thunder.

I swung open the heavy glass door and was immediately thrust into the hyper-busy and buzzing world of fashion. The usual soundtrack of hip-hop music was playing in the background, and I could see Charlotte's brother Charlie in a meeting with a client through the glass wall of his office across the room. He gave me a quick wave as I walked in and asked Emily at reception if I could see Charlotte. All the bookers, including Jazz, sat at two long, adjoining tables in the middle of the main room. Headsets in place, fingers tapping at their computer keyboards, they were all concentrating on the booking task at hand, occasionally looking up to wave or smile or blow a kiss at the various models walking in and out of the room.

While I waited for Charlotte, I wandered over to the wall of zed cards behind the booking tables. I'd finally had a proper zed card printed after I came back from New York, but seeing images of myself all made up with perfect hair and makeup, in color on a professionally printed glossy card, still kind of freaked me out.

"Axelle, Charlotte is ready for you," Emily said as she bent to greet Halley. "Would you like a cup of tea?"

I thanked her and accepted the offer of tea (peppermint), then followed her to Charlotte's office.

Charlotte waved me in with one hand. Her other hand was holding her cell phone to her ear. Her mane of red hair was free, her heels high, and her clothes black. This was Charlotte's preferred uniform.

"So, Axelle," she said after setting her phone down on her large chrome-and-glass desk, "first things first—we're in luck. I've just heard back about Gavin's brief. I had to call in a favor because no magazine gives out details from its shoots—at least not before the story has run. But don't worry," she continued quickly when she saw my look of concern, "the favor was long overdue. Anyway, Gavin was indeed hired by *Harper's Bazaar* to shoot a profile piece on Johnny Vane. It's meant to coincide with the upcoming anniversary—it's twenty years since Johnny opened his first shop in Marylebone—just downstairs from where you'll have your casting tomorrow morning, in fact."

I started to interrupt her and she smiled. "Yes, I did get you a casting appointment, but it doesn't look like Johnny's going to be there, unfortunately. He'll be at Big Sky Studio all day tomorrow overseeing the shooting of his autumn-winter ad campaign, but you should do the casting regardless."

"That's fine," I said. I could ask questions whether or not he was there.

"Anyway," she continued in her deep voice, "to get back to Gavin's booking for *Harper's Bazaar*… According to my source, there was absolutely nothing in the brief about Johnny's childhood. What *Harper's Bazaar* did specifically ask for were a few good new portraits of Johnny, as well as some shots of him working. They have plenty of photographs from his early days in their own archives."

My mind was running in circles as the information buzzed through my head. So Gavin hadn't been asked to shoot the old photo for the *Harper's Bazaar* job. What was it about that picture that I was not yet seeing?

That thought promptly raised another one. How had Gavin gotten hold of the photo in the first place?

Of course, the most obvious answer was that he had snapped it at Johnny's house when he'd taken Johnny's portrait. But then why wasn't it in a silver frame, like the other photos I could see in the background of some of Gavin's pictures? And why was there a manila envelope underneath it? And if he had snapped it at Johnny's house, had someone shown him the photo? If so, why?

"Axelle? Is everything okay?" Charlotte asked.

"I'm sorry. Yes, Charlotte, everything's fine. And you've been a huge help. It's just…your information got me thinking about other things I must look into." As I smiled and tried to slow the thoughts whizzing through my mind, Emily knocked on the door and entered with my peppermint tea and a biscuit for Halley.

Changing the subject, I asked, "Charlotte, what can you tell me about Johnny's childhood? And his sister, Georgiana?"

"Johnny's childhood? Hmm… Well," she said as she turned to her computer and googled him. (At least I presumed that's what she was doing.) "I know that his parents were a bit grand—although of slightly diminished means. Johnny himself likes to come across as edgy and bohemian, but he can be quite posh when he decides to be. Apart from that, I know he suffered some early tragedy—deaths in his family…"

She was momentarily quiet as she read her screen. "Yes, here it is. His parents and twin brother died when he was young. How sad. How he's managed to overcome so much, I don't know." She turned away from her computer and continued.

"I know he went to Central Saint Martins, and of

course, his mother was a real fashionista before the term even existed. As for Johnny, I think the word 'partying' probably sums up his early adulthood. He was constantly in and out of clubs, but still designing all the time. When he started really applying himself, the business grew, and today he's considered a pillar of British fashion. He's mentored a new wave of designers, including Jorge Cruz. If he continues as he has, he'll probably get a knighthood or an award from the Queen."

As I finished my tea, Charlotte leaned across her desk and said, "And that's why you need to tread carefully, like I said earlier. If you *are* working on a case, then as your modeling-detective agent"—she smiled at her job description—"I'm asking you to please remain tight-lipped and totally discreet until you're absolutely sure of your facts. I need hardly to tell you that fashion people often have huge egos. An accusation of any kind—especially a false one—will not be taken lightly. Okay?"

"Yes," I answered, and I meant it. The last thing I intended to do was jeopardize my detective career with an ill-informed accusation. In the gossipy world of fashion, I'd be more untouchable than polyester within about a minute.

She paused for a moment, then continued. "Is there anything else I can help you with?"

I nodded, pulling myself together. "Georgiana."

"Right. She's a bit of a dark horse—and by the way, everyone calls her Georgie. I don't know her very well.

She keeps out of the spotlight. She works at Johnny's in publicity, in the building where you'll be going for your casting tomorrow. And, honestly, considering how long she's been at her job, she can't be all that good. In all the years she's worked there, she's never advanced beyond her present position."

Hmm…I wondered if there would be some way for me to "accidentally" meet Georgie tomorrow at the Vane headquarters. For a moment I entertained the thought of using my school magazine, the *Notting Hill News*, as an excuse to interview her. But would a member of a famous fashion family really give me a few sound bites for a school magazine? I doubted it.

"Other than that, I don't know anything about her. She certainly doesn't go out and about."

"Thanks, Charlotte." Then remembering another question, I changed tack. "By the way, does a muse get paid?"

Charlotte laughed. "That came out of nowhere!" I watched as she got up and walked to the bookcases behind her desk and pulled out a book.

"Well, there's Amanda Harlech, she's a muse to Chanel's creative director, and she has some sort of salary. But this," she said as she handed me a book, "should answer any questions you may have about what a muse is or does. The exhibition was fab, by the way."

I took the large-format, hardcover book from her hands. It had been published by Yale University Press, and the title said it all: *Model as Muse: Embodying Fashion*. It was actually the catalog for an exhibition some years ago at the Metropolitan Museum of Art in New York City. The entire book was about models who were also muses to the fashion elite.

"Take it and read it," Charlotte said. "You can bring it back when you're finished with it."

"Thank you, Charlotte."

"You're welcome. I hope it helps…" Her voice trailed off as her direct line rang. I watched her as she took the call. "Great, thanks," she said as she looked at me and gave me a thumbs-up. "I'll tell her now."

She hung up and said, "Good news, Axelle. That was Jacky calling to book you for the *Teen Chic* shoot with Josh Locke. You'll work for three hours tomorrow afternoon at Spring Studios."

My mouth dropped open. Booked? Me? For *Teen Chic* tomorrow? With *Josh Locke*!

Argh!

Why? Why was I booked when he and I clearly didn't get along and when Jacky Sykes had barely acknowledged my existence at the casting?

"Jacky says you met Josh at the casting, you lucky girl! How could you keep that a secret?"

Easily, I thought, because (A) I never imagined I'd be booked for the job; (B) Josh Locke is painfully arrogant; and (C) I had a case to solve—and therefore other things to think about.

Speaking of which, the case was shaping up to be a really meaty one, so I was going to need every minute I could get to solve it before Gavin was targeted again—but now my week was filling up with bookings!

"Axelle, you're the only model I know who'd look so miserable after hearing such fab news," Charlotte said, laughing. "But I'm sure you'll have fun at the booking. After all, everyone loves Josh Locke."

Grrr…

I needed to vent, so after leaving the agency I called my BFF and neighbor Jenny Watanabe for some support. As I walked to the Tube, I told her all about my *Teen Chic* casting and how Josh Locke's fame seemed to affect everyone in his orbit.

"You should have seen them. The models were preening, the reptilian editor was giggling, and a dozen people were listening at the door!"

"Yeah, but, Axelle, he's Josh Locke," Jenny said. "He's famous! Of course people watch his every move and hide behind doors listening to him."

"But it's like a circus around him…and he just acts like that's normal!"

I could feel Jenny rolling her eyes on the other end of the line. "He can't help it. It's a by-product of what he does—which, may I remind you, is write and sing songs that millions of people love. Cut him some slack."

"Jenny, you weren't there, but trust me, the atmosphere around him is weird—plus he knocked me down flat and then said it was my fault! The guy's ego is ridiculous, and I'll be stuck working with him all afternoon!"

"Do you always have to take things so seriously? I mean, come on, any girl from our school would love to spend an afternoon with him."

"Well, I'd be happy to swap places with them."

I heard Jenny sigh loudly. "You know what I'm thinking right now, Axelle?"

"I'm not sure I want to."

"I'm thinking that you're the one always saying that there's more to people than you see on the surface. That most people have an entire inner world that we can only guess at."

"Thanks, Jenny—but that's when I'm talking about people's motives and actions. As in a mystery."

"Yeah, well, how would it be if you applied that logic to people in general—whether or not they're suspects in a case? Does someone have to commit a crime before you really want to talk to them?"

"No, but it helps." I couldn't keep from smiling.

"You're twisted, Axelle," Jenny answered with a laugh. "Do yourself a favor and cut those of us who haven't committed a crime some slack, will you?"

I took the Tube back to Notting Hill Gate and walked home from there. Then, after feeding Halley and making myself a cup of tea, I went upstairs to my bedroom and lay down on my bed.

Thoughts of Gavin, Johnny Vane, and the images on

the flash drive were on my mind as I flipped through the book Charlotte had lent me.

But I snapped out of my thoughts with a start when the doorbell rang a while later, setting Halley off down the stairs barking. I instantly knew who it was.

Sebastian.

My heart began to race as I vividly recalled the last time we'd been together: on top of the Empire State Building—kissing. And, although it had taken us a long time to get to the viewing platform on the eighty-sixth floor (the lifts are old and slow, and there are various checkpoints to go through), our kiss had lasted way, way longer. And then, when we'd finally stopped, laid out all around us was the most amazing sunset ever. The entire city had shimmered in the orange light.

But that was three months ago…before Sebastian returned to Paris and I came home to London. And although we'd Skyped a lot between then and now, video calls didn't have the same romance factor. It wasn't the same as *seeing* someone, was it? How easily *can* you see someone who lives three hundred miles away in a whole other country—not to mention the time zones? (Okay, so there's only a one-hour difference, but still.)

But now finally Sebastian was here to see me. He'd arrived late this afternoon on a Eurostar train. We hadn't been able to arrange anything sooner because of my exams, so we'd been planning this trip for a long time.

I got off my bed and went downstairs, nervous about what to expect. I ran a hand through my hair, took a deep breath, and opened the front door.

He stood at the top of our steps, just as tall, broad-shouldered, and biker-boy cute as I remembered, hair tousled, leather jacket on, smiling at me. And although there was a bit of shuffling around and eyeing each other as I invited him in (FYI: seeing the person you fancy like mad for the first time after months apart is *weird*), soon enough, we were standing face-to-face, close enough that I could smell him.

And suddenly it was as if time and distance had never intervened. Sebastian reached out and pulled me to him. I'd be lying if I said I didn't go weak in the knees. He had that kind of effect on me. After a long hug, he pulled back and gently pushed my hair behind my ears as he smiled at me in that slow, tender way he has. "I've missed you, Holmes," he said. But I didn't get a chance to answer because his hand suddenly dropped from my face as if it were a hot coal and his eyes darted to something behind me.

"Why, Sebastian! How lovely to see you!"

Of course. It was my mom.

Honestly, I thought as I listened to their small talk, what was the point of finally being in the same city if we couldn't even have five minutes alone together?

"So, are you excited about seeing the London sights?" Mom asked.

Sebastian's eyes darted to me quickly before he politely answered. "Uh, yes, Mrs. Anderson, thank you. I'm looking forward to it."

"Anything in particular? Which exhibitions do you have lined up?" I bit my tongue as I heard my mom quiz Sebastian. But as always, he was prepared.

"Well, I'm especially looking forward to seeing Rubens at the National Gallery, and Tracey Emin at the Hayward Gallery."

"Well, that sounds like a good plan," Mom answered. She was smiling but I could tell she was surprised—even pleased—by his perfect answer. She quickly moved on. "And how do you like Bloomsbury? Axelle tells me you're staying there with an aunt…" The chitchat continued for a few more minutes until Mom's phone rang and she answered it.

There was a moment of awkward silence as my mom left the room. It was as if she'd broken the spell. But then Sebastian suggested we grab a bite to eat, an idea I jumped on. I was hungry, in need of some fresh air, and eager to escape from Mom.

"I'm starving," he said. "I only had a sandwich on the Eurostar. Can we get a burger anywhere near here?"

At least one thing would never change, no matter the distance between us, I thought ruefully: our mutual love of a good burger and hot fries. "Absolutely, Watson. Follow me."

I made for the door as quickly as possible after a

quick good-bye to Halley. (London is not Paris. You can't just walk to a local restaurant with your dog and sit at a table together, unless you're outdoors. In Paris, it's *jamais un problème!*) But if I was hoping Mom would let us go without sticking her oar in again, I was wrong. Her head popped around the kitchen doorway as we were making our escape.

"Not longer than two hours, please, Axelle. You have to be in Mayfair for your show fitting with Belle La Lune at eight thirty a.m. We'll have to leave at seven forty-five to get across town in time. Sebastian, it was lovely to see you—though I'm sure I'll see a lot more of you this week."

Believe it or not, my mom said that bit about seeing Sebastian all week without the tiniest trace of a corny smile or wink.

While she'd been thrilled when I first met Sebastian in Paris, now after months of watching us struggle to spend time together—and not really succeeding—my mom had finally intervened and told me that she felt I was too young to have a boyfriend who lived so far away.

"You should be going out and having fun, Axelle—here and now—making the most of your opportunities and making new friends, not glued to your phone waiting to speak to someone who lives three hundred miles away…"

That was the part of her argument that always made me roll my eyes, because what seemed to fly completely over my mom's head was the fact that I'm not glued to my phone waiting for Sebastian to call. I'm glued to it hoping someone will call with a new mystery for me to solve.

Grrr! Mom!

We shut the door behind us and walked out through the front gate and onto the street. As we turned right and walked past St. Stephen's Church, I realized we were the only people around. The street was empty. Sebastian must have noticed too, because he grabbed my hand and pulled me into a huge rosebush that was growing wild over a wall. He dipped his head toward mine. My heart skipped a beat (okay, maybe a few)… But just as we were about to kiss, the vicar from St. Stephen's appeared as if from nowhere. "Axelle, good evening!" he called from across the road. "What a lovely time of year. Summer's in the air, isn't it?"

I was red in the face and flustered, only able to nod and wave as the vicar went on his way, but Sebastian just laughed. "And I thought being in the same city would make kissing easier," he said. "Come on, let's go get a burger."

Two minutes later I pushed open the swinging door to my favorite local hamburger joint, the Lucky Seven Diner ("the most authentic diner experience this side of the Brooklyn Bridge"), and let the smell of cheeseburgers, fries, and milk shakes waft over me for a moment before sliding into the nearest available booth (which was, in fact, the only available booth).

Sebastian and I placed our orders—cheeseburger with Kraft cheese for me, a bacon cheeseburger with Monterey Jack cheese for Sebastian, and a side of fries for both of us. I couldn't wait to tell him about the new case. It would no doubt take Sebastian by surprise and definitely mess with our sightseeing plans. Apart from the exhibitions he'd told my mom about, we'd planned to go on the London Eye, see a play that a friend of his aunt's was performing in, and take a day trip to Oxford. But regardless, I was certain he wouldn't mind. After all, he was as eager to be a crime journalist as I was to be a detective—and since both occupations complemented each other, solving cases was fun to share.

"Your eyes are sparkling, Holmes. And as much as I'd like to think it was due to me, I think there's more to it than that, isn't there?"

Of course I wasn't immune to the way his gray-blue eyes crinkled at the corners as he smiled at me from across the table, or how his tousled, light-brown hair looked totally touchable... Then again, a case is a case—and romance aside, it was time to get working.

"Actually, Watson, someone came to see me this morning..."

I'd brought my laptop along, so after bringing Sebastian up to speed on my meeting with Tallulah that morning, we started on our vanilla milk shakes while scrolling through the images on Gavin's flash drive.

"How do you start figuring this one out?" Sebastian

asked as we stopped at the last image—the photo of the old photo. He ruffled his hair and leaned back in the banquette opposite me. "From everything you've told me, this case seems about as murky as the Thames."

"Hmm…it could be, yeah…but on the other hand we're lucky to have a fixed location."

Sebastian raised his eyebrows at me.

"We know more or less where Gavin was attacked, and we have specific times for where he was that morning."

"Not that that tells us much…"

"Well, not yet, but still, I think it's safe to deduce that the location by the Thames must have some kind of link to what happened—especially since his shoes and jeans were wet."

"You think he stepped into the river?"

"Maybe…" I suddenly remembered a thought I'd had earlier. I typed *Thames tides* into Google. A few moments later I clicked onto a site that listed the precise times for high and low tides for the entire year. "Look… the tide was at its lowest that Sunday morning." I turned my laptop so that Sebastian could read it. "I know it's possible to get right down to the waterline if the tide is low and you're in the right place. And there must be a few points with direct public access to the water near Westminster Palace. I just don't know where exactly."

"That's something I can look into tomorrow," Sebastian said.

"Thanks. That would be great."

"And what about Johnny Vane? Have you ever met him or worked with him?"

I shook my head. "Not yet—but I've already been warned to be careful around him." As I pulled my laptop back toward me and started bringing up information on Johnny Vane, I quickly told Sebastian about my conversation with Charlotte. Sebastian slid onto the banquette next to me and watched as Johnny's Wiki page came up. Trying to ignore Sebastian's warmth and his nice smell (leather, trees, and adventure, mixed with a light touch of French sophistication), I sat next to him as we read the piece I'd looked at on the Tube earlier in the afternoon.

"So he lost his father, his twin, and his mother in quick succession. How horrible," Sebastian said as he came to the end of the piece.

"True…but…" There was something I found odd now that I was rereading Johnny's entry.

"But?" Sebastian said.

"Well, at least his father's death has a clear medical explanation: 'heart attack,' right?"

"Yes."

"And it states that he died at his club after supper…"

"So?"

"So his brother 'drowned' and his mother 'died in an accident at their home.' Those descriptions both sound fairly vague, don't you think? Like, *where* did Julian drown? And what kind of accident did Clarissa have? And take a look at this…" I clicked onto Clarissa Vane's page and waited while Sebastian studied the photos of her early modeling career and read about her jet-setting days as a fashion muse.

"She was beautiful," he said.

"She was. But again there are no specific details about the way she died."

"Should there be?"

"Well, if Johnny's father's death was clearly documented, then why not the deaths of Johnny's mother and brother?"

Drowned. The word kept turning in my mind. I went back to the file with Gavin's pictures and scrolled down to the old photo. "I mean, look. I'm pretty sure the boys are standing in the Thames here. And the fact that Gavin focused on this particular image makes me wonder whether that's where Julian drowned."

"You're thinking it could have happened near Westminster? Where Gavin was found?"

"Something like that, yes," I said before turning back to my computer. "Maybe that's why Gavin was there. Maybe there's some connection."

Sebastian raised his eyebrows at me.

"You don't have to give me that look, Watson. I know I'm leaping to a lot of conclusions," I told him. "Of course, for all I know Julian could have died in the bathtub at home. Either way, I think we should find out what exactly happened to him and his mom. Old newspaper clippings might be a good place to start. The deaths must have been reported somewhere." Quickly I checked the references at the bottom of the Wikipedia article.

"Hmm…" I said as I motioned to Sebastian to look at my screen again. "For the deaths of his mother and twin brother, they list an old article in *Vogue* as their reference. But"—I rapidly scrolled down to where they mentioned his father's death—"here they list the *Times*."

"So?"

"So his father's death came first, right?"

Sebastian nodded. "I think I see what you're getting at, Holmes. No newspaper—and certainly not the *Times*—would have let the subsequent deaths of James Vane's son and wife go unreported. Three tragedies make too good a story to miss, and the journalists couldn't have resisted linking them together. So the *Times* archive must have the details of all three deaths."

"That's exactly what I'm thinking, Watson. Let me have a quick look…"

I tried searching for old articles about the Vanes—with no luck.

"It's not that easy," Sebastian said. "To access old material, you need to subscribe to the archive that's storing it or ask them directly. But that's something I'm good at. I'll access the *Times* archive online first thing tomorrow morning and start with that. Anything else I can do?"

I nodded as I finished my milk shake. "It would help if you could find out more about Gavin's background, friends, and so on. I know the police have been looking into it—although Tallulah is convinced they're only going through the motions—and I've been through his phone and emails, but there may be something we've both missed, or that he kept well hidden."

"I can look into his background, no problem."

I went back to studying the old photo again. I just couldn't seem to leave it alone. There was part of a brownish ring in its upper left-hand corner that I'd noticed when I was on the Tube earlier. Now, in the bright-neon light of the diner, it looked like a stain from a cup of coffee or tea—and it didn't look old. To my eye, the ring appeared too dark and well defined to have been made years ago.

"You're convinced there's something more to this picture, aren't you, Holmes?"

I shrugged. "Well, why did Gavin include it on the stick when it wasn't part of his *Harper's Bazaar* brief?"

"Maybe he just liked it?"

"Tallulah said the photos on the stick were an edited selection. He sent the same choice of images, minus the old one, to *Harper's Bazaar*. She checked his emails."

"The old one really wasn't part of the shoot then…so why include it on the stick?"

"Exactly, Watson."

Sebastian had finished his milk shake and sat quietly watching me. "What are you thinking about now, Holmes?" he finally asked.

"Still the past, Watson."

Sebastian waited silently for me to continue.

"Let's assume for a moment that Gavin discovered something thanks to the old photograph, that maybe the photo is a clue to something important that happened around the time it was taken…"

"Go on."

"Well, maybe someone wants to keep Gavin's 'discovery' hidden. Maybe *that's* why he was attacked. Maybe it was about more than just stealing the flash drive—maybe they were trying to silence him."

Sebastian's expression was grim. "You're talking about attempted murder."

"I know," I said. Hearing Sebastian say out loud what had been floating at the back of my mind for a few hours sent a shiver down my spine, but it meant this case was now even more urgent. I had a sudden thought. "Do you think you could find out if anyone besides close friends and family has called the hospital or tried to visit Gavin?"

Sebastian raised his eyebrows at me.

"Better to be safe than sorry," I said. "If they tried to get him once, surely there's a chance they'll try again."

"Good point, Holmes," Sebastian said, turning toward me, his voice low. "But if you're right about Johnny's brother and mother, how do you solve a mystery that happened in the past?"

"I don't know, but I guess I'll have to find out."

As we spoke I continued to search online and noticed something that had escaped me while I'd been researching on the Tube earlier: *Clarissa Vane's only sibling is the fashion stylist Caro Moretti (née Carolyne Ryder).*

I knew Caro! I'd met her when I was in New York doing the shows (and solving my last case). She's been styling for Jorge Cruz since he first began designing and would no doubt be in London to help him with his resort collection show later this week. There was even a good chance I'd see her tomorrow at my Jorge Cruz fitting. But what a surprise to learn that Clarissa Vane was her sister! Even Charlotte hadn't mentioned it. Then again, their names were so different, and Clarissa had died so long ago that I supposed not many people knew or remembered.

Caro was also the only surviving relative of Johnny and Georgie mentioned online. Could she have become their guardian after Clarissa died? If I could find a moment or two during my fitting, I definitely needed to ask her some questions.

"So, what's the plan?" Sebastian asked after I'd told him about Caro Moretti.

"Well, it's important to establish who the children in the picture are, and I should have the perfect opportunity to do that when I see Caro tomorrow."

"And what about finding out where it was taken?"

"I looked a bit today, but maybe tomorrow one of us can go farther up and down the river…perhaps at the end of the day sometime."

"That's fine with me. By the way, Holmes, can I have my own copy of the photo?"

I pushed my copy of the old picture to him.

"Thanks. So I'll start with hunting down the newspaper reports. That seems to be most important. And what about you? Do you have lots of appointments?"

"I have a fitting with Belle La Lune first thing. I'm hoping that, knowing the business as she does, she might be able to tell me something about the Vanes."

"When will you see Caro?"

"After Belle, I go straight to my Jorge Cruz fitting. I expect Caro will be there, so I'll take another copy of the photo with me."

"And after that?"

"After that I'm off to Marylebone to the Johnny Vane head office. Johnny won't be there, but I want to check out his headquarters. I may able to ask a few questions and hopefully find a way to meet his sister, Georgie. Anyway, my castings are all in the morning. Then in the afternoon, I have a three-hour booking across town for *Teen Chic*." *With Josh Locke*, I reminded myself. *Argh!*

Sebastian nodded. "Good. So while you're doing that, I'll look into Gavin's background and check out the situation at the hospital. Shall I try to find out exactly where Johnny grew up?"

"Yes, Watson, that would be helpful." I thought again of how Johnny had grown up in Notting Hill. "He can't have lived far from here. Hopefully the address will be given in the reports you'll find. And…"

"Yes?"

"Maybe you could try tracing the Vane nanny too. Apparently she's still very close to Johnny. Ellie said her name was Jane."

Sebastian nodded. "Will do…" Then he went quiet for a moment before asking, "And what about actually spending some time with you? Is that going to happen at all?"

His voice was teasing—but his eyes weren't. A pang of guilt shot through me as I looked at him. I thought again of how often I'd complained lately about us never seeing each other…and yet here he was, in the flesh and right in front of me—and I had a case to solve! I wanted to be with him—badly—but I also had to get Gavin out of danger. *Argh!*

"How about meeting for lunch and going over whatever new leads we'll have gathered by then? I'll have some time between my morning castings and the *Teen Chic* shoot."

"Perfect. I'll take whatever I can get," he said, smiling. "I suppose this is what happens when you date an undercover model. So where should we meet?"

"That depends on what we find out between now and then…and where it leads us next."

"Good point, Holmes. So it sounds like we have a plan."

"Yes, we do, Watson." I smiled.

What we didn't have a plan for was how to say good night.

As we left the diner, Sebastian slipped his leather jacket gently around my shoulders. He took my hand, and we walked the short distance to my house in silence.

At first it was a bit uncomfortable standing outside my house with him. Saying good-bye in person and saying good-bye on Skype are two very different scenarios—and we were more used to Skype. But finally Sebastian stepped forward and gently ran his finger down the side of my face, cupped my chin in his hand, and gave me *that* look. I nearly melted under his touch.

He slowly ran his hands down my sides until they settled around my waist. Then he leaned into me and kissed me hard. This, I thought as I felt his lips move over mine, is what it should be like to be with someone—so much better than lots of wishful thinking over a cold computer screen.

Even though I really, really liked Sebastian, I didn't like how little time we spent together, and how that made both of us upset. Have you ever spent three months apart from the person you like? And is it possible to stay together with someone when you know that you'll only get to see them for a few days every couple of months at best? I got depressed just thinking about it.

We finally pulled apart and stood gazing at each other—or rather, Sebastian gazed at me. I was too fidgety and couldn't hold his stare. The night was bright. The high moonlight overhead illuminated the houses and church on my street with a pale, silver light as we stood in the shadows thrown by the rosebushes that grow like wild-haired sentries on either side of my gate.

"I'll look into everything we discussed," Sebastian said. We both edged out of the shadows and into the bright light of the pavement as he spoke. "And then meet you for lunch."

"I'll send you a message as soon as I've finished my appointment at Johnny Vane, speaking of which—"

He interrupted before I finished my sentence. "Don't worry," he said quickly. "I know, if I find out anything important I'll message you. Right away—I promise."

I smiled. It was nice to work with someone who knew me so well.

"Good, thanks."

I slipped his jacket off my shoulders and handed it back to him. He leaned into me quickly and kissed me on the cheek.

"*À demain*, Holmes."

"*À demain*, Watson."

I watched him turn and leave before I started toward my door.

But as I reached for my key I heard him call out to me softly. "Axelle?"

I turned back and faced him.

"It was nice to see you tonight." Then he smiled and disappeared.

Same here, Sebastian, I thought as I pushed open my front door and Halley hurled herself at me.

WEDNESDAY MORNING

Seen from the Side

As I woke up bright and early, the images from Gavin's flash drive kept flitting through my mind—although Halley's enthusiastic morning greeting did push them out of focus for a few minutes.

Waking up with Halley always involved lots of dog kisses all over my face and ears, as well as some excited jumping around on my bed. I tried to get into the shower before too long, however, because as cute as Halley is, West Highland white terrier saliva smells quite strong when it dries on your face.

Foremost on my mind as I got ready was how I was going to manage to meet Johnny Vane. Charlotte hadn't sounded too positive about me actually seeing him at his offices today, but I needn't have worried. As it turned out, Belle La Lune arranged an introduction.

Belle—like Jorge Cruz and Marc Jacobs—was in London to present her resort fashion show. Fashion houses sometimes travel to other cities to show their resort and pre-fall collections in between their normal spring-summer and autumn-winter collections. For example, Chanel and Christian Dior, both Paris-based fashion houses, have shown their resort and pre-fall collections in cities far from home, like Vienna and New York City—even Dubai.

This time around, Belle was opting to show the La Lune resort collection in their new London store, which was why my appointment to meet her was at the very fashionable Connaught Hotel, just around the corner from her store in Mayfair. She'd brought a large part of her in-house team with her. Belle wasn't just staying at the Connaught; she was holding her castings and fittings there too.

As my mom drove down Porchester Road and cut through Hyde Park, I read the message Tallulah had just sent me:

> Any progress? I'm going to see Gavin later. I'll let you know how he is… PS: I didn't know you were going to Chic House yesterday—looks like you had fun!

Fun? What was she talking about? I wrote back:

> Some progress, yes, but expect more later today. I'm following a couple of strong leads. And yes, I was at Chic House yesterday—for a casting.

I refrained from mentioning that "fun" was the last word I'd use to describe the tedious meeting with

Jacky—followed by my annoying encounter with Josh Locke.

Tallulah wrote back right away:

> **Great news. I definitely want to hear more info as soon as you have it...BTW since when do castings involve holding hands with major pop stars?**

Now what was she talking about? I wrote back and she answered with a link. I clicked on it and found a photo of myself, cropped at the knees and shown from the side. If you knew me well, you could tell it was me. Otherwise, I was hard to identify. But one thing was clear: it looked as if Josh and I were holding hands and gazing, love struck, into each other's eyes. Worst of all was the caption underneath the photo: *Does Josh Locke have a new mystery love?*

We must have been snapped by the paparazzi just after he pulled me up outside the revolving door. I was standing on my own two feet, but I remember he'd held on to my hands while I regained my balance.

What would Sebastian think if he saw this photo?

ARGH!

"Axelle, is everything all right?" my mom asked. "You've gotten awfully quiet."

As if I didn't have enough on my plate between my new case and all the castings and bookings Thunder kept throwing at me—now I had this to deal with too!

The only bright spot in the whole mess was that I was unidentified. Besides upsetting Sebastian, the last thing I wanted was a team of paparazzi following me around as I tried to fly under the radar and search for clues.

In answer to my mom's question, I held out my phone to show her the picture.

"Darling, it's Josh Locke! You didn't tell me you knew him—and judging by that photo, I have to say it seems you know him quite well. When were you going to tell me?"

It took all my self-control not to jump out of our car. "Mom, I met Josh Locke yesterday *accidentally* at my *Teen Chic* casting. I spoke to him for, like, five minutes, because he ran into me and knocked me over just as I was stepping outside. Some random paparazzo must have been lurking behind a car or something and taken these pictures with a telephoto lens."

"It certainly looks romantic.… Does Sebastian know?"

"I hope not. And, unfortunately, I'm going to work with Josh Locke today. For some bizarre reason, *Teen Chic* booked me for the job."

"Then he must like you." Mom smiled at me.

I looked at her. Honestly, what planet did she come from? And could she ever—*ever*—see things from my perspective for just one minute? "Mom, he's so arrogant. Trust me, we did not get along. I couldn't believe it when Charlotte confirmed the booking, because the editor hardly stopped talking on the phone long enough to take a proper look at me."

"Oh, Axelle, I've heard Josh Locke is absolutely charming. I'm sure he's not arrogant. He's famous—that's different."

I rolled my eyes. My mom was such a closet celebrity fan that it almost hurt. "Anyway," she continued, "at least you're not mentioned by name, so I doubt you'll have any paparazzi following you around today—or jealous fans." She giggled. "He must have masses."

I hadn't even thought of the jealous fan scenario. I was quiet for a moment before answering. "Well, that's something anyway." *And that's how it's going to stay*, I thought. As soon as I saw Josh, I planned to give him a piece of my mind. The last thing I wanted was the extra attention that having my name linked with his would bring.

I'd never been to the Connaught Hotel before. It was a grand old brick-and-stone building with a spotless facade and liveried footmen standing at attention by the elegant door. The Connaught is located on a small, pretty square called Carlos Place and looked like it had come straight out of an old black-and-white film. If Audrey Hepburn had stepped out, impeccably dressed in one of her Givenchy frocks, I wouldn't have been surprised. Along with Claridge's, it was one of the two London hotels that discerning fashionistas preferred. Both hotels are located in Mayfair, just around the corner from some of London's most expensive shops.

"Don't forget to say hello to Belle for me," Mom said as we pulled up in front of the Connaught's discreet columned entrance. "And I would love to see the show," she added with a pointed smile.

This was her hint that I was supposed to ask Belle for a ticket to see her resort show. Of course, knowing Belle, she'd already have one reserved for my mom. Since I saved her life in Paris, Belle had taken a strong interest in my life and career—my *detective* career, that is. Not that she ignored my modeling work. The casting request was proof of that. But Belle understood that for me, modeling was just a way to (hopefully) solve some juicy fashion mysteries—and I loved her for that.

"And, Axelle, love?"

"Yes, Mom?"

"I know you're upset about the photo, but it's not as bad as you think. No one will recognize you. Call me if you run into any problems, all right?"

"Thanks, Mom."

I walked into the hotel, gave my name at the reception desk, and was directed to a suite of rooms on the top floor. Once there, the hushed calm of the elegant hotel came to an abrupt end.

I was ushered into an enormous suite vibrating with music, frenzied chatter, and laughter. It was crowded with clothes and people, some holding folders and notebooks, others with pins in their mouths, others talking into their phones or taking photos. And there in the middle of the friendly storm was Belle, bent over and snipping into a dress with long steel scissors while the model wearing it watched her with wide eyes. A pair of seamstresses stood by, and Belle's long blond hair kept falling into her eyes, until one of the seamstresses tied it back for her.

"Axelle, *bonjour*," Belle said as she got up to hug me. "Great that you're here! Julia, would you show Axelle her outfit, please?" she asked in her lightly lilting French accent before turning back to me and adding more quietly, "And you are not to leave until we've had a moment to catch up, all right?" Before I could answer, she'd been whisked away by yet another assistant.

As I slipped into a featherlight, multicolored tunic, I couldn't help checking my phone in case Sebastian had found something out. *Then again, Axelle*, I told myself, *it's not even nine o'clock yet. How much could he have unearthed by now?*

The stylist finished fastening the tiny buckles on my coral suede heels, and I walked across to see Belle.

"What's going on, Axelle?" she asked. "You look like you have something on your mind. Am I right?" She looked me in the eyes and smiled as she adjusted a belt round my waist. "Is it to do with work?"

I pursed my lips slightly and Belle laughed.

"Ahh!" she said teasingly. "Might it be something along the lines of what you did for me in Paris?" she asked.

"Maybe."

"And is there some way I can help you?"

I nodded slowly. "Actually, yes there is. I need to talk to Johnny Vane, but he's on a shoot today—their autumn-winter campaign. I've got a casting there later this morning, but I won't get to see him and I really need to. He's linked to the case I'm following up. Anyway, the sooner I can talk to him, the better. Even today might be too late…but he mustn't suspect anything. Have you any idea how I can meet him?"

"Well, I think I can help. In fact, I know I can," she said as she swapped the coral shoes I was wearing for a pair of gold, strappy heels. "There, that's better," she said as she stood back and admired her styling adjustment. "It needed that touch of sparkle. Anyway…listen, Axelle. Are you free this evening?"

"Um…yes, I think so," I said hesitantly. I felt a pang of conscience and hoped Sebastian hadn't already made any plans for us.

"Good, because tonight I'm hosting a summer party and auction at Kensington Gardens to raise money for the La Lune Fashion Design Foundation. Anyone who's anyone in London fashion will be there, along with a good handful of musicians, actors, It girls, our biggest clients, buyers, and…Johnny Vane. If you came, I could make sure to introduce you to him. Would that help?"

Was she kidding? Was black the new black? "Definitely," I said, smiling with gratitude.

"Good. I'm pretty sure Ellie's coming. She's on the guest list. You weren't automatically invited because I know fashion parties aren't really your kind of thing," she said with a laugh.

"True," I said, smiling, "but in this case I'm willing to make an exception." I thought for a moment, then asked, "Belle, could you invite Sebastian too?" I couldn't very well leave him on his own when he'd come all the way to see me, and it would definitely help me to have an extra pair of keen eyes along. Besides, Belle's family has known Sebastian's father, Inspector Witt, for years. Sebastian's hardly a stranger to her.

"Is he in town?" She looked at me, head tilted to the side.

I nodded.

"So I presume he's helping you? On your case?" She added the last question in a whisper.

I nodded.

"Fine. Then why don't you bring him with you this evening, and I'll make sure they let him through."

"Great!" I said as I tried to walk a few steps in the sparkly shoes. "And Belle?"

"*Oui.*" She had a couple of pins in her mouth and was standing back from me, examining the tunic I was wearing through narrowed blue eyes.

"Thank you."

She looked at me and smiled. "It's the least I can do for the person who saved my life, don't you think?" Then she laughed and signaled to me to walk the length of the room.

Belle gave me my hair and makeup times for her show on Thursday, and it was confirmed by Thunder just as I left the Connaught. I stepped out of the hotel feeling as if I was making progress. Okay, maybe *progress* was a bit of a strong word, but I was pushing forward anyway, and that felt good.

Unfortunately the feeling was short-lived. A few minutes later my phone rang. It was Tallulah.

"Axelle, I have some bad news!" she said quickly. "Gavin's life-support machines were found disconnected just before five this morning!" The panic in her voice shot across the airwaves like a live current.

"Is he all right?"

"Yes—for now anyway. He's stable, but it was close. Fortunately, the nurse on duty was immediately alerted by an alarm."

"How did it happen?"

"The hospital doesn't know…" Her voice trailed off. "But I have a bad feeling about this." She was quiet for a moment before saying, "Do you remember what you told me on Tuesday morning?"

"That if given the chance, whoever attacked Gavin on Sunday might try to attack him again?"

"Yes—well, as far as I'm concerned you're right. You have to hurry, Axelle. Please!"

Keeping my voice calm, I promised her I was moving as quickly as I could and then said good-bye.

Panic spread through me as I hung up. It was just as I'd discussed last night with Sebastian. Until I could identify Gavin's attacker, his life was still in danger.

After putting my phone away, I continued the short walk to my appointment for Jorge Cruz. He and his team had just arrived from New York City and had chosen a suite of rooms at Claridge's. And while they were super excited about being in London to show their resort collection at Hampton Court Palace, I was focused on getting a few minutes of question time with Caro. Fortunately, as soon as she saw me, she called me over to her.

"Hi, Axelle," she said as she gave me the fashion double air-kiss and asked what I'd been doing since I last saw her in New York. "I've just seen your pictures for French *Elle*, by the way, and they look great."

Those were the photos I'd shot during my first week of undercover model work, while I'd been in Paris solving my first mystery. I thanked her and tried to get a question in, but it wasn't easy.

Caro had to be in her early sixties, but you'd never have known it. That's the thing about fashionistas—the ones who really know how to put clothes together tend to look timeless. You can't peg their style to any definite age or trend.

For example, Caro was well known for the way she mixed Chanel jackets and hip-hop-inspired sportswear. Furthermore she loved a heavy gold chain and a good ear cuff. If I'd gone by her jewelry alone, i'd never have guessed how old she was. Her raspy voice spoke of years smoking cigarettes, although she'd actually quit some time ago.

"It was so hard," I'd heard her say once. "I was almost

at the point where I would have willingly worn velour just to have a smoke."

But now she was telling me all about how this Jorge Cruz collection had been inspired by Bloomsbury, and how so many other editors and designers were still inspired by Bloomsbury writers and artists such as Virginia Woolf and Vanessa Bell.

Ah! I thought, just the moment I'd been waiting for. Without delay I jumped right in. "Clarissa Vane was a huge inspiration to designers too. She was your sister, wasn't she?"

To say I'd caught Caro by surprise was an understatement.

"Wow, you have been reading up on your fashion history, haven't you?" she said.

I nodded as she hung various earrings in front of my ears and stood back, squinting at her options through narrowed eyes. I told her about the book Charlotte had lent me. Her sister figured prominently in it—not that her connection with Caro got a mention.

Caro didn't seem interested in talking about Clarissa. Then again, she was in the throes of last-minute before-the-show adjustments. Finally I asked, "Did you and your sister ever have the chance to work together?"

Her answer came quickly. "No." It was brief, but nevertheless I thought I detected a touch of irritation (with me?), jealousy (of her sister?), and exasperation (perhaps with us both?).

So much for this line of questioning, I thought. But I wasn't about to leave without having another try—even at the risk of being pushy. So, as she asked me to change into another dress, I reached for my shoulder bag and quickly took out the photograph of the two boys in the water. I'd made a new copy that morning. But then I hesitated. On one hand I was hoping that if I showed it to Caro, she could confirm who the boys were. On the other hand, I didn't want to stupidly put myself in harm's way. After all, if my suspicions were correct, Gavin's attack had something to do with this very photo.

I thought of my granny. Sometimes—especially when we were watching *Midsomer Murders* on television—she would become frustrated when the detective was too timid. "Flush him out! Provoke the villain!" she'd say to Inspector Barnaby as she passed me the crystal bowl full of hard candies she kept next to her favorite armchair. "Show him you're on to him. Make him move!" Granny said that a clever villain would often only make a mistake when provoked or under pressure. "Surprise can be a useful element when laying a trap. You just have to be sure to follow up quickly."

I took a breath. The call from Tallulah had proved it was definitely time to move things forward—and maybe an element of surprise was exactly what was needed here. I quickly changed into the outfit Caro had given me, and with the photo clasped in my hand, I walked over to her.

While she looked me over and made a few minor styling adjustments—a tug here, another one there—I handed her the photo. She took it, looked at it, and said, "Why are you giving me this?" She seemed confused.

"I thought you might be able to tell me something about it."

Caro shook her head.

"You don't know the boys in the photo?"

Exasperation crept into her voice as she said, "I don't see what this has to do with anything, Axelle. Can you concentrate on what we're doing, please? I have other models waiting for my attention."

At that instant an assistant interrupted us to say that Jorge needed Caro's "eye" for some last-minute style adjustments on a dress he was finishing for the show. Caro looked back as she followed the assistant. "See you on Thursday, Axelle," she said as they left the room. Clearly my question time was over.

It was only as I packed my bag a couple of minutes later that I realized Caro had kept the photo.

As I left Claridge's and walked to the nearest bus stop, Tallulah's phone call kept circling through my mind. The pressure was mounting with every second that ticked by, because I now had no doubt that her brother's attacker would try to get to him again—and soon.

Hopefully I'd be able to meet Georgie next. But would I get any further with her than I had with Caro? I was so sure that the boys in the photo were the Vane twins. Was I wrong? And if I was right, why didn't Caro admit that she knew them?

Just as I hopped onto a bus my phone vibrated. It was a message from Sebastian:

> I've found the Vane address in Notting Hill: Dawson Place. And the nanny's name is Jane Wimple. How's it going with you?

Dawson Place? That was right on the border between Notting Hill and Bayswater, and within easy walking distance from where I lived.

I answered him:

> Fab news! Well done, Watson! I know Dawson Place—we should check it out at lunch. And find out whatever you can about Jane, please. I'm meeting Johnny Vane tonight—you're invited too! Have just met Caro, but found out nothing. On my way to see Georgie now (hopefully). Any details on the deaths?

Sebastian replied:

> Not much to go on from the news archives so far, but your hunch was right—Julian died in the Thames. Not sure exactly where yet.

Hmm…at least now it was clear that Julian did

indeed drown in the Thames. I couldn't help but feel it must have happened near where Gavin was attacked.

> Well, that's something. And Clarissa?
> Nothing more so far, but I'm still chasing info down. I've got the name of a handyman quoted in a couple of the reports though.

That was interesting…

> Who is it?
> Juan Rivera, former handyman and gardener. He worked at the Dawson Place house. I don't know if he's alive, but it might be worth looking him up. The last address I found for him was in Notting Hill. Reports also mention a housekeeper, but no name is given.

I started to buzz with excitement at the thought of speaking with someone who could give me a firsthand account of life with the Vanes—and perhaps even details of Julian's drowning and Clarissa's accidental death… Although first I had to find out if Juan Rivera was still alive and in the neighborhood—and if he was willing to talk to me. I wrote back to Sebastian:

> Definitely worth looking into. If we find him, he might lead us to the housekeeper too. See if you can trace him. Otherwise I have an idea who I can ask. We'll do it at lunchtime. Do you have an address for Jane?

Sebastian:

Still searching.

Me:

Maybe I can find something out at my appointment at Vane HQ...

We exchanged a few more messages, and I learned that so far Sebastian's inquiries into Gavin's comings and goings of the last few weeks weren't bringing much up. I'd put Sebastian in contact with Tallulah, and he'd asked her for more information. He'd also spoken to Gavin's agent and the friend who'd had his laptop, but he'd gleaned nothing new. On the other hand, while checking out Tallulah and Gavin's flat (from the outside and unbeknownst to Tallulah), Sebastian had asked around in the local shops and cafés about Gavin, but found out most from the barman in the pub.

Apparently, Gavin had ducked into the pub on Saturday night on his way home. He'd been in a bit of a state because he thought he was being followed but had no idea by whom. Then, after a drink, Gavin had seemed to calm down and wasn't sure if his mind was just playing tricks on him, the barman said.

I wrote to Sebastian that I'd send him a message after my visit to Vane HQ. We'd decide where to meet then.

Then I put my phone away, and for the last few minutes of my bus ride, I looked over my notes:

> The photo. Gavin chose to include a photograph that was not part of his job brief on a flash drive of images that otherwise fit the job description. Furthermore, someone seems to be trying to steal the flash drive from him. Why? Because of the photo? If so, what is it about the photo that someone wants to keep to themselves?
>
> Gavin. So far no skeletons in Gavin's closet and no new information, apart from the fact that at one point last week he thought he was being followed... By the person who attacked him? Or...?
>
> The family: Johnny Vane, Georgie Vane, Caro Moretti, and Jane Wimple (technically not family, but close to them). These four people seem most likely to know something about the photo. Will questioning them about the pic reveal why someone wanted it hidden? And will that put me in harm's way?
>
> Water. A recurring theme. Gavin's trousers and shoes were wet at the time of his attack. Why? Furthermore, he was attacked near water (on the Embankment near Westminster Bridge). Johnny and his brother, Julian, were photographed standing knee-deep in water. And Sebastian has confirmed that Julian, Johnny's twin, drowned in the Thames.
>
> The past. Can't help returning to this because

my gut tells me Gavin's attack was linked to the old photograph. I need to keep digging.

Tragedy. Unusual to lose sibling and both parents so young. Did Gavin stumble upon something to do with Johnny's childhood: a secret or cover-up, for instance? Could "accidental drowning" or "accidental death" in fact be...death by design?

The hairs on the back of my neck stood on end at this thought. I'd never dealt with a case that concerned someone's death—past or present. And with the threat to Gavin, this was proving to be my most dangerous case yet. I put my notebook away and asked, *Where do I start?*

Right where you are, I told myself as my bus came to a slow and careful stop in the heart of Marylebone, two hundred yards from Johnny Vane Ltd.

After getting off the bus, I made my way as quickly as possible to the Vane offices and presented myself at the reception desk. I was led into a showroom full of models. There I tried on a dress and walked for the casting director, then posed for a quick picture before changing back into my own clothes. The casting went well and quickly. But I wasn't about to leave without first trying to meet Georgie.

As I left the showroom, I stopped an assistant and quickly mentioned that I had an interesting photo I wanted to show Georgie Vane. "Would it be possible," I asked, "to see her for a few minutes?"

The assistant seemed to buy this. "Sure," she answered. "I'll give her a call and see if she has time."

She rang Georgie and, keeping her eyes on me, told her what I'd explained.

"Exactly. Axelle Anderson. Hmm…no time? Okay, I'll tell her."

I put my hand up and loudly said, "Tell Georgie it's an old photo of her brothers. I think it'll interest her."

I'd been hoping Georgie would hear me—and my idea must have worked because next the assistant said, "Yes," and then after a few seconds' silence, "Fine, I'll send her up right away."

Ha, I thought. *Now let's see if I can get anything out of her.*

The assistant got off the phone and called a lift for me, directing me up to the fourth floor.

Georgie didn't say anything as she opened the door to her office and motioned for me to come in. She was wearing ill-fitting trousers, a silk blouse of nondescript color, and a cardigan that was way too small. Her medium-brown hair was tied back in a ponytail, and a large pair of glasses perched on the end of her nose. She looked about as unfashionable as a person can look. Charlotte's comment about Georgie never moving up the ranks of the company came to mind. I wasn't surprised. Fashion publicists are normally the most fashion-conscious people you'll ever meet.

She sat watching me across a messy desk piled high

with files and papers. A vase of wilting flowers and various half-finished cups of coffee only added to the disorder. On the shelves behind her, knickknacks and mementos made a busy, colorful background. Books lined some of the walls, some of them obvious favorites, if the slips of paper sticking out of them were anything to go by. In fact, the only stylish-looking thing in her office was a silver-framed photo of her brother, Johnny. Decked out in his usual black-leather biker jacket, black jeans, and studded fingerless gloves and silver rings, he seemed to be keeping an eye on me. For a moment it mildly freaked me out.

"Hi, Axelle," she finally said as she reached across her desk to shake my hand. "I'm Georgie. Millie says you've got something to show me. An old photo?"

I nodded and sat down as she motioned to the empty chair opposite her. I pulled my tablet from my shoulder bag and brought the photo up on the screen. With a quick prayer to the detective gods that Georgie wasn't the person who'd attacked Gavin, I handed her the tablet.

She sat quietly for a few moments, looking carefully at the photo. Meanwhile, I quickly scanned her desk. I was looking for something—and I saw it just as she cleared her throat and passed me my tablet. She sat back, saying nothing, and loudly clicked a pen she held in her left hand.

"Do you know anything about the photo, Georgie?"

She nodded. "It's of my brothers when they were

very young." *Ah!* I thought, finally I had confirmation that the photo was indeed of Johnny and Julian.

After a moment Georgie asked, "Where did you find it?"

I was scared of saying too much—I didn't want to end up unconscious on the Embankment like Gavin—but I had to push the case forward. I took a quick breath and said, "A friend, the photographer Gavin Tempest, gave it to me. Do you know him?"

Georgie answered right away. "Yes, of course. He shot a reportage piece on Johnny recently. But why did he give you that photo? Do you know him well?"

I shrugged my shoulders. "He thought I might find it interesting. He gave it to me before he was taken to the hospital on Sunday…after he was mugged."

"Oh no," she said as she stood up abruptly. Then, with her back to me, she looked out the large window to the right of her desk. Without a moment's hesitation I reached for the "something" on her desk that I'd noticed a few minutes earlier: her address book. "Where did it happen?" she continued. Her voice sounded constricted, as if she was having trouble getting the words out.

I opened the address book quickly. *T, U, V, W…W…* Wimple. There it was! Jane Wimple. "On the Embankment near Westminster Bridge," I said. "I thought you might know… Word tends to travel fast in the fashion world."

Jane Wimple, 16 St. Leonard's Terrace, Chelsea. There it was! And I knew the street. I memorized the address and put the book back on Georgie's desk just as she turned around.

"I haven't heard a word," she said, looking right at me. "Is he all right?"

I nodded and tried to look innocent. "Sort of. He suffered a head injury. But they're hoping he'll be out of the hospital by the beginning of next week." I watched her for a moment before I continued. "I thought you might be able to tell me something about the photo, like where it was taken."

She looked at me but didn't say a word.

"Or perhaps how Gavin would have gotten hold of it."

Still she said nothing, but she started clicking her pen again. After a moment she said, her voice taut, "Why are you showing me this photo, Axelle?"

I didn't want to tell Georgie about the stick, so I kept my answer vague. "Curiosity. I'm assuming it's a personal family photo…so how did Gavin get hold of it?"

Still she said nothing, so I pushed further. "He seemed to think it was important. I thought that you might be able to tell me why."

Georgie shrugged her shoulders. "You'll have to ask him when he gets out of the hospital. I'm sorry I can't be more helpful."

She looked at her watch and said, "I'm afraid I have to get going, Axelle. I have an appointment in ten minutes. But it was lovely to meet you, and thank you for showing me the photo."

WEDNESDAY AFTERNOON
Mega-Mansion and Megastar

Sebastian saw me first. He was waiting on the westbound platform of the Hammersmith & City line. I'd sent him a message as soon as I'd finished at the Vane offices, and since he wasn't too far from where I was in Marylebone, we agreed to meet at Baker Street station. "No surprise seeing you here, Holmes," he said, smiling as he jumped into my car, sat next to me, and gave me a quick kiss.

"Very funny, Watson," I said. Sebastian was referring to the fact that Sherlock Holmes had supposedly lived on Baker Street.

We sat side by side, and as the train left the station, Sebastian quietly fleshed out the information he'd given me earlier.

"Well done, Watson. You seem to have good sources no matter what city we're in," I whispered as I thought of how he'd tracked down vital information in New York while working there on our last case.

He shrugged his broad shoulders and turned to smile at me. "If I'm going to be a crime reporter, it's in my interest to find good sources. Then again, I've been learning the tricks of the trade since I was knee high." As the son of the Chief Inspector of Paris, he certainly had a point.

"And you'd be surprised," he continued, suddenly putting on a thick French accent, "'ow much it 'elps to be a foreigner in your country."

In fact, Sebastian's English was excellent. His accent was so slight that it was barely discernible.

"People get very tired very quickly of heavy accents," he explained. "All I have to do is repeat myself slowly a couple of times, and they lose their patience and end up telling me everything I want to know as quickly as they can just to get rid of me. Works every time." He smiled.

I brought Sebastian up to date on all the new information I had—the invitation to the La Lune party at Kensington Gardens and what I found out in my meetings with Caro and Georgie. I also told him about Tallulah's call. "It's proof that Gavin is still in terrible danger. We need to move faster."

"It's just like you said last night. Someone wants to silence him for good. Poor Gavin," said Sebastian, suddenly looking serious.

"I know," I said. "We've got to work fast."

I pulled my notebook out and opened it for Sebastian to see. "There's this too," I said.

"Jane Wimple's address? How'd you get that?"

"Ah, Watson, you're not the only one with good sources."

But Sebastian didn't buy it. He leaned back and narrowed his eyes at me. "That didn't come from 'a source.' No, no, no," he teased. "My gut tells me, dear Holmes, that you *took* that information. Nobody gave it to you, did they?"

I didn't say anything.

"I knew it! You even made a point of saying that Georgie's desk was messy. You were practically bragging. That's where you got it, isn't it? I bet you sneaked a look in her address book, didn't you?"

"Well, I can't help it if she just leaves things lying around. And anyway, what's the big difference between your tactics and mine?"

"Ah! Well, my tactic is called *sourcing*—and it requires finesse. Your tactic, on the other hand, is simply…stealing."

"Trust me, it took a lot of finesse to get that information, considering Georgie had her eyes glued to me for nearly our entire meeting!" I stuck my tongue out at Sebastian and he laughed.

"So where do you want to start?" he said.

"Well, I thought we could take a look at Dawson Place. It's literally a ten-minute walk from home. We can pick up Halley and grab a bite to eat on our way there. We should have just enough time before I go for my *Teen Chic* booking. Did you manage to trace the housekeeper or handyman, by the way?"

"No. My search dead-ended."

"No problem. I might know someone who can help, but let's check out the house first."

Then Sebastian reminded me of his plan to visit the hospital while I was at my booking. "I would say it's urgent now. With a bit of luck, maybe I can unearth some nugget of information to add to what we have."

I agreed.

"But going to the hospital," Sebastian explained, "means that I won't have time to get to the Thames—if we have to be at the La Lune party in the early evening. What do you want to do?"

"Hmm...well, I definitely need to see the river at low tide."

Sebastian looked into his jacket pocket and pulled a folded piece of paper from his notebook. "This is the timetable," he said as he studied the columns of tiny numbers. "The tide will be low again at...22:51. Could we go then? After the party?"

I nodded. "Perfect, Watson. And maybe we can stop by Jane Wimple's house on the way there. It's on the way to Westminster from Kensington Gardens."

"So if we leave Belle's by around nine p.m. and walk to Notting Hill Gate Tube station," he said, studying the Tube map just to the left of the train door. "Stop by Jane Wimple's..."

"That would be Sloane Square."

"And then continue to Westminster, we can get to the river with time to spare. Which reminds me—I was thinking about a boat trip." Sebastian pulled his phone out and looked something up. "The last boats going up and down the Thames leave at eleven p.m. It could be romantic."

"'It *could* be romantic' is very different from 'It *will* be romantic,' you know."

"I like your attitude, Holmes. You keep me on my toes."

I rolled my eyes. "Thank you, Watson."

"Any time."

I didn't say anything, but Sebastian was looking at me. "What?" I finally asked.

"Aren't you going to tell me what you like about me?"

He looked seriously cute, but I wasn't about to get off course. "I'm afraid you'll have to wait, Watson," I said, smiling. "In case you've forgotten, we have a case to solve—and that's what we should be discussing now. Speaking of which, I'll have to think of something to tell my mom—about why I'm out late, I mean—something that won't make her suspicious. Westminster isn't exactly in my neighborhood, plus she doesn't like me staying out late on a weeknight."

"Blame it on me," Sebastian said. "Tell her that I'd like to do some sightseeing—London at night by boat."

I nodded. "Okay. Although, just so you know, if I get home too late, my mom will definitely send Scotland Yard after us." I smiled.

"By the way," Sebastian said a minute later, "I did

find out a bit about Jane Wimple and Caro Moretti." He pulled out his notebook and read from it. "According to *Vogue* magazine, Jane has been a major influence on Johnny's life. She used to work for"—Sebastian stopped to look through his notes—"ah, yes, Ossie Clark. She met Clarissa Vane there, and after they got to know each other, Jane started working for the Vanes as a private secretary.

"Later, apparently after Johnny and Julian were born, she became more of a nanny. I'm not sure why she left Ossie Clark's design studio though. She's never married or had children, and according to another recent *Vogue* article, she remains very much involved in Johnny's life. It sounds like they're still really close."

That, I thought, jibed with what Ellie had told me the previous day. "Good work, Watson. And what about Caro Moretti?"

"Well…" I watched as he flipped through his notebook. "When her sister died, she became Johnny and Georgie Vane's legal guardian. Incidentally, she was already living with them—Clarissa and the kids, I mean—and had been since James Vane died."

Hmm…so why hadn't Caro admitted to me earlier that she knew the boys in the photo?

"You know what, Holmes?" Sebastian suddenly asked as our train pulled into Royal Oak station. "It feels quite nice to be able to tell you something you don't already know—especially on your home turf." He was grinning broadly.

"Yeah, well, don't get too excited, Watson. It might be a while before you get another chance," I teased back. Then we jumped off the train and headed for home.

On the way to my house I quickly ran my eyes over my TBLI list and found something I'd forgotten to ask Tallulah: did she know where Gavin had found the old photo of Johnny and Julian Vane? I reached for my phone and called her to ask just that.

"To be honest, I don't know for certain," she explained, "but a few days after he'd done the shoot at Johnny Vane's, an unmarked envelope was slipped under the street door of our apartment building. Gavin's name was on it, but nothing else. I remember giving it to him and him disappearing with it. When I asked him later what had been in the envelope, he said, 'It's just something I've been asked to look into.'

"Again, I can't be certain it was that photo, and Gavin does get lots of mail and packets and stuff. I suppose that's why I didn't think the envelope was important. I'd never have thought about it if you hadn't asked. I'm just guessing that's where the 'old photo' came from. That probably doesn't help you much, but it's the best I can do, I'm afraid."

On the contrary, I thought, *it does help…*

"How can knowing—or rather *believing*—that Gavin was sent the photo possibly help?" Sebastian asked when I told him what Tallulah had said.

Having picked up Halley (and made yet another copy

of the old photo), we were now on trendy Westbourne Grove, the two of us eating warm paninis we'd ordered from the takeout place on the corner. We were a short walk from Dawson Place. "Well, I'm just kicking ideas around, but I have to start somewhere…"

"Go ahead."

"The fact that the photo was delivered anonymously has given me an idea," I answered. "Rather than simply stumbling across something on his own, maybe Gavin was helped or maybe even prompted into uncovering something."

"By whom?"

"Maybe someone who's frightened or, less possibly, has a score to settle."

"Why less possibly?"

"Because if what's happened to Gavin was caused by a forty-year-old dirty secret, someone has waited a very long time to settle that score. Furthermore, asking someone else to do your dirty work is an oddly subtle way to get even. I mean, isn't the whole point of revenge that your intended victim knows that *you're* the one bringing grief upon them? Think about it. All the best retaliation leaves the victim in no doubt as to who's gotten even. Sending a photo anonymously on the other hand—"

"How do you know the sender didn't identify themselves? There might have been a note with the photo."

"Remember: it was an unmarked envelope quietly slipped under the door, which suggests to me that even if there was a note inside—and there probably was *something* confirming the boys' identity—it wasn't signed. If they'd been willing to sign it, what would be the point of secretly hand delivering it?"

"Ah, I see."

"Which reminds me…" I took my phone out and quickly sent Tallulah a message asking if she knew where the photo Gavin had received was, or if she'd come across a note anywhere that might have been sent with it.

She answered back right away:

No. Nothing, sorry.

Hmm…I wondered briefly if the person who'd broken into her flat had perhaps come across the note and taken it.

"Anyway," I continued as I put my phone away, "this anonymity—this secrecy—seems a very timid approach, which leads me back to my first theory. I think someone is frightened. Perhaps they sent Gavin the photo hoping he'd help."

"Help?" Sebastian laughed. "They must be desperate if they need to randomly ask a young fashion photographer to sift through the past for them."

"Well, they probably are desperate."

"How do you mean?"

"When you were researching today, you didn't find

many reports that mentioned Johnny and Georgia Vane's childhood, did you? Or Caro Moretti's connection to them? Or much about Jane Wimple either? And certainly no photos?"

"True—I didn't dig up much about their past. But maybe they've always been discreet because of the tragedies. They're not exactly the sort of thing you want to shout about."

"I know and I agree, but that would make it even more likely that the photo came from one of the Vanes or someone who was close to them at that time—their nanny or guardian, for instance."

"Good point. And…?"

"So leaving aside the possibility that some unknown troublemaker is involved for the moment, I think it highly likely that one of them sent the photo to Gavin."

"Okay. But if it was one of those four, what was their motive for sending the photo?"

I shrugged my shoulders. "Again, I can only guess… but if I wanted to be dramatic with my theories—"

"A touch of drama never hurt anyone, Holmes."

I cleared my throat loudly. "As I was saying, Watson, if I want to kick flamboyant ideas around, I'd say maybe one of them knows something—a secret, a lie, some cover-up concerning the family. And maybe knowing this—even after all these years—makes them very frightened."

"But why?"

"Well, look at what happened to Gavin."

"Another good point, Holmes."

"So if I continue with my dramatic theory, sending this particular photo of Johnny and Julian confirms my earlier suggestion that there was something suspicious about the drowning."

"Okay…"

"So let's suppose that having been tipped off by the photo, Gavin did indeed discover that something odd had gone on by the Thames the day Julian drowned. And let's also say that one of the four people mentioned—Johnny, Georgia, Caro, or Jane Wimple—was Gavin's attacker. And that perhaps this person has also found out how *and with whose help* Gavin uncovered his knowledge. Remember, my theory also presumes that the photo was sent to Gavin by one of those four people because they would have access to old family photos."

"Okay, I'm following you."

"Which means that at this moment Gavin's attacker could be closing in on the person who gave Gavin the photo." I stopped and turned to face Sebastian. "So wouldn't you be frightened too?"

Johnny Vane's childhood home was enormous and creepy. Furthermore, it looked neglected. Standing on the corner of Dawson Place, it was a large, white stuccoed building that dominated the end of the street. Any movie producer hunting for the perfect setting for a horror film would have no need to look further. I got the chills just looking at it.

A short flight of stone steps led to a grand portico entrance. The house's imposing facade was punctuated with large windows, all dark and inscrutable from where we stood. Four large stone eagles—one at each corner of the flat roof—added a touch of spooky drama. An untamed collection of evergreen shrubs completed the forlorn image.

"The house looks ready for Halloween," Sebastian said. "If a witch opened the door, I wouldn't be surprised." At that exact moment, a black cat walked past the place. Halley strained at her leash to chase after it.

"True," I said as I imagined growing up in such a house.

"So what's next?" Sebastian asked.

"Follow me," I said as I crossed the road, then let Halley off her leash. I pulled a bright-blue ball out of my pocket and threw it along the pavement for her to chase.

"Are you about to do what I think you are?" Sebastian asked, eyebrows raised, smile playing at the corners of his lips.

I nodded. "Uh-huh," I said as I took the ball from Halley's mouth and then drew my arm back. With all my might, I threw the ball into the front yard of the house. Halley ran toward the house and slid to a stop as her nose pressed up against the low wall that encircled it. She started barking and didn't stop until Sebastian and I had reached her.

I attached Halley's leash to her collar, then walked

to the front gate and opened it. Once inside, Sebastian and I headed up a short stone-flagged path that led to the flight of steps.

"Why do I feel as if we're being watched?" Sebastian asked as we stood on the top step under the portico.

"Because maybe we are," I whispered. A bay window protruded on each side of the front door. The windows were covered with thin muslin curtains that had probably been white originally, but were now yellow with age. Even so, they blocked the view through the windows effectively.

The door knocker was enormous and jutted out aggressively. Like the statues on the roof, it also took the form of an eagle. I grabbed the large bronze circle that it grasped firmly in its sharp beak and swung it. The knocker creaked before hitting the door with a loud thud. I banged a few more times, then stood and listened. But the house remained silent. No sound, no light ruffled its dark interior.

Then just as we turned to leave, I could have sworn I saw a curtain twitch in the left bay window. Sebastian brushed my arm to show he'd noticed the movement too. I pressed my nose up against the window, but I couldn't see anything through the muslin fabric. Who was in there?

I motioned to Sebastian and we walked back down the steps—but I wasn't going to leave without having a look around. "I can always say that we tried to ask permission, but no one was home," I said as we turned right at the bottom of the stairs and walked to the side of the house. But the windows along that wall were too high up for us to look through, so after finding Halley's ball, we walked around to the other side, where we could see a little more.

The first two windows we came to were positioned close to each other and were much taller than the others I'd seen so far. Because the second one was placed higher along the wall than the first, I thought they might light a staircase—not that we'd find out. Even if they'd been low enough, we wouldn't have been able to see through the stained glass.

We continued farther along the side of the house to the next set of windows. From there, through the large gap between the drawn curtains, we could see into a library. I turned on the flashlight on my phone, then swept its beam of light over the room.

"Talk about a creepy time warp," Sebastian said.

"I know, right?" The room's faded decor was old-fashioned, and it looked as if it hadn't been lived in for decades. Otherwise everything appeared relatively tidy. Nothing looked out of place, and even the cushions were plumped. "It's weird. It's as if someone left the room about forty years ago and everything has stayed exactly the same since then."

"Yeah, like the room is just waiting for them to walk back in," Sebastian said as we stepped away from the window and moved back toward the front of the house.

"We have to find out who owns the house now," I

said as we walked out through the front gate and turned right. "There's something very odd about this place."

"I agree. I can start tracking down the details online…"

"I don't think you'll have to," I said. As we came to the first street corner, I pointed to the building just opposite us: the Notting Hill Gate Library.

"What? There? Since when do local libraries keep documents of land ownership?" he said as we crossed the street and walked up the short flight of stairs that led into the large, white house that was now the library.

I laughed. "Since never. But our librarian is very knowledgeable on local lore."

"Meaning?"

"Meaning that she—Mrs. Sobecki—might be able to answer some of our questions and help us trace the Vane handyman or cleaner." I tied Halley up just outside the door, and Sebastian and I went in.

"Hello, Axelle," Mrs. Sobecki said when she saw me walking up to the front desk. I said hello back and introduced her to Sebastian. This provoked a widening of her large, dark eyes and a quick, knowing smile. She was almost as corny as my mom.

But before she could say anything to embarrass me I asked her if she knew of a local man named Juan Rivera.

"Ah!" she said with a broad, warm smile. "So we're working on a new case, are we? Is this another investigation for your school paper?"

"Sort of," I answered. Sebastian gave me a nudge from

behind, and I knew he was trying not to laugh. Mrs. Sobecki had no clue that I'd taken my detective work up a notch (okay, maybe a few notches) since I'd started writing for the *Notting Hill News*. And frankly, she was such a gossip that I planned to leave her in the dark.

"Hmm…Rivera," she said as she tapped her fingers on the counter. "Well, I do have a Mr. Rivera who comes in here very regularly. But I doubt he's the person you're looking for."

"Why?"

"Because he's old—very old."

"Then he's probably just the person we're looking for. We need information on the history of our neighborhood, which is why he was suggested to us."

Mrs. Sobecki looked at her watch. "Well," she said as she peered at us over her glasses, "in that case, Axelle, it seems you're in luck. Mr. Rivera should be here any moment. He comes every day at about one o'clock. I'll introduce you as soon as he's—" Mrs. Sobecki didn't finish her sentence because at that moment Mr. Rivera walked in.

She introduced us, and a few minutes later Sebastian, Mr. Rivera, and I were sitting together in the large bay window overlooking the street. Halley, meanwhile, was still tied up just outside the door, where I knew Mrs. Sobecki would keep an eye on her. "And let me know if he helps you with your case, Axelle," Mrs. Sobecki said with a quick wink before getting back to her work.

If anyone looked as if he knew about the past it was

Mr. Rivera. He was wrinkled and his back was bent, but he was friendly and quick to smile. Fortunately, he was more than happy to answer a few questions about "the old days" in the neighborhood, as he put it.

It turned out that eighty-year-old Mr. Rivera was an avid reader, which is why he was often in the library and knew Mrs. Sobecki so well. In fact, I realized as I looked at him that I'd seen Mr. Rivera in here many times before. More significantly for my immediate needs, however, was the fact that he had lived and worked within a two-block radius of this library ever since he'd arrived here from Spain as a child. He knew the history of the neighborhood better than anyone.

"So, Axelle, what can I help you with?"

I took my freshly printed copy of the old photo out of my backpack and showed it to him.

"Ooh," he said. "That's old. Where did you find it?"

"I'm writing an article on Johnny Vane for my school magazine, and I found the picture through a photographer. I believe it's of Johnny Vane and his brother, Julian…"

Mr. Rivera confirmed that it was indeed the Vane twins.

"I knew the family well, you know," he continued. "I worked as their handyman for many years—well, until they left anyway. Those two were lively little boys—Johnny especially." He stopped to peer closely at the photo. "I'm not a hundred percent sure, but I think this one's Johnny," he said as he pointed to the figure that stood behind, engulfing his brother in a big bear hug. "The boys were identical twins, you know. It was nearly impossible to tell them apart. I didn't always manage.

"I can see them as if it was yesterday." He smiled. "They loved to go mudlarking. Absolutely loved it. As soon as the sun came out, off they'd go. With their nanny, of course. But that all ended when Julian died."

"What is mudlarking?" I asked.

Mr. Rivera handed me back the photo and smiled again. "That's something you kids don't do anymore. It used to be very popular. I think you'd call it treasure hunting or beachcombing now. You know that the Thames is a tidal river?"

I nodded.

"Well, when the tides go out every day they leave beaches uncovered."

"Beaches?" said Sebastian.

Mr. Rivera nodded. "Yes, beaches. Now I'm not talking fine white sand and palm trees, but nonetheless, when the tide's out, the Thames does have real beaches—rough, pebble beaches. A long time ago—and I'm talking one hundred to two hundred years ago—poor children would comb the beaches at low tide searching for trinkets and anything of value. That's what they called 'mudlarking.' Lots of stuff fell or was thrown into the Thames, you know—some of it valuable, or at least valuable enough to be worth the search. The kids would sell whatever they found and earn some money that way."

"But the Vanes were quite a wealthy family, weren't they? Why would the boys go mudlarking?"

"They just did it for fun. A lot of kids did back then. Down by the Tower of London and along Grosvenor Road, for instance, you'll find some small beaches when the tide is out. If you're lucky, you might pick up an old Victorian clay pipe. I hear lots of them still wash up. Just like the one Sherlock Holmes used to smoke!"

"If I wanted to go mudlarking now, today, where would I go?"

He rubbed his chin. "I used to have a friend—a black-cab driver—who went on his day off. He'd even take a metal detector with him. He did it out of the Westminster Boating Base. I think you might need a license nowadays, but I'm not sure. The Port of London Authority should be able to tell you that. But, Axelle, if you do go out, be careful. The tides fall and rise by about twenty feet, twice a day. The water comes in very quickly, and the currents of the river can be very, very powerful."

"Is that what killed Julian?" I asked.

Mr. Rivera looked down at his hands. "Yes, poor boy. He was caught out when the currents were coming in and didn't make it to the steps in time. Small as he was, the strong currents pulled him under. Johnny tried to help him, but there's no beating the river if it wants to take you. By the time the nanny reached the boys, Julian was dead." Mr. Rivera went silent for a moment, then said, "But that won't happen to you if you're careful.

"Anyway, I'm not surprised that Johnny's gone on to be such a success in fashion," Mr. Rivera went on. "He was always drawing and always particular about what he wore—even at that tender age. His brother was more introverted, quieter. He liked drawing too, mind you. But nice boys, both of them, always playing in the garden. I was their gardener too, you know. Their mother was always away. She traveled nonstop after her husband died. Grand she was. Beautiful too. So sad the way it all ended."

"And Georgie?"

"Yes, poor girl," said Mr. Rivera. "Her father died before she was born, and she was still very young when she lost her brother and mother. And after the deaths they—Johnny, Georgie, and their nanny—kept very much to themselves. They had an aunt, their guardian, who lived with them. She'd moved into the Dawson Place mansion after Clarissa's husband died. What was she called…?" He rubbed his chin for a moment before it came to him: "Yes, Carolyne. Carolyne Ryder."

She's Caro Moretti now, I thought.

I listened with particular interest as Mr. Rivera told us about her. "Carolyne was Clarissa's sister, although you wouldn't know it from looking at them. Carolyne was always in Clarissa's shadow. After the accidents, Carolyne and the kids—and the nanny too—became very secretive and you hardly saw them anymore. Not long after Clarissa died, they moved away. Carolyne went to New York City, I think, and

I know Johnny and Georgie were sent to expensive schools, and their nanny did everything for them. But I never saw them after that—not while they were young. I've heard Georgie works for her brother now."

"I read that Clarissa died accidentally in the house," I said. "But I don't know how…"

Mr. Rivera looked at me and slowly nodded his head. "She had a terrible fall."

"Where?"

"The house has a large staircase in the hallway. She fell all the way down from midway up. The stone floor at the bottom broke her fall."

"Do you know how it happened?"

Mr. Rivera shrugged. "I wasn't inside the house at the time, but everyone said she'd slipped or tripped or something. It's true that the stairs in that house are terribly slippery. I always said you could ice skate on them if they were flat!"

It took me a few moments to digest this information, and I couldn't help wondering if the stained-glass windows we'd tried to look through had been witness to the fall.

"By the way, I've read there was a housekeeper who worked at the house…but I don't have a name. Would you happen to know if she's still alive?"

Mr. Rivera shook his head. "You must mean Mrs. Underwood, but she died about ten years ago."

Hmm…a dead end (no pun intended), I thought.

I had one last question before we needed to leave. "Mr. Rivera, you said you never saw the Vane children again when they were young. Does that mean you've seen them as adults?"

He nodded.

"Where? Here? Do they still come back?"

He nodded and smiled. "They moved away but they never sold the house. In fact, they kept me on as their handyman until a few years ago when I retired. Johnny and Georgie inherited the house, and later when they were old enough to decide what they wanted to do with it, they insisted on keeping it as a way to remember their brother and mother."

No wonder the room we saw looked like such a creepy time warp, I thought. *It probably hasn't been touched since Clarissa died.*

"I sometimes see the two of them go in—Miss Wimple too, in fact. That's the nanny," Mr. Rivera continued. "Not often, but it does happen. Come to think of it, I've seen Georgie at the house a couple of times in the last month. It's a shame they don't keep it looking better on the outside. They could get a fortune for it if they sold it now."

We thanked Mr. Rivera before turning to leave. "I'll want a cut of the treasure if you go mudlarking," he called after us with a wave.

Sebastian came home with me but then headed off to visit Gavin in the hospital. "I'll get to the party as soon as I can after I've showered and changed," he said. "Although, frankly, *ma chère* Holmes, I'm most looking forward to the boat trip afterward."

"Me too, Watson."

I wasn't running late yet, but it would take me a while to get all the way across town to Spring Studios, where I was due for a shoot that afternoon. The studios are in north London, and I had to take the Tube and a bus to get there. As I sat watching the views whizzing past the bus windows, I turned over in my mind everything that Mr. Rivera had told us.

Once I finally arrived at the studios, I pushed all thoughts of the case to the back of my mind and focused on the booking in hand—and Josh Locke. I checked in at reception and walked into Studio IJ, the largest at Spring Studios. I said hello to the team and the other models (they'd shot all morning and were now ready to leave)…or at least I tried to. Josh Locke's fame hung over the studio like some kind of transparent fog, making it nearly impossible to hold eye contact with anyone, let alone speak to them. It didn't matter who I tried to chat with, they all seemed to have an eye over my shoulder looking to see where Josh was, what he was doing, or who he was talking to.

As for Josh, I couldn't have gotten close to him without a struggle even if I'd wanted to. He was surrounded by models and studio crew. He seemed to enjoy the fuss everyone made over him though. Light banter came easily, and he seemed to hold the models and studio crew enthralled with everything he said.

It wasn't my sort of thing.

I quietly headed over to the hair and makeup area and set down my shoulder bag, but before sitting down, I went to the buffet table laid out with an assortment of salads and finger foods and filled a small plate with some squares of potato frittata, a yummy-looking prawn salad, and a couple of veggie sides. It already seemed like ages since Sebastian and I had eaten our paninis, and working on a case always seemed to make my appetite voracious.

With the loaded plate in one hand, I took as many toothpicks (speared fish cakes—yum!) as possible with the other. I was looking forward to sitting down for hair and makeup so that I could think through the morning's discoveries while I ate. But as I turned away from the buffet table I bumped—hard—into someone. This time, unlike the collision by the revolving door yesterday, my lunch plate took the shock of the blow. I watched as my prawn salad went flying off my plate and landed all down the front of Josh Locke's jacket.

"Yesterday you nearly take me down in the revolving door, and today you accessorize me with a selection of salads. I'm clearly a walking target whenever you're around," he said. His voice was stern but his eyes were smiling.

"Trust me," I said, "you're the last thing I've been aiming for." I felt a little guilty about the salad though, so when I saw he was looking for something to wipe his jacket with, I put my plate down, found a roll of paper towels, and helped him clean himself up. Then I picked up my still half-full plate and left.

He followed me as I walked over to hair and makeup and asked, "So, are you going to go all prickly on me again today?"

I could see some of the crew watching us as we headed toward the far end of the studio. "Prickly?" I stopped and looked at him. "How would you be with someone who'd just sent you flying?"

"Well, *perhaps* a bit prickly at first," he said, smiling, "but afterward, once I'd seen that they'd clearly bumped into me *accidentally*, I think I'd lighten up."

"Then I guess that's the difference between us."

"What?" He looked confused.

"I'm not about to lighten up." I continued walking, hoping that he'd leave me alone. I had to admit that I hadn't been especially friendly with him yesterday, but we'd hardly met under the best of circumstances—and I'd been really irritated by all the preening and fame-worshipping that surrounded him.

I thought again of the half-dozen people who had been listening at the door during his meeting with Jacky, not to mention her outrageous eyelash batting. Josh had seemed to revel in it. All that fuss made it hard for me to take him seriously. I had no idea where Josh the pop star ended and Josh the person began.

"Is there something I'm doing or saying that you don't like?" he persisted.

"You're being very direct today."

"That's because I'm trying to start a conversation with you, and so far, I have to say, it's not been easy."

I shrugged my shoulders and put my loaded plate down on the hairdressing table.

"You know, Axelle," he said, "I actually *asked* to work with you today—hard though that may be to believe. I'm starting to ask myself why."

He clearly meant to compliment me, and maybe most people would have taken it that way, but his words had the opposite effect on me. *Famous Josh Locke wants to work with a particular model so he clicks his fingers, and said model magically appears in the studio and is supposed to be flattered. Is he serious?* I thought. Did he really think that just because he wanted to work with me, I would jump at the chance of working with him?

I tried my best to keep my anger in check, but that only lasted about a second. I turned to face him.

"You *what*?" I said.

"I asked to work with you."

"And so now I'm supposed to be *grateful*? Because you *chose* me?"

To his credit, he looked confused.

"Because if that's the deal, then you're totally mistaken. I'm not like some dish in a restaurant that you just pick off a menu!"

Sam, the hairstylist, pointed to a chair and I sat down in a huff.

"That's not what I mean—at all."

"Yeah, well, that's what it sounds like. *I* didn't ask to work with *you*. I was put on option, accepted the job, and now here I am. I certainly wasn't told that I'd have to be extra excited about the job just because I was your choice!"

Josh looked furious. "Clearly, I made a mistake. That wasn't my intention at all—but you're obviously too stubborn to understand that."

I honestly didn't see how else I could have interpreted his behavior. Because of his fame he'd (A) been given the option to decide which model he'd like to work with and (B) assumed the model—in this case, me—would be excited or flattered to work with him.

"Good," I said. "So now that that's clear, why don't we just decide to ignore each other and get on with our afternoon as best we can?"

"Fine," he said and walked away.

"I hope the two of you are good actors," Sam said as he started brushing my hair.

"Why?"

"Well, I don't know if you've seen the storyboard yet, but you're supposed to be a young, romantic couple." Sam laughed lightly as he caught my eye in the mirror.

Grrr!

After that, the prep time progressed as normal. Sam

finished my hair—it was stick straight and very 1960s—and then Priscilla, the Italian makeup artist, carefully applied foundation, concealer, contour, and blush before giving me cat's eyes. This involved drawing a thick line of black liquid eyeliner—with a nice flick at the end—on my upper lid, and then generously adding false eyelashes, each one applied individually with a pair of tweezers. The effect was amazing—I hardly recognized myself.

I changed into the 1960s-inspired outfit the stylist from *Teen Chic* had chosen for me—a short, icy-pink dress and some really great, very high chunky heels in a zingy green. Ten minutes later I was on set…and in Josh Locke's arms.

Josh and I stood quietly embracing (per the photographer's and *Teen Chic*'s instructions) on the pristine set, while one of the photographer's assistants moved around us taking light readings. Behind us, the freshly painted, white background dazzled in the afternoon light, while from the side of the set Sam adjusted the strength of the air from the fan that was blowing directly on my hair. I couldn't believe we had to stand romantically embracing each other like this—and Josh couldn't help a snide comment.

"Well, you asked for it," I reminded him through gritted teeth.

At that moment the photographer yelled out, "Could the two of you get friendly with each other, please? Remember the storyboard! These pictures are supposed to be romantic, okay? Tell yourselves that you're in love."

"You know," Josh whispered into my ear (which, by the way, he was way too close to), "we have to do two shots like this, so why don't we make the best of it and find a subject we can talk about without going for each other's throats?"

"Fine. I'm all for calling a truce. But do you think you could pull back from my ear a bit?"

"That's exactly what I'm talking about. And who says I want to be this close to your ear anyway? In case you didn't hear the photographer's directions, I was told to stand like this."

The photographer yelled out again, "Friendly, please! Remember: you like each other!"

"What do you suggest we talk about?" I asked Josh.

"Why don't we just start with what we're doing."

"What? Modeling? You want to talk about modeling?"

"Why not? It's neutral."

I shrugged my shoulders. "Fine." I thought about what Jenny had said about giving people a chance to show me more of themselves than just a first impression and decided, reluctant though I was, to give Josh his chance.

"So how did you start?" Josh asked as he leaned in to me and rested his hands on my waist.

"That's better!" yelled the photographer.

As we stood on set, shifting our weight to one leg, then the other, I told Josh about how I fell into modeling while I was in Paris for Fashion Week. Yes, our conversation was stilted at first. We practically had to squeeze our questions and answers out through our gritted teeth, but we were eager to continue because any conversation—even a challenging one—made the romantic poses we had to do easier.

Gradually, we slipped into a more natural rhythm, until suddenly I realized that—probably because I wasn't entirely concentrating on what I was saying (we were working, after all)—I'd told Josh about how I'd found missing French fashion designer Belle La Lune while I'd been in Paris, although I didn't mention anything about becoming a model so I could work undercover. Instead I made sure to emphasize that I fell into modeling—and finding Belle—accidentally.

Josh asked me lots of questions as we stood there on our own. (Well, sort of on our own. A crew was watching us, but—and this may sound strange if you haven't done it before—when you're on set, you feel as if you're in a bubble because there's generally music playing so loudly that unless someone shouts at you, you can't hear them. Plus, the photographer is hidden behind a camera, and everyone else is standing in the shadows at the sides of the set.)

Slowly, I began to forget that I was talking to Josh Locke, the famous singer, and started to feel as if I was just talking to Josh, a nice guy I was modeling with. After a while, I think Josh and I were both a bit surprised by how smoothly our truce seemed to be working.

The spell broke when the photographer yelled at us to take a break before the next shot. There was a bit of weirdness as we walked back onto the set and settled into our next romantic pose—this time we actually had to stand and look at each other as if we were about to kiss—but within a minute we picked up where we'd left off. Josh knew a lot about modeling. He was familiar with the globe-trotting rhythm of castings, go-sees, and bookings—both editorial and commercial—that a modeling career was comprised of. I couldn't help teasing him about how he must have dated a lot of models.

"Actually," he said, "I haven't dated any models." That was a surprise. I'd pegged him as a playboy, judging by the way he'd been flirting with the group of models earlier. "Although," he continued, "you could say it's in my blood."

"So how is it that you don't date models, and yet it's in your blood?"

"It's not that I have something against dating models," he said, laughing. "I would if I met the right one. As for my modeling connection, that's easy. My mom and granny were both models. My granny was even quite famous. So, I've heard about modeling my entire life."

That took me completely by surprise, and before I knew it, I was hearing all about how his mother had worked during the heyday of supermodels like Cindy Crawford, Christy Turlington, and Linda Evangelista.

"She wasn't quite in their exalted league," said Josh,

"although she wasn't that far behind. The thing is, my mom didn't want to leave London, and at that time London was definitely not the place to be if you wanted to hit the top of the modeling pyramid. Plus she had me fairly early on, so my arrival sort of nipped her career in the bud. My granny, on the other hand, was a real supermodel—although the term didn't exist at that time.

"Ever heard of Jodi Lipton? She was modeling in the late 1960s and early 1970s, and at that time London was really happening, so her career got off to a good start. Eventually she did end up spending a lot of time in Paris and New York. She worked with the best magazines, editors, and photographers of the time, and she was friends with all the supermodels of her day like Jean Shrimpton, Twiggy, and Veruschka."

As I listened to Josh's story, I'll admit I felt a twinge of guilt about the way I'd behaved just an hour earlier. In fact, I was learning a lot. Josh was interesting, and once he was on his own without his fawning fans getting in the way, it was as if the fame cloud evaporated and I was just talking to another friend.

As I got sucked into his story, I began to ask more and more questions. A thought started to flit through my mind… Could Josh's grandmother have known Clarissa Vane? From what Josh was saying, his grandmother had modeled in the same circles. I had an urge to ask Josh if I could meet his grandmother, but after our rocky start, why would he want to help me?

I waited until we needed touching up before I decided to ask him. Josh and I stood quietly on set while Priscilla and Sam finished working on us. Then, as we slipped back into our pose, I opened my mouth to speak, but the words seemed stuck in my throat. I wanted it to seem as casual as possible, to avoid any difficult questions. The photographer's assistant hovered around us for a minute or two, measuring the light, before I finally managed to say, "Josh, I'd love to meet your grandmother and talk to her about her modeling days."

My question took Josh so much by surprise that he pulled back and looked at me. The photographer loudly reminded us that we were supposed to be in a romantic pose. We both laughed. "Well, I can't say that we're romantic exactly," Josh said as he pulled me closer to him and looked into my eyes again, "but at least we're talking now."

"That's great!" the photographer called.

"So you want to meet my grandmother?"

I nodded. "Uh…yes, please, if you think she'd be up to talking about her past to a perfect stranger."

"She would be if I introduced you, and I'll happily arrange it. But can I ask why? Why would my grandmother's fashion past interest you so much?"

Great. Exactly the question I'd been hoping he wouldn't ask! "You've underestimated my passion for fashion, Josh!" I answered. It didn't quite ring true—and to his credit Josh picked up on that.

"Really? Even though you fell into modeling 'by accident'?"

I didn't say anything.

He looked at me through narrowed eyes, a smile playing on his lips.

"That looks great!" the photographer interrupted. "Keep your eyes narrowed just like that, Josh!"

I couldn't help giggling.

"Fine, don't tell me," Josh said, "but be warned." He smiled as he leaned in closer. "I plan on figuring out all your secrets."

"Okay," I said. "But I'm afraid you'll be sadly disappointed."

He laughed. "I'll be the judge of that."

We finished our second shot and the day came to an end. While the photographer and his assistants began to put the equipment away, and Sam, Priscilla, and everyone else started packing up, Josh phoned his grandmother, true to his word. As he hung up, his eyes found mine. A smile played on his lips as he said, "It's all set up. She's more than happy to speak to you. And she'll even do it in person…that is, if you'd like to. At ten tomorrow morning, if that works for you. If it does, I can pick you up and take you there," he said as he put his phone back in his pocket.

I wasn't sure how to answer. It was super sweet of Josh to organize the meeting—and of his grandmother to even agree to speak to me, let alone actually meet me!

I was thrilled to have found a potential new source of info on the Vanes but surprised that I'd be meeting her together with Josh. It almost felt like a date. When he saw me hesitate he quickly said, "Think about it, and you can let me know tonight when I see you."

"Tonight? When I see you?" What was he talking about?

"At Belle's party. She told me you'd be there."

I should have seen that one coming, I thought. Belle was a huge fan of Josh. "When did you see Belle, by the way?"

Josh smiled. "Earlier today. I had a fitting just after you were there for yours."

"What? You had a fitting for the show? Are you going to be in it?"

Josh laughed and shook his head. "No, not for the show—for my next tour. Belle will be making some of my suits." He stood watching me, smiling. "Axelle, don't look so surprised. I am a singer, you know. I do have a band. And I do go on tour."

It had been so normal just talking to him, alone on set, that I'd completely forgotten about Josh the superstar. Furthermore, the idea of going to see his grandmother with him still hadn't sunk in. I mean, that was totally normal, right? Like it or not, I was starting to see Josh in a different light.

I had a twinge of conscience as a thought suddenly popped into my mind. Was I becoming one of the fans I'd been so eager to keep myself apart from?

"I think I'd forgotten about the whole singing and pop-star side of your life," I said.

"Well, if forgetting about all of that helps you to talk to me, then please put it out of your mind, okay?" he answered as he leaned in to me. "I look forward to seeing you tonight."

I didn't know what to say. As he walked from the room, throwing me an over-the-shoulder smile, I stared down at my backpack and started busily packing my things away.

Within a few minutes I was out of the studio and in a cab. (I'd never make it across town in time to change for the La Lune party otherwise.) It pulled out of the parking lot and turned a corner, and I caught sight of Josh in the distance. He had a beanie pulled down over his head and a guitar case over his shoulder. (I hadn't even realized he'd brought a guitar with him to the studio.) He was walking home on his own—he'd told me he lived a twenty-minute walk from the studio.

"No, thank you," I'd overheard him say when the editor from *Teen Chic* offered to call him a car. "I could use the fresh air. Besides," he'd continued as he pulled the beanie and sunglasses out of his backpack, "with these on I should make it to my front door unnoticed." That didn't seem like superstar behavior at all.

Hmm...Jenny's words came back to me again. Maybe she was right. Maybe it's not just criminals who have more sides to them than the eye—or my eye anyway—can see.

I think I *was* becoming a fan.

WEDNESDAY EVENING
Moonlight on the River

"Axelle, are you ready? We should get going. Ten more minutes, all right?" my mom called from downstairs.

"Yes, fine! I'll be down in a few," I called back.

While I'd been at the studio working with Josh, Belle had sent me a super-cool trouser suit to wear to her party. (She'd called my agency to organize it.) The skinny black pants were topped off with a La Lune tuxedo jacket. I wore it with a white T-shirt I'd found a couple of weekends earlier at Portobello Market. It had a loud, multicolored design down the front. I finished the look off with a pair of Converse.

Hmm…I took a last look at myself in the mirror on the inside of my closet door and realized there was no way my mom was going to let me through the door with the Converse on—not if I was wearing a T-shirt. (She'd no doubt have something to say about that too.) On the other hand, I needed the Converse for the boat trip later—and I preferred them anyway.

A compromise came to mind, and I quickly kicked off my Converse and put them into my favorite black-leather clutch bag. It had large gold studs all over it and was one of the few designer pieces I really liked. Most importantly, it could just hold my pair of Converse, my phone, and my lip gloss. Then I dug a pair of red satin strappy sandals with heels (a gift from Belle La Lune) out of my closet and slipped them on. Yes, I thought, they'd do. They stood out against the black of my suit and picked up on the red on my T-shirt, but most importantly, they'd please my mom. They were, in fact, perfect for an early-summer garden party, but I'd change into my Converse as soon as I could.

I ran my hands through my hair. It looked fine—surprisingly. Often after a shoot, it would end up a mass of hair product and leftover hairstyles. Combing and washing everything out could take a while. But Sam hadn't put much product on my hair this afternoon, even though he'd straightened it. It fell brown, glossy, and straight to just past my shoulders.

My makeup, meanwhile, still looked fresh, and although it was heavier on the eyes than I'd usually like, Priscilla had applied it with a light touch. Even my mom thought I should leave it, so I did. A swipe of lip gloss was my only personal contribution to my look for the night. Before leaving my bedroom though, I remembered to squash my glasses into my clutch. After all, I never knew when I might want to blend into the crowd.

I flew down the stairs, and sure enough, before we'd

made even made it out of the house my mom asked me if I had to wear a T-shirt.

"Cara Delevingne always wears one," I answered, which instantly silenced Mom. I secretly thanked Cara yet again. Because of her, I get away with a lot of sartorial choices that my mom would otherwise veto. Cara Delevingne is a super-successful model, and clearly wearing Converse, beanies (another of Mom's pet peeves), and T-shirts hasn't affected this. In fact, it may have helped.

I kissed Halley good-bye, got in the car, and fifteen minutes later, Mom was dropping me at the Orme Square Gate leading into Kensington Gardens.

"Have fun and don't forget to thank Belle again for my ticket to the fashion show tomorrow. And call me if you're going to be back later than ten thirty, okay?" Mom said.

I assured her I would, then stepped out of the car just as Ellie arrived.

It was a warm evening and the sky was clear. Soft orange turned to a pale hazy blue as purple clouds scudded high above. The large topiary yews decorating the impressive palace orangery cast their shade in the gentle June twilight. Kensington Gardens are attached to Kensington Palace, the London home of the Duke and Duchess of Cambridge. Was I likely to spot the young family as I walked through the royal park? No, probably not. Were the gardens beautiful? Yes, absolutely—and a perfect setting for Belle's soon-to-be-unveiled *Alice in Wonderland*–inspired resort collection.

Like the palace, the Orangery is built of brick and has white-framed windows, and despite being part of the royal residence, it can be rented as a private venue. An excited murmur of laughter and chitchat drifted out on the cool evening breeze as Ellie and I approached the party. Twittering birds and clinking glasses were the only other sounds in this beautiful green haven, smack in the middle of London.

A large and elaborate bunny cage—from a distance it resembled a bird aviary—stood underneath one of the large yews. Shaped like a fanciful castle, it housed several white rabbits that were busily munching on fresh lettuce. Waiters in exquisite costumes—some dressed as the Mad Hatter, others as the Queen of Hearts—carried trays of canapés.

On any other day I might actually have enjoyed the party. But now that the day's modeling was done, thoughts of Gavin and the threat he was under crowded my mind. I was impatient to find out how Sebastian had gotten on at the hospital. And of course my whole reason for being at the party was to meet Johnny and see if I could figure anything out. Small talk and exotic juice drinks were not what this night was about. *Not for me anyway*, I thought as I watched Ellie. We'd just arrived and she already had a large glass of sparkling cranberry juice in one hand, a plate full of nibbles in the other, and a well-known Italian fashion designer on her arm.

A moment later, a voice I knew well surprised me from behind.

"Here you are!"

It was Chandra Rhodes, supermodel (and someone I met while working on my last case). She was wearing the most amazing silver strapless jumpsuit. Its spare lines and sparkly shimmer set off her tanned skin, untamed hair, and amazing face to great effect.

She'd just flown in from New York City, where she was based, and was here to do the La Lune fashion show, along with a couple of other big jobs. Knowing how familiar Chandra was with the fashion business, I couldn't help asking her about the Vanes. Caro—whom I'd spotted in the distance—seemed like a good person to start with.

"Have you seen Caro, by the way?" I asked, nodding in the direction of a group to our right where Caro stood, dressed in an all-white trouser suit.

Chandra nodded. "I did and she looks fab in white. We're actually working together tomorrow, shooting an editorial for *Love* magazine."

"By the way," I said, "I bet you didn't know that Caro is Johnny Vane's aunt."

"I had no idea! Are you sure?"

I nodded. "Caro was even Johnny and his sister's guardian after their parents died."

Chandra slowly shook her head. "Wow. I never would have guessed. I've done some of his shows, you know, and I'm on option for his upcoming perfume campaign." She smiled suddenly and said, "You know how he's always wearing those fingerless gloves and silver rings, right?"

I nodded.

"Well, apparently he never takes them off. I've heard his skin is so pale underneath that when the gloves are off, it just looks as if he's swapped them for white ones." Chandra shook her head and laughed.

"Has he always worn them? The gloves, I mean."

"I think so…"

"But why? There must be more to it than just fashion."

Chandra shrugged her shoulders. "I doubt it. Everyone likes a trademark look, after all. Besides, the gloves really set off his rings."

Just as Chandra said this, Ellie wandered back over and immediately positioned herself between us, stretched out her long arm, and took a picture.

"Party or no party," she said, as Chandra noticed a makeup-artist friend and moved on, "I have to feed my Instagram beast. And soon, Axelle, I promise you—you'll start loving it too."

I was a newbie to Instagram. The idea had come from Thunder. Charlotte and Charlie had made it clear to me in our first meeting that having an active account where fans could follow was a determining factor in a model's career.

"Not that it's a factor that's easy to measure…but

all things being equal, when a client has two girls on option, they'll check which girl has more followers—and that's the model they'll book," Charlotte had said. I'd found that hard to believe, but after talking to other models, Charlotte and Charlie didn't seem to be exaggerating. They'd opened an Instagram account for me that same day.

"Come on," Ellie said, as she slipped her phone into her tiny clutch. "I think it's time someone introduced you to Johnny Vane. I know Belle was going to do it, but that could take all night." She nodded across to where Belle stood surrounded by journalists and bloggers. "And this," Ellie continued, "is the perfect time to interrupt him. I happen to know that the shoe designer who's cornered him against that tree is not someone he wants to speak to. Shall we go?"

I nodded and linked my arm through Ellie's. Together we walked to where Johnny was standing.

He was indeed relieved to see Ellie and me. "Ah! You've been taking our small world by storm, haven't you?" he said to me after Ellie introduced us.

He was dressed as usual in one of his iconic, black biker jackets. Heavy black boots, black jeans, and a T-shirt completed his look. And while that may all sound a bit rough and rocker, on him, with his graying stubble and hair, it looked edgy and cool. His hair stood on end in soft spikes, and last but not least, on his hands he wore the studded fingerless gloves showing off his many silver rings.

"I've been enjoying myself. Modeling is much more interesting than I'd ever imagined," I answered. We made friendly chitchat for a few minutes until I gave Ellie the signal to leave by coughing. As soon as she'd moved away, I turned to Johnny and said, "I'm actually writing a story about you for my school magazine. With your big anniversary coming up, I thought the timing was perfect. Plus loads of the girls at my school absolutely love your biker jackets—not that we can afford them! I wondered if I could ask you a few quick questions now, if you could spare a moment…?"

"Go ahead," he said. "Ask away."

"Well, like I said, I've been doing some research on you, and I came across this photo. I wondered if you could tell me a little about it." I pulled my copy of the photo out of my clutch bag and handed it to him.

Whether he was more unsettled by the sight of the photo or the fact that I had a copy of it, I didn't know, but he swiftly turned his look of surprise into one of interest.

Then he teasingly said, "Well, now I'd like to ask you a question…" His eyes and voice could pass as lighthearted, but he still held the photo firmly in his hand, I noticed.

"Okay."

"Where did you find this photo?"

"A friend of mine, Gavin Tempest, gave it to me."

"Ah, Gavin. He just shot a story on me for *Harper's*

Bazaar. How clever of him to help you out with your story," he added.

"Yes," I answered. "He's nice that way…"

"And do you know where he got the photo from?"

I shook my head. "I have no idea. He just said there was something very interesting about it. I thought perhaps you could tell me what it was."

Johnny looked at me sharply.

"Listen, Axelle, I'm happy to answer questions that deal with my work. Anything other than that, and I'm afraid this is not the time and the place, all right?"

He turned to leave, but I didn't want to let him go without pushing more. Forgetting what Charlotte had told me about not throwing false accusations around, I quickly said, "It almost sounds as if you're trying to hide something. Are you?"

He stopped in his tracks and slowly turned back to face me. He watched me for a moment, his eyes dark and intense. "Axelle, since you don't seem to have understood, let me be blunt. You're being incredibly pushy about things that have absolutely nothing to do with you. I don't know what you're after, but my advice to you is this: keep your thoughts and questions to yourself. Do you understand?"

At this moment we were joined by a highly respected fashion journalist and another fashion designer. Before turning to them, however, Johnny spoke under his breath to me. In a menacing growl, he said, "Take care,

Axelle—and I do mean that." Then he thrust the copy of the photo back at me. "You'd better keep this. After all, you seem to find it more interesting than I do."

What was that all about? I thought as I reeled back from Johnny. I watched as he stood, all smiles, talking to the journalist and designer. Aggressive one moment, all nice the next—talk about night and day. He was just like Charlotte had said.

I was feeling unsettled after questioning Johnny. His words were close to an outright threat. But why? Gavin came to mind, and thinking of him lying in the hospital didn't help. I was suddenly thirsty and headed toward the nearest waiter, but before I reached him, both Sebastian and Josh found me.

Sebastian was wearing a black suit with a white shirt and black tie. His hair was tousled in that way I liked, and I could see from his eyes that he had a lot to tell me. But at exactly the same second that he approached me with a glass of cranberry juice, Josh greeted me with a glass of sparkling elderflower water—and a plate full of nibbles.

I saw Sebastian bristle slightly, and he was just about to say something when Josh acknowledged him with a slight nod before turning to me. "I thought you might be hungry," he said. "And you look absolutely stunning, by the way."

Sebastian's expression went from initial surprise as Josh hijacked "our" meeting to outright irritation. I carefully took the food from Josh and the drink from Sebastian.

"Thanks for these, Josh," I said. "I'm starving. I haven't eaten since we had those snacks at the studio."

"You mean when you accessorized me with your prawn salad?" He laughed.

I saw Sebastian turn to leave, but I pulled him in by the arm and said, "Josh and I worked together today for *Teen Chic*."

Sebastian nodded curtly. "And did you have a good day?" he asked.

"Actually, yes," I answered.

"You sound surprised, Axelle," Josh said, laughing again. "Personally, I knew I'd have a good day as soon you were confirmed for the booking." He looked at me as he said it, and I could feel the color rise to my cheeks. Sebastian nearly snapped the stem of the glass he was holding, and right then, I would have given nearly anything to disappear into one of the Queen of Hearts costumes. Josh, on the other hand, was smiling broadly. "And I'm looking forward to taking you to see my grandmother tomorrow morning," he added.

I felt Sebastian tense up, but I had to answer Josh. After all, he was doing me a favor. I was really hoping it would make a difference to the mystery—but how was Sebastian supposed to know this? Obviously, I couldn't say that out loud now, here, in front of Josh.

"She's really curious to meet you, you know," Josh continued. "I've never brought any girl friend of mine to her house, so don't be surprised if she asks you a few questions too."

Argh! Why did *girl friend* and *girlfriend* have to sound the same? Sebastian looked at me, eyebrows raised.

"Well, I'm really looking forward to meeting her too, Josh," I said lightly. "It's really sweet of you to take me to see her." Turning to Sebastian, I quickly added, "Josh's grandmother used to be a model in the sixties and seventies, so I'm going to ask her about what it was like working back then."

I hoped that with this veiled explanation Sebastian would understand that all this was for the sake of the case…but my words didn't seem to register as I'd hoped. He turned and said, "Why don't I leave you two to talk about it? I'll find you later, Axelle."

He was gone before I could say anything.

I wanted to run after Sebastian, but I couldn't just leave Josh. He was talking about how and where it would be best to meet the next day. Why was everything so complicated? Josh chatted for a few minutes more (I wasn't really listening because I kept trying to look for Sebastian over his shoulder), and then we were joined by Chandra and a few other models.

As soon as I could, I slipped away and found Sebastian. He was talking to Belle. Not forgetting her promise, she immediately asked me if I'd like her to introduce me to Johnny Vane. I told her that Ellie had introduced us, and after another minute she left to greet some late arrivals.

"Well, someone is certainly into you," Sebastian said as soon as Belle left us. He was fiddling with his shirt cuffs and wasn't looking at me. Clearly he was referring to Josh.

"I doubt that very much," I answered. "Josh and I could barely stand the sight of each other when we started work this afternoon."

"Well, you seem to have moved on since then." He looked at me, his eyes dark.

I shrugged my shoulders and looked away for a moment before turning back to him. I was annoyed. I mean, Sebastian and I hadn't seen each other for weeks on end, and now, suddenly, because he was in town, I couldn't talk to anyone else—even when it might help me solve my case? "We're friends, Sebastian, and absolutely nothing more. Besides, I only met him yesterday!"

"Ah!" he said, his eyes still on me. "So you do acknowledge that if you got to know him better you could be more than friends?"

"Huh? No, that's not what I meant."

"But it's what it sounded like to me."

I sighed. "Sebastian, could you please stop pairing me up with Josh Locke? He's a new friend I made at work today, okay? Nothing more." Was it always like this with famous people? That as soon as you talked to one, people immediately had to pair you up with them? "Although," I continued, "I'm really curious about meeting his grandmother. I'm hoping she can shed some light on Clarissa Vane's past for me."

Sebastian was watching me in that way he had, his light, gray-blue eyes piercing in their directness. His hands were deep in his pockets as he stood, feet apart, and looked at me from under his tousled hair. I couldn't really tell what he was thinking, but it felt as if a giant question mark hung in the air between us. *What was that about?* I thought. Ellie would have said that Sebastian was feeling more than a touch of jealousy. But the idea of Josh and me being an item was ridiculous. I mean, we barely knew each other.

I bit my lip as I remembered how I'd felt when I'd thought that Sebastian was seeing someone else in New York. We'd both been there at the same time, and I was certain that the gorgeous model he kept meeting was his new love interest. It turned out I was wrong, but seeing them together had not been easy. At all.

Argh! At the rate I was going, I'd soon need a neat Clue-like solution to my relationship with Sebastian too.

I took a deep breath.

Axelle, I told myself, *you're at a beautiful party. You have a case to solve, and a photographer's life will remain in danger until you do so. Don't think so much, and just do what you need to do. Now.*

"Sebastian?" I said.

"Yeah."

"Can we talk about the case, please?"

Sebastian gave me a weak smile and then, taking me by my hand, led me to a wrought-iron gate. It was embedded in a stone wall, behind which lay a hidden, sunken garden. He tried the gate and it opened. Still holding hands, we descended through a couple of thickly planted terraces until we reached a large, rectangular water basin. The only sound was a gentle splattering from the small fountain at its center.

We found a bench and sat down. The heady scent of the early summer blooms was especially fragrant in this space, and the garden was so quiet that the party could have been miles away. Sebastian was still holding my hand, but he let go of it as he started to speak and we were back to being detectives.

"First things first," he said, reaching into an inner pocket of his jacket, pulling some folded slips of paper from his notebook, and handing them to me. "I managed to track down a few more newspaper reports, and you were right. The *Times*, among others, did report on Julian and Clarissa Vane's deaths—and they said a lot more than the Wiki entries we looked at last night."

I unfolded the reports and read through them. The details on Julian's death were pretty sparse, and disappointingly, they still didn't tell us where along the Thames Julian had drowned.

As for Clarissa, the accounts in the paper were a little more sensational than Wikipedia's or Mr. Rivera's:

Clarissa Vane died tragically yesterday afternoon after falling down the stairs of her Notting Hill home. She died instantly. There is no suspicion of foul play... Vane had been seen at various parties all week, including one the night before...

Several of the articles hinted somewhat dramatically that Clarissa might have been partying too much and that had contributed to her fall.

"Thank you for this, Watson," I said as I handed the articles back to him.

"I've also found out a little bit more about Jane Wimple," Sebastian said after a moment. "She grew up in Lyme Regis where her parents owned a shop. She left when she was quite young and seems to have come straight to London and started modeling quite quickly. She's never married, but she has five brothers—or at least she had five brothers. I don't know whether they're all still alive. Frankly, I couldn't find much on her at all. She wasn't a famous model, and apart from a couple of early fashion magazine interviews that mention her—and then only in connection with Johnny Vane—I didn't find anything else about her."

Despite her lofty fashion connections, Jane was a bit of a dark horse, I thought. "It'll be interesting to check out her house tonight. At this point, just catching a glimpse of her through a window would interest me." I still hadn't even seen a photo of Jane. Till now I'd heard little about her, and although I was hoping that Josh's grandmother would enlighten me with more details the next day, I still wanted to see her, but just seeing her house was better than nothing.

I often find that looking at a person's house—the way it's decorated, its location, the overall feel and vibe that the place gives off—can give away a lot about a person's preferences and lifestyle. I looked up at the sky quickly. Ideally, we'd check the house out once the sun had set. The darkness would help us to spy, as long as there were lights on inside and the curtains weren't closed!

"Did you make it to the hospital?" I asked Sebastian.

"Yes," he answered. "Apparently there's no big improvement in Gavin's condition, but he's stable. And from what I saw, it would be difficult for anyone to get to him again. He's being checked on often, and any visitors are strictly accounted for. I was actually asked to leave. Even so, it would help if the nurses and receptionists could keep an eye out and let us know if anyone else even tries to see him. Do you think you could ask Tallulah to talk to them?"

"Good idea." I took my phone out and sent Tallulah a quick message while Sebastian studied Google Maps. "What are you looking for?" I asked.

"Well, instead of taking the Tube, it might be more fun to walk from Jane's place on St. Leonard's Terrace down to the river. From there we could get a clipper to the Embankment." He looked at me. "What do you think, Holmes?"

I smiled. "You said earlier that a boat trip *could* be romantic…"

"And I'm saying now that it will be romantic. Come on, Holmes, time to go."

In one swift movement Sebastian stood up and offered me his hand. I took it and together we walked out of the hidden garden and back into the excited fray of the party.

We made our way to the Orangery, where I changed my heels for the Converse in my bag, while Sebastian went to find Ellie to tell her that we were leaving. I was sitting on a bench under one of the large topiaries, just tying my laces, when I felt someone sit down next to me. It was Josh. I looked up and immediately noticed that Josh's fame cloud was in full force. We were getting lots of surreptitious glances.

"So are you all right with me picking you up tomorrow, Axelle?" he asked.

I'd only fleetingly thought about Josh's offer of a lift to his grandmother's. Sebastian wouldn't like it, but then again, it would save me time—something Gavin and I were desperately short of at the moment. Without much more thought, I nodded. "Yes, I am. What time?"

"Well, we have to be at my grandmother's at ten, and she's in Marylebone…so how about nine thirty?"

"Fine. And thank you."

"Are you always like this?" he asked suddenly.

"Like what?" I asked as I finished tying my Converse.

"Different?" He was leaning back on the bench, an amused smile on his lips.

"How do you mean?"

"Well, we're at an amazing fashion party and yet

you're putting on your Converse, getting ready to leave early and go who knows where. You're not going to another party, are you?"

I didn't say anything. And Josh laughed. "And that's another thing—you don't talk just for the sake of talking, do you?"

"Why would I?"

"Because a lot of girls do around me." He was quiet for a moment. "Anyway, go ahead and keep me in the dark…but I'll see you in the morning. You can share the juicy details of your mystery outing then."

"Very funny."

He stood up and offered me his hand. I didn't take it.

"I don't bite." He smiled.

"How do I know?"

"There's only one way to find out."

I laughed, then reached up and took it—but Josh didn't let go after I'd stood up.

"Are you sure you have to go?" he asked.

I nodded. "Positive. But I'll see you tomorrow," I answered as I slipped my hand out of his.

Then I said good-bye and went to find Sebastian.

I didn't really know what I was feeling as I walked away. Maybe a bit thrown—because the more I spoke to Josh, the nicer he seemed to be.

From the Orme Square Gate, Sebastian and I walked to Notting Hill Gate Tube station and caught a train for Sloane Square, the nearest station to Jane Wimple's address. I quickly sent Mom a message to say that Sebastian and I were leaving the party to go for a walk along the Embankment. I also made a point of explaining that we'd catch a cab home together and I'd be back just before midnight. She answered saying no problem as long as we stuck together, and that she'd wait up for me.

As soon as we sat down, I told Sebastian about my meeting with Johnny and then compared it to my interviews with Caro and Georgie.

"All I can say, Axelle, is that you'd better be careful. You may have flushed the beast out, so to speak," Sebastian said. "Johnny sounds quite threatening. And Caro's reaction was odd as well."

"I know, but I had to provoke them. I've got to start getting some answers soon."

"Fine. But from now on, don't wander about on your own. Remember what happened to Gavin? You'd better stick with Ellie or me at all times."

"I will," I said. "But it's not only myself I've put in danger. Whoever sent Gavin the photo could be at risk too. Let's presume they wanted Gavin's help and sent the photo as a clue. They most likely wouldn't have told the others that they'd sent it. But now that I've shown it to everyone but Jane and told them all how it came to be in my hands, well…they—Johnny, Caro, and Georgie—must be asking themselves which one of them sent it."

"Shouldn't you let Jane know somehow that you

have the photo? It would be interesting to see how her reaction compares to the others. Maybe she can be provoked into saying something," Sebastian asked.

"Yes, Watson. Good point. I think I might try my luck when we get to her house." I looked at my watch. By the time we got there, it would be about ten p.m. "If I see she's up, I'll try knocking on her door."

"And show it to her in person?"

I nodded. "I'll need some kind of excuse though. It is a bit late to just turn up at someone's door. But who knows? If she's there, she might be willing to answer some questions."

The walk from Sloane Square to St. Leonard's Terrace was a short one. The mild, dry weather had held and the pretty square was busy. To our right as we left the station, people were sitting outdoors at the Colbert and Botanist restaurants. King's Road was lively; people were window-shopping or chatting at the small tables set up on the pavement outside some of the restaurants. I couldn't, however, shake off the feeling that we were being followed by someone and had been since we left the La Lune party.

"Funny you should say that..." Sebastian said when I told him. "I sort of had that feeling when we left the party too, but I haven't actually seen anyone. Have you?"

"No...well, apart from a shadow that I just caught out of the corner of my eye, but then again, it could have been anything. I'm probably just thinking too much about the case."

"And? Any idea yet who might have sent the photo to Gavin in the first place?" Sebastian asked as we walked past the Saatchi Gallery.

I shook my head. "No, not enough of an idea anyway. And there's always the chance that some random troublemaker is behind this. Johnny is famous enough to have them. Although attacking Gavin is pretty sick. But if one of the four did send Gavin the photo—and I'm assuming one of them did—then their reactions haven't helped me much so far. I mean, Caro seemed uninterested, nearly dismissive, and then she was bustled away before I could ask more. Georgie didn't say anything, but I got the feeling she knows something. Then again, I could say that about Caro. The way she was so dismissive about it might tell us something…"

"You mean perhaps she's just a good actress?"

"Umm-hmm, something like that. On the other hand, Johnny was aggressive. He growled and thrust the photo back at me. Of all of them, he definitely seemed the most rattled—but why?"

"Could be any number of reasons," said Sebastian.

"Well, at least I have a better idea of who Caro, Johnny, and Georgie are now. If we could just figure out who sent the photo, that would help us to work out what secrets they're covering up."

"What? Secrets? Now you think there might be more than one secret?" Sebastian asked.

"Possibly. There were two 'accidental deaths' after

all." Just as I said this, we reached St. Leonard's Terrace. Jane's dainty house sat more or less in the middle of the pretty and elegant block. Built of red brick and with large sash windows on the first and second floors, her house was the smallest on the street. Or to put it another way, her house seemed to be the only one that had kept its original Georgian proportions. No rooftop additions or side extensions marred its dollhouse dimensions. The windows were lit, and even in the evening light, the house sparkled with cleanliness and order. Two neat topiary obelisks in black cast-iron urns sat on either side of the short flight of steps that led to her bright-red door.

"Does she own this house?" I asked.

"I didn't look into that," Sebastian said. "But I can… Why?"

"It's an expensive address. A house like hers—even if it is small—must cost a fortune." I knew the street well. My mom had redecorated one of these houses for a rich banker. "If she owns it, I'd like to know how—with her modest beginnings and working as a fit model, private secretary, and then nanny—she was able to afford such a upscale address."

Sebastian nodded as he quickly scribbled something in his notebook.

Suddenly we caught sight of an old lady moving in what looked like the sitting room. "That must be her!" I said. "She's still up. I'm going to try knocking on her door now."

"Have you thought of a good cover story?"

I nodded as I pulled a small pen and my copy of the photograph out of my clutch bag. "This," I said, as I quickly waved the photo in my hand, "is my cover. Not that it's a great one, but it's the best I can do right now." Then, using my clutch bag as a writing desk, I rapidly scribbled Jane's name and address on the back of the photo and the names Johnny and Julian Vane on the front.

"What are you doing?" Sebastian asked.

"You'll see," I said before leaving him behind and quickly crossing the street to her house. I opened the dainty gate that led into Jane's front yard and walked up to the front door. An old-fashioned wall light illuminated the door. I found the buzzer and rang. To my surprise, the door opened almost immediately.

The lady I'd seen through the window was standing in front of me. Tall and slim, she was dressed in trousers and a jacket. A large, colorful brooch was pinned to her left shoulder. It looked like one of the pins I'd seen on the accessories table at Johnny Vane's.

"Jane Wimple?" I asked.

She had a curious way of looking at me. Almost as if she couldn't see me—and yet it felt as if she was carefully taking in every detail of my appearance. "I was expecting someone else entirely," she said. "And, yes, I am Jane Wimple, although I don't think I can do anything for you. Do your parents know you're out?"

She wasn't unkind, just brisk and very sure of herself.

She started to close the door, but I pushed my arm against it and quickly said, "I'm sorry it's late, but I have an old photo here that I came across this evening. It has the name Jane Wimple and this address written on it. Here..." I handed her the photo. "I thought it might be yours."

At once she stood still, opening her door wider to get a better light. She studied the photo, but without budging from the threshold.

Meanwhile I quickly looked into her hall. An oriental rug in hues of faded oranges and blues lay on the stone-flagged floor. In front of me a staircase ascended, and through the door to the left, I glimpsed a pretty room decorated in tones of yellow. Beside the bottom step of the stairs, a large polished-brass umbrella stand held a small collection of umbrellas and canes, each a different color, pattern, and length. Beyond that, the house seemed to be as neat on the inside as it was on the outside.

After a few moments she said, "I'm afraid my eyesight is poor. Why don't you tell me what it shows?"

I described the photo to her, but she said nothing. Frustration was beginning to gnaw at me. Why would no one tell me anything about this picture?

"I came across it when I was researching an article about Johnny Vane for my school magazine. I heard that you raised Johnny and his brother, that you were close to them—and Georgie too." I saw her stiffen when I said this.

"Close?"

Now I didn't know what to say. She was prickly, and if I said the wrong thing, I clearly ran the risk of turning her off. I tried being as vague as possible. "Yes, well, sort of—"

"There was no 'sort of' about it," she hissed.

Ah, so she wanted me to know she had been close to them. Good, then I'd push the opposite way. Hopefully I could provoke her into talking. "Well, I was surprised to hear that you could have been so close to the Vane children, because I know how much their mother, Clarissa, was loved and admired. From everything I've heard and read, it seems she must have been really, really lovely—"

"She was lovely, that's right," Jane interrupted, "but she was also a vain, flighty creature who was tortured by demons of her own making. I'm the one who kept that household together—not Clarissa. I'm the one the children were close to—not Clarissa. She has never been close to them."

"You mean, she never was," I corrected her quietly.

Jane's eyes were blazing. For someone who had trouble seeing, she could certainly focus when she wanted to—and right now she was focused on me.

Suddenly my phone vibrated. It was a message from Sebastian:

Leave now

He gave no details, but he surely had good reason for telling me to get out. It was unlike him not to use punctuation; speed was clearly of importance.

"I'm sorry, but I have to go. My parents have just rung for me. Bye!" I didn't wait for an answer before I rushed down the steps. But as I neared the street, I spotted a figure heading toward me, and I instinctively ducked into the shadows afforded by Jane's neighbor's large shrubs. From there, I saw Johnny Vane walk past me and into the house. *So that's who she'd been expecting*, I thought.

"Thanks, Watson," I said to Sebastian as I joined him across the street. We quickly fell into step as we headed for the Thames. Along the way I told Sebastian about my exchange with Jane.

"Funny," Sebastian said, "how Caro and Georgie didn't react too much—or at least tried not to—yet Jane and Johnny reacted very aggressively."

"I know. So does that tell us that Johnny and Jane have something to hide? Or just that Caro and Georgie are better actors?"

"Good questions, Holmes. I don't know."

"Neither do I—yet. But I look forward to finding out."

After a few minutes we reached the Chelsea Embankment and bought tickets at the booth on Cadogan Pier. We were a little early for the next departure, so after boarding, we found the seats we wanted and I pulled out my phone and searched online for images of Johnny Vane. Slowly I scrolled through the images. Johnny looked the same in nearly all of them—even the ones dating back twenty years to his graduation from Central Saint Martins. Leather biker jacket, boots, and a T-shirt: these were the basics. Sometimes there was a scarf or a chic turtleneck, but always worn with a good dose of irreverence. Even in the few photos showing Johnny in a tuxedo, his ability to twist a classic form shone through. And always there were the fingerless gloves and silver rings.

"What's so important about those images?" Sebastian asked as he sat on one side of me and watched my fingers zoom from one picture to the next.

"No special reason…it's just something Chandra said. She said Johnny never takes his gloves off. And if these images are anything to go by, she's right."

I held my phone out for Sebastian to have a look. "Maybe he just really, really likes wearing them. Besides, by now they're clearly a part of his look."

"That's what Chandra says, but I'd get tired of wearing gloves all the time."

"Yeah, well, you don't live and breathe fashion."

"True…but things aren't always what they seem, you know—as my grandfather often liked to say."

"Okay, but how can wearing studded, fingerless gloves be anything other than what it seems?"

"Well," I said, laughing, "I won't know unless I keep looking, will I?"

Finally the boat's engines revved to life and we slowly pulled away from the dock. The air on the Thames was invigorating and the view splendid. London's lights danced on the water's surface, and from the river, the buildings seemed totally different—more beautiful even. It was fun, standing on the prow of the boat, leaning on the railing, and watching my lovely city go past.

Sebastian pulled a folded map out of the inner pocket of his jacket and spread it out on the broad metal handrail. He'd placed red crosses on a few spots up and down the river.

"The red crosses represent the places where, according to the London Port Authority, small beaches appear when the tide is low. Considering that the Embankment is well lit, we shouldn't have any trouble finding them, even if we can't reach them all on foot."

In fact, from the boat and even in this light, we could see a few of the narrow, rocky, but very real beaches that Sebastian had highlighted on his map. Despite the romantic view from the boat, I was excited and wanted to get off and explore one of the beaches. "I have to know what it feels like to walk on one of them, and I'd like to feel the water too," I said.

"Fine, Holmes. Let's get off at Westminster. It would make sense to try to retrace Gavin's steps."

I nodded as I looked at the map. There was one beach that seemed a likely destination for Gavin on Sunday morning. I pointed to it. "That's the one," I said, just as the boat's intercom system called out "Next stop: Westminster Pier!"

We got off the boat, and once again, I had the sensation that we were being followed. Covertly, we checked behind us, but nothing or no one caught our attention.

"Well, if someone is shadowing us," Sebastian said, "then they certainly know how to do it."

"That doesn't make me feel any better about being followed, Watson."

Annoyingly the shadow had moved so quickly and lightly that I hadn't had a chance to make out a distinct shape. Was it Gavin's attacker, maybe? Or someone who didn't like me questioning the Vanes? Could it even be one of the Vanes themselves? Unless I got a good look I'd never know.

There wasn't much we could do except stay alert, I thought, as Sebastian and I reached Westminster Bridge. Once there, we crossed to the south side of the river and left the bridge by the flight of steps on the right. From here to Lambeth Bridge, the Embankment was accessible to pedestrians only. After a few minutes (I was timing it), we stood in front of a simple loading dock. The beach I wanted to see was directly below us.

The loading dock was between an ice cream stand and a tour boat company. On the opposite side of the river and a bit farther down, to the right from where we stood, was the Palace of Westminster. It was spectacularly lit up, and I couldn't help but stare at its reflection rippling on the water's surface.

But after a moment, we stopped admiring the view and walked down the short flight of stairs that led to the dock. Nothing was closed off—although, of course, the small office on the dock was shut for the night. We passed some loading equipment and crates, and then climbed down a ladder that led right onto the surface of the pebbly beach. I was surprised to find that we were not alone. A couple of flashlights shone farther along the pebbly shore as a small, chattering group combed the beach. They were mudlarking!

It was amazing to think that I'd never noticed how much the Thames rises and falls. The river had a life of its own that I'd been entirely ignorant of. I bent down and swished my hand through the water. The current had changed, and from this moment on, the tide would begin coming in—not that I could see any discernible change at that moment. The surface of the water seemed as impenetrable as ever. But from what I'd read and heard, it was underneath the surface that the tugging of the current could really be felt. The water swirled around my hands, inky and opaque. I watched, mesmerized by the fact that I'd never touched the Thames water before. Suddenly I felt something wrap itself around my hand. With a soft yelp I jumped to my feet.

"What is it?" Sebastian said, concern in his eyes.

I laughed as I lifted my hand and revealed an old

shoelace entwined around my fingers and wrist. *Not the most stunning start to my first mudlarking experience*, I thought as I continued walking along the water's edge. The going underfoot was rough and I was thankful for my Converse.

A few minutes later, however, it was Sebastian's turn to call out. He wasn't up against a mere shoelace, however. He was well and truly stuck!

I thought he was joking at first, teasing me for the way I'd jumped when the shoelace coiled around my hand. But by the time I ran to him, I'd noticed two things: (A) he was standing with both his feet in the water—how had that happened? And (B) judging by the way he kept twisting and turning, he was in serious trouble.

"My left foot's caught. I can't get it loose," he cried out.

I plunged my hands into the water and tried to free him.

"It's a roll of wire fencing," he said. "I could see it at the waterline and I jumped onto it without thinking. Stupid! As soon as I put my weight on it, it slid down into the water. I don't know if it's the bottom of my pants or one of my shoelaces that's caught on the wire. But I'm definitely stuck."

"Hold on to me," I said as I continued to feel around under the water, hoping to find a way to loosen him from the wire's grip.

The tide was coming in fast now, and the spot where

we were standing would shortly be submerged. I looked around, but there was no one else on the beach. The treasure hunters had disappeared back onto the Embankment.

"Sebastian, you have to wait here for a minute, all right? I'm going to go back onto the dock and find something I can use to cut the wire," I said.

I ran back along the beach the way we'd walked and up the ladder onto the dock. Then I dashed up the stairs that led to the Embankment in the hope of finding a passer-by who could help me. But it was quiet, and I saw no one nearby. As I turned, however, I saw a figure flit behind the ice cream stand to my left—and he or she moved with the same lightning speed and lightness of foot as the shadow I'd seen earlier.

"Hello!" I called. "I need some help!"

No response. I'd definitely seen someone run behind the ice cream stand, so either they hadn't heard me, or they were deliberately keeping away from me. In that case, I was even more sure that whoever was hiding was the person who had been shadowing us since Sloane Square—or probably since we'd left the party.

I ran to the ice cream stand, but as I reached it, I saw the figure peel away from the shadows and start to run toward the bridge. There was no point in following—I'd wasted enough time already. But at least I'd seen a distinct shape: tall, athletic, and male. That didn't tell me much, but I wouldn't have applied that description to Johnny, Georgie, or Caro. So who was it?

I ran as fast as I could back to the dock. Once I reached the loading equipment, I turned on my phone flashlight and frantically searched among the crates, forklift, and machinery for scissors, a crow bar, a hammer, anything that might be sufficient to cut the wire holding Sebastian. But there was nothing!

I started picking up some of the empty crates and tossing them around, hoping to find something useful lying forgotten underneath—but there was nothing. Then, just as I was about to run along the Embankment and call again for help, a glint of something metallic caught the light of my flashlight. It was on the floorboards of the forklift. The machine's tiny cab had a covered roof, but was otherwise open to the air, and I saw no blinking light signaling an alarm. Without further thought I reached in and grabbed the tool by its handle. It was a chisel. It wouldn't have been my first choice, but perhaps it would do.

On my own, I didn't have the strength to hit the wire mesh with enough force to break through. I quickly ran my eyes over the crates and equipment. I didn't see what I was looking for, but surely I would find something on the beach.

I ran back to the ladder and climbed down it again. As my feet touched the beach I searched around me, my eyes taking in the varied surface of the shore until they rested on just the thing I needed—a heavy stone. I picked it up and hurried back to Sebastian.

He was up to his knees in water now. "I can feel the current coming in from behind me," he said, a note of panic in his voice. "It's quite strong."

"Well, hold still," I said. "I hope this will work."

We positioned Sebastian's leg so that I'd (hopefully) be able to break the wire around his left ankle without hurting him. Then he repositioned his free leg for maximum balance.

"I thought you said this was going to be a romantic outing," I said, trying to lighten the mood.

"Technically, I think I said it *could* be romantic—which I actually feel it's becoming."

"And how can you possibly get that feeling?" I asked as I lifted the rock in my right hand and held the chisel with my left.

"Well, there is something quite romantic about being saved by a good-looking detective at night under the moonlight, don't you think?" He stopped talking as he watched me aim the first thwack. "Of course, most romantic would be if you could get me free without breaking my ankles."

"Very funny, Watson. You're entirely in my hands now, so I'd start being nice if I were you. And stop distracting me and look somewhere else, will you?" I didn't wait for an answer but let the stone fall onto the chisel handle. It felt like the wire bent, but it didn't break. I repeated the same procedure again and again. Soon, however, my hands were submerged under the water, and I could see that Sebastian was getting more anxious. The water was above his knees now, and I had to get up to my shoulders in the water to reach his ankle. (I thanked the detective gods that it was Belle La Lune who'd lent me the suit I was wearing. She was the last person who'd be angry with me for ruining it.) It was getting more and more difficult to hit the chisel. But finally I broke through enough of the wire around his foot to loosen it.

"Stand up, Axelle, and get out of the water," Sebastian said. "You're getting tired—"

"I am not!"

"You are…" He stopped talking as he wriggled his foot. "Besides, I think you've done it."

I took another step deeper into the water so that Sebastian could hold on to me more easily. My legs and arms were now completely sodden with river water (not to mention my suit!). I began to shiver as I stood next to Sebastian so he could lean on me for support until he finally his foot pulled free.

With a hop and a skip we splashed our way out of the water, only stopping to pick up my clutch bag from the edge of the beach as we dashed back to the ladder. We climbed to the dock and collapsed onto a concrete barrier between the loading dock and the steps leading up to the pavement. Neither of us said anything as we caught our breath.

"Well," I said finally. "I think we've figured out how Gavin got his legs wet."

"You think he got stuck in some wire?"

"No, I doubt he would have had the same brilliant idea as you."

"It's nice to know, Holmes, that even when you're half soaked with germ-infested river water, your spirits aren't dampened."

"Clearly, Watson, you haven't heard that old saying, 'Look before you leap.'"

"And clearly, Holmes, I'm never going to live this one down."

"Probably not." I laughed. "But seriously, I think Gavin might have come down here for the same reasons we did: to test the water, to know what the incoming current feels like."

"This is the closest 'large' beach to where he was found, so timing wise, it fits perfectly with his actions on Sunday morning—better than any of the others I've marked on the map."

I nodded. "Yes, and that's given me a theory. Remember that Gavin told Tallulah he had to check on something, and that she also had the feeling he was planning to meet someone. Let's assume he was checking on the tides and currents, and while he was down there, he maybe looked at his watch, realized he was running late for the prearranged meeting he'd made with whoever, and got out of the water. He ran the five or six minutes to the Embankment on the other side of the river and confronted his 'date' with whatever he'd discovered about the past, thanks to that old photo, and the person hit him hoping to silence him."

After a moment Sebastian said, "So what do you think he discovered?"

I shook my head. "I only have a few vague ideas at the moment."

"That you won't share?"

I laughed as I upended my Converse and watched a stream of water pour out. "Don't you think it's time we got home?"

Sebastian did the same to his shoes, then took my hand and pulled me up. As our hands touched I felt a tingling sensation race through me like a jolt of electricity. I'd forgotten how good we were at dealing with dangerous situations together. I'd almost forgotten how good we were together period. I was spending more time with him now than I had in three months, and it made a welcome change from our tension-fraught long-distance Skype calls.

Living three hundred miles apart was a killer (no pun intended), but being together—even drenched in stinking river water—felt, well, right somehow.

As we stood on the loading dock and gazed at Westminster Bridge, Sebastian suddenly made a small gasp.

"What is it, Watson?" I asked.

"Holmes, did you save the old photo to your phone?"

"Yes, I did," I answered, pulling my phone out and searching through my album. I found the picture quickly and, standing next to him, held up the phone so we both could see it.

Sebastian studied the image for a moment and then said, "Follow me." He led me back to the end of the dock, down the ladder, and onto the beach. The water had risen, but hadn't yet reached the riverbank wall. With our backs to the wall we retraced our steps to near where he'd been stuck.

"Look," Sebastian said, as he pointed out over the Thames in front of us. "The photo must have been taken from this beach. Do you see?"

"I think you're right, Watson," I said as I zoomed in on the image. The background matched up perfectly with the fuzzy detail we could see in the photo—which I could now see was in fact the western edge of the Palace of Westminster! But we'd never have noticed it if we hadn't come down here.

"No wonder we couldn't work out where the photo was taken," I said. "You'd have to stand in this exact spot, looking from this angle and at low tide. It seems even more likely now that Gavin came here on Sunday morning. The photo must have led him to this beach." I paused, thinking hard.

"You've gone quiet…"

"Sorry. I'm just thinking. The photo has led us to this beach, but so what? What does it tell us? We don't know where Julian drowned exactly—and it doesn't seem that we'll find out either. Mr. Rivera didn't tell us anything specific, and we got hardly any details from the newspaper reports. Furthermore, the four people who probably could help us haven't given anything away so far. So how could Gavin have found out more than we have?"

"Maybe he didn't."

"True. And like I said, he could have come down here because he'd figured out the location of the photo, but the location may not be all that important. Maybe this location"—I waved my phone around to indicate the area where we were standing—"has nothing to do with the motive for Gavin's attack. Maybe there's something else in the photo, some other little clue we're still missing."

"Like what?"

I shrugged my shoulders. "If I knew, we wouldn't be standing here, dripping and shivering…but…but maybe Gavin found out some intriguing detail about Julian's death. Not that it necessarily happened here on this beach. But the photo must have prompted him to investigate…"

I felt a chill run up my back, and not just because of my wet clothes.

What had Gavin seen in the photo? What had tipped him off to the idea that something wasn't quite right?

My grandfather's trusty mantra flickered through my mind: *Things aren't always as they seem…*

What had Gavin seen that I hadn't?

"Before we get you back home, there's something I'd like you to do, Holmes."

We were back by the dock, alone. I looked at Sebastian, my eyebrows raised.

"Take your wet jacket and T-shirt off—you can wear mine." I started to protest, but Sebastian wouldn't have any of it. "You're going to catch your death if you don't," he said, "and you've a case to solve. That's not a good combo."

He had a point. "Okay, fine."

"Oh, and Holmes?" he said with a smile as he pulled off his jacket and shirt.

"Yes?"

"I promise I won't look."

I rolled my eyes at him as he held his jacket up as a screen for me to change behind. After I peeled off both my T-shirt and jacket, Sebastian handed me his shirt. It was warm and smelled deliciously of him. I put it on and he took a step toward me, holding out his jacket so that I could slip my arms into it. But I couldn't take that as well.

"Sebastian, keep it. You can't walk around half naked. Then you'll be the one stuck indoors with a fever, and I need your help to solve this case. Please. I'll be fine with just your shirt."

"Axelle—"

"I promise."

I watched as he slowly slipped his jacket back on.

And can I just say, he looked gorgeous, standing in front of me, torso bare and bathed in moonlight. I couldn't take my eyes off him.

And then Big Ben struck.

"Your mom," Sebastian said with a laugh.

Grrr!

I knew he was right. The last thing I needed at the moment was to be grounded for getting home too late. Quickly, we turned and left the dock.

We'd just reached Westminster Bridge and were standing waiting to cross the road, when I noticed someone vaguely familiar on the other side of the crosswalk. With a jolt of surprise I realized who it was. Gently I signaled Sebastian to follow me away from the crossing and toward a group of tourists taking London-at-night photos with Big Ben in the background. I didn't want the person I'd spotted to see me. I watched as the lonely figure stood and waited for the lights to change before heading across the bridge. I followed at a safe distance, but she didn't go far. She stopped in the middle of the bridge and, arms on the stone wall, looked out over the black Thames.

"Axelle, who is it?" Sebastian asked.

"That is Georgie Vane."

As we walked on toward the Tube, I couldn't help but wonder what she was thinking about...her dead brother, Julian...and Johnny maybe? Their childhood? And had she come because of something she knew? Or, like us, because of something she was trying to find out?

THURSDAY MORNING
Model Manipulation

"Axelle!" called my mom from downstairs. "Axelle, you need to get down here and take a look at this!"

A few minutes later I was standing in our kitchen in shock. Both of the morning papers my parents read included photos from last night's La Lune party at Kensington Gardens. And while that in itself wasn't shocking, the following was: an image of yours truly, cozily ensconced on a bench with Josh Locke. Either the photographer had found an angle that made it seem as if Josh and I were practically joined at the mouth and sitting on each other's laps, or some photoshopping had been done. Either way, the effect was the same. It definitely looked as if Josh and I were more than just good friends.

Was that why my phone was buzzing with messages this morning? I took it out of my pocket and looked. I had over fifty direct messages on Instagram!

I was starting to feel queasy.

At that moment my mom's phone rang in her basement office. We listened as the answering machine picked it up. "Hello, Mrs. Anderson? We're calling from the *Daily Sun*. We'd just like to confirm that your daughter, fashion model Axelle Anderson, is in a relationship with Josh Locke. We'll try you again later. In the meantime, if you hear this message, please call us back at…"

I read some of the DMs and sank further into shock. Some of the comments were really nasty; a few even threatened violence.

> **I hate you!!!**
> **Don't think it's gonna last. Josh Locke went out with my friend and…**
> **I'm going to find you, YOU B****!**

Josh certainly wouldn't need to bother hiring bodyguards, I thought. All he had to do was unleash a few fans, and he'd be more than safe.

"Mom, I swear—it was nothing like this! Josh and I sat together on the bench. That much is true, but we weren't anywhere like this close to each other in real life. We were just talking. Besides, Sebastian was there with me!"

My explanation was cut short by Primrose, who helps in the house in the mornings. Actually, it wasn't Primrose herself who offered a fresh distraction, but rather what she was carrying. "Axelle, this is for you. It was on the doormat. It's unmarked—it must have been delivered by hand."

I took the envelope and looked at it. It was manila, A5-sized, and it had my name handwritten on the front in black ink. I didn't recognize the handwriting. I hesitated to open it. Was this some kind of threat from yet another crazed Josh Locke fan?

"Shall I open it for you, darling?" Mom asked.

"No, that's all right, Mom," I said as I ripped into the envelope.

The contents caught me completely by surprise. "So what is it?" Mom asked, peering at what I was holding.

"Oh, nothing to worry about. It's just a note about school," I lied. "I'll take it upstairs." All thoughts of Josh were pushed to the back of my mind as I sprang up the stairs two at a time. "I'll be right back," I called down.

I sat on my bed, Halley next to me, and emptied the envelope. Inside was a photo of what I presumed to be the entrance hall of the Dawson Place mansion—I recognized the stained-glass windows. Attached to it with a paper clip was a note.

> Help!
> At the time everyone asked me about what I could see, but not about what I could hear. I'm so, so tired. And the nightmares don't stop.
> Help me.

I looked at the photo again. The word "Hall" was handwritten in the top left-hand corner. The picture was printed on normal photographic paper, recently it seemed—if the crisp edges and ever-so-slightly sticky surface of the image were anything to go by.

Holding the photo up to the light coming through my window, I carefully studied the word in the corner. Like the writing on the envelope it didn't seem to be particularly masculine, feminine, old-fashioned, or unusual in any way. I certainly didn't recognize it.

The thought running through my mind, of course, was that whoever had sent this to me had sent the old photo to Gavin.

I picked the envelope up again and looked at it carefully. Hmm…it looked similar to the one in the background of Gavin's photo. I got up and went to my desk. On top of it lay the four copies of Gavin's photograph that I'd printed first thing that morning. (I'd figured that at the rate I kept handing them out, I should make several.)

Was it a coincidence that both of our photos had been delivered to us in the same way? I doubted it.

So who'd sent them? And why?

In my head I imagined someone frightened and haunted by the past. Maybe they'd stayed quiet for so long that now they were desperate to speak out. About what though? Something they knew? Or, as their note suggested, something they'd heard?

They were probably terrified of being found out by whoever had threatened or frightened them into staying quiet all these years. Hence, perhaps, the anonymous clue and the plea for help?

Yesterday I'd made it clear to Johnny, Georgie, Caro, and Jane that I was delving into that part of their past. Perhaps whoever had sent Gavin the clue had realized they had another chance of releasing the truth... through me.

But which one of them was it? Assuming the sender was one of those four people, of course...and it now seemed more likely than ever that it was. Tallulah, Sebastian, and I had searched every possible lead in Gavin's agenda and phone and had got nowhere.

I looked at the photo again. Why an old picture of the hall? There had to be a connection with Clarissa Vane's death... The newspaper reports and Mr. Rivera's account all told the same story. Clarissa Vane had fallen as she'd walked down the stairs in the hall of her Dawson Place mansion. Death had been instantaneous. There'd been no suspicion of foul play, although the newspapers had made a point of saying that she'd been at a party the night before, insinuating that perhaps she'd been under the influence of something. It all added to the feeling of an untimely tragedy.

I reread the note:

> Help!
> At the time everyone asked me about what I could see, but not about what I could hear. I'm so, so tired. And the nightmares don't stop.
> Help me.

So who was there when the accident had happened? I had to find out.

It was time to get working on the case—and the first thing I had to do was call Mr. Rivera to ask him if we could meet early that evening. Fortunately he agreed.

A million thoughts seemed to be going through my mind, and the most distracting, annoying, and just plain stupid one was about the photo of me and Josh in the newspapers. As if having that maliciously manipulated image weighing heavily on me wasn't enough, I kept being reminded of it by the way my phone was vibrating relentlessly. If I hadn't needed to be available in case Tallulah or Sebastian called, I would have turned it off altogether. I'd already received a good number of texts from girls at school—including ones I only vaguely knew (how did they get my number?)—commenting on how amazing it was that I'd kissed Josh Locke. *Argh!*

I sent them all the same reply:

> **I DID NOT KISS HIM!!! The photo has been manipulated! We sat on the same bench and were present at the same party—but that's it!**

Another worry circling my mind was what Sebastian was thinking. Yesterday I'd insisted numerous times that Josh and I were only friends. I needed to talk to him about the photo of the hall...but dreaded having to discuss the photo in the papers. *Case first, Axelle, case first*, I told myself. *Gavin and Tallulah are depending on you, remember?* While I was brushing my teeth I decided to send Sebastian a message. I kept it as simple as possible, in the hope that he hadn't read any of the papers:

> **Where are you?**

His answer came back right away:

> **I can't sing or write songs—are you sure you have the right person?**

Grrr! I wrote back:

> **I'm sorry about the photo, but can we please talk about it when I see you? It's not how it looks.**

Sebastian:

> **Now you're paraphrasing yourself: "Things aren't always as they seem."**

Me:

> **You're in fine form this morning, aren't you? I have a case to solve. Are you up to helping me? Or not?**

Sebastian:

> Oh, so you can solve it without my help?

Me:

> Just try me.

Sebastian:

> Still tough, Holmes. I like that. Anyway, I plan on watching you solve it—from up close. When and where?

Me:

> After La Lune show, Bond Street Tube station in Mayfair—westbound platform of the Central line. At 4-ish. Will message you when show is over. Need to go to Notting Hill Gate, meeting Mr. Rivera again at 5. Can you bring notes re Clarissa's death? Also, interesting development this morning…image to follow.

I took a photo of the picture and note I'd received and sent them to Sebastian before texting again:

> Hand delivered to my address this morning. Let me know what you think.

Now didn't seem like the moment to remind Sebastian that I had a meeting with Josh Locke's grandmother, so I didn't say anything about it, although knowing him, he would remember anyway.

Sebastian:

> I'll be there at 4. No need to message me unless plans change.

Then:

> Just saw the image you sent… I'll have a proper look and get back to you. Assume you've had some thoughts already?

Me:

> Sort of…

Sebastian again:

> By the way, I still don't sing or write songs.

Me:

> With your voice, it's probably better that way.

Sebastian:

> Ouch! Now who's in fine form?

I was smiling as I put my phone down, but it didn't last long. A quick glance out the bedroom window gave me my second big surprise of the morning. Thanks to my supposed romance with Josh Locke, there were now paparazzi standing outside our house!

I pulled back quickly. Here was a situation I absolutely had not thought about. I grabbed my phone and texted the number Josh had given me the previous day. There was *no way* I could let him drive me to his grandmother's now. I'd have to insist on a change of plan—one that didn't include me going anywhere with him.

The whole fame thing freaked me out, frankly. I don't know how Josh could deal with it—even if, as Jenny insisted (and she did have a point), it was a part of his life that he couldn't really do much about. I, however, could do something about it. I could get myself, by myself, to meet his grandmother.

Josh picked up on the first ring, and fortunately he understood my point. He apologized for the situation he'd put me in and said that normally these things blew over within twenty-four hours. If it didn't, he promised he'd get his publicist to write a brief statement saying there was no truth in the rumor. He said he'd already spoken to his lawyers about getting some kind of official apology from the newspapers in question and wanted them to make it clear that the photo had been manipulated.

I didn't realize I'd been holding my breath while he'd

been talking, until he began to explain that he'd be insisting on some kind of accountability from the newspapers.

"That would be great, Josh," I said as I let out a long, slow breath. "I'd really appreciate that. And I know my parents would too."

"It's the least I can do," he said. "I'm only sorry that now when we've got over our rocky start, I've really given you fair reason to hang up on me and say goodbye for good. Will you give me another chance?" As he said that, I thought how he'd looked the previous day and the way he'd left the studio, beanie pulled down low, guitar slung over his shoulder. That, I thought to myself, was the real Josh Locke.

When I suggested it might be best to meet him at his grandmother's, he tried talking me into meeting him around the corner from my house. "The paparazzi don't know we have plans to see each other this morning. They'll probably think you're going out for a booking or something. They won't follow you far."

He had a point, but how could I be sure they wouldn't follow me as far as his car—no matter where he parked? And honestly, I didn't want to run the risk of being followed while working on a case. I was and needed to remain an undercover model…not that I could explain any of that to Josh.

Finally, realizing I wouldn't budge on this, Josh agreed to give me his grandmother's address. I'd meet him in the lobby of her building.

"Why do I have the feeling that being stubborn is your MO?" Josh asked as our conversation wound down.

"Probably because it is," I said, laughing.

Mom rapped on my door just as I hung up, and I quickly told her what Josh had said. Although Mom is a major celebrity fan, she was not thrilled about the photos in the paper. In fact, she'd already called our family lawyer and my dad. "Using manipulated photographs is just plain dirty," she said. "We've even got paparazzi outside, Axelle! Anyway, Primrose can help you get past them. You'll need to disguise yourself a bit today. You'll get more attention at the La Lune show because of the photo."

That, I thought, was a good point. "Well, I'll be ready for it, Mom," I said as I put my glasses on.

"When are you going to get rid of those, Axelle?"

My mom was just as bad as Jenny. "Um…never. I've kept them for situations just like this morning's. Perfect disguise, don't you think?"

"Absolutely—I can barely see half of your face. Oh, by the way, I spoke to Charlotte at Thunder. She was as surprised by the photos as we were, and she's written a statement the agency can give out if anyone calls them for information. She says to ignore messages from enraged fans. She thinks it'll all calm down in a day or two. If it doesn't, then you're to get her to deal with it, okay? Anyway, I can't wait to see you in the show! Bye, darling! And call me if you need anything, okay?" She kissed me and left.

Before going downstairs I took a look at my list for the day:

> 10:00 a.m. Meet Jodi Lipton, Portman Square. Ask about Clarissa Vane and Jane Wimple.
> La Lune resort collection fashion show at their newly redecorated London flagship store and showroom premises on Mount Street, Mayfair. Hair and makeup at noon, show at 2:00 p.m. Finished by 4:00 p.m. (latest).
> Meet Sebastian after the show.
> Meet Mr. Rivera in the library at 5:30 p.m.
> Go back to look at Dawson Place mansion?
> Dinner with Sebastian and Ellie.

As Jazz had said when she'd given me my details, "It'll be a full day for you, Axelle." And she'd only been talking about the La Lune show!

Halley's sharp bark woke me from my thoughts. "You're right," I told her as I fluffed my still wet hair with my fingers, "it's time to go…and I think I need your help this morning." The paparazzi were probably expecting me to look like a model—not a dog walker, I thought as I adjusted my large black glasses and looked in the mirror. Yes, they really did the trick. Well, the glasses and my hair, which was quickly drying to look like a tumbleweed—the stuff you see rolling across desert canyons in Westerns.

As for the rest of my outfit, because I couldn't turn up to Belle's show looking too shabby, I chose a loose-fitting, gauzy cream-beige cashmere pullover (Christmas gift from my parents), some faux black leather jeans (Topshop), and a large, featherlight, La Lune multicolored scarf. I slipped into a pair of hand-painted DIY Converse, and a bright-blue Mulberry shoulder bag completed my look.

But then again, as a dog walker, I couldn't look too glam. So, instinctively, I reached for the one thing that would add just the right touch of anonymity: my scruffy old trench coat—the one at the very back of my closet (as opposed to the new one up front). I slipped it on and tied the belt. Then, before leaving my bedroom, I remembered to add the classic accessory of any urban disguise: a beanie. Pulling my scruffiest one out from the back of the shelf, I stood in front of the mirror, pulled it down over the top of my tumbleweed, and watched as my hair was squashed into submission. *Perfect*, I thought, as I dashed down the stairs.

Before heading out of the door, I quickly sent Josh a message asking if I could bring Halley. His answer came back right away:

No problem!

"Halley, it's time you started doing undercover work too," I said as I attached her leash to her collar. I had a quick chat with Primrose, and we made an exit plan. I then went out through the garden and walked around to the side of the house and sent Primrose a quick text. After a moment Primrose opened our front door and made her way down the path to the street, diverting any attention away from Halley and me as we slipped out a tiny side gate and into the mews alley that runs along the side of our house.

"Now that," I told Halley, "is what I call a clean getaway!"

Except it wasn't.

We'd left the mews behind us and had just stepped onto Westbourne Park Road when a tall girl, her ginger hair tucked into the collar of her bright-blue parka, jumped out in front of me. "Gotcha!" she hissed as she blocked my path. "You think you can get away with everything, don't you?" Slowly she began to advance on me, every step hitting the ground with a solid thud. I had no idea what she meant, but clearly she had an ax to grind.

She took a loud breath before saying, "I saw you sneaking around last night, trying to cover your tracks…"

Could she be the person—the shadow—who'd followed us from Kensington Gardens to the Thames?

"And I couldn't believe my eyes…" she continued. Yes, I thought, as she continued her slow advance, her silhouette could match the one I saw running away. "Who do you think you are?" she asked as she continued to block any attempt I made to get around her. "*Who?*"

I recognized the tall frame, blousy jacket, and athletic build. Last night, however, I'd had the impression we were being followed by a man, maybe because she'd had her hair tucked into her jacket collar, like now. *Things aren't always as they seem.* So who was she? And what did she have to do with Johnny Vane? There was only one way to find out—and judging by the truculent look in her eyes, the sooner the better.

"How do you know Johnny Vane?" I asked as calmly as I could.

Her eyes looked confused, and for a second she turned around as if to check whether I'd been talking to someone else. "Johnny Vane? Who's Johnny Vane?" She continued moving toward me.

"Johnny Vane—the fashion designer. And Jane Wimple. You followed me to her house last night…"

Her eyes widened with anger. "You never stop lying, do you? Well, that's exactly why I'm here. I'm going to show Josh Locke what a lying cheat you are!" She suddenly lunged at me. I ducked her enormous arms just as they were closing around me and managed to hold Halley back at the same time. "Don't think I didn't see you last night. You were at that party with Josh but then you left with another guy. I saw you go down to the beach with him, you nasty little…"

Blah, blah, blah. I listened to her screeching for a moment, but I'd soon heard enough. She may have been following me last night, but she had nothing to do with the case. She was one of Josh's overzealous—*deranged* may have been a better description—fans. Trying to explain anything to her would just be a waste of my time.

I took a couple of quick steps backward as Halley started to growl. The girl swung toward me and I sidestepped out of her way, spun on my heels, and hightailed it down Westbourne Park Road. Halley and I didn't stop running until we reached Portobello Road—and even then we only slowed down after slipping into a little shop I know that has shelves and shelves of tea sets. Halley and I hid behind a shelf of patterned china cups and looked out through the shop window while we caught our breath. I hoped I'd lost the girl for good.

After a few minutes we left the shop and made our way—undisturbed—to Notting Hill Gate Tube station.

When I reached Josh's grandmother's building, I stood in front of the grand arch and gazed upward. I definitely had the right address—the enormous numbers carved into the stone arch couldn't be wrong, I thought. It was just a surprising place for a former supermodel to live. Somehow I'd expected something with more of a downtown kind of vibe, not this incredibly grand building. In fact, it reminded me of some of the apartment buildings I'd seen in New York City. The ones that lined Fifth Avenue, with liveried footmen and large, dark lobbies.

I turned left after the arch, into the building's elegant and muted entrance. Josh was waiting for me. To his credit he didn't mention the bush-like apparition sticking out from under my beanie—although I did notice his eyes widen a touch. He was quiet about the glasses too. Josh was definitely scoring points.

"It's quite a grand place your grandmother has," I said as I took in the stone interiors, elegant runners, marble floors, and low lighting.

"I know what you mean," Josh said. "But don't worry, my grandmother isn't at all stuffy or formal. She's kept her nonconformist approach to life, although"—he continued as he led me and Halley up a short flight of stairs and to the lifts—"as she gets older she seems to keep moving to more upscale neighborhoods.

"Actually, she earned quite a bit in her day—she was one of the first models to have an exclusive cosmetics contract—and then she made a few wise investments. She moved here after my granddad died. Actually, he wasn't really my granddad. He was her second husband, but he always seemed like a granddad to me. Anyway, she wanted to be near restaurants and shops, somewhere that wouldn't get too quiet after dark, but that was still safe."

We got out on the sixth floor and knocked on a mahogany door opposite the lift. Jodi Lipton answered the door, and as soon as I saw her, I knew what Josh meant. The building might be very posh and formal but she wasn't. She was tall and still slim, her finely honed features topped with a head of thick gray hair. She wore jeans, a black cashmere pullover, and colorful sneakers. She had a large gold cuff on each wrist—they looked almost tribal—and didn't seem to be wearing any makeup. A pack of small dogs swarmed around her ankles.

"Let yours loose, please," she insisted as soon as she saw Halley. "We can leave them all in the kitchen together. Tina, my assistant, is in there now. She'll be able to keep an eye on them and give them a few biscuits." She was a striking woman, and I suddenly realized that I recognized her. She'd recently done a series of ads for a major British retailer. The campaign had featured English women of all ages and professions. She'd been labeled "The Original British Supermodel."

Josh introduced us, and Jodi led us to what she called her sitting room, although it seemed more of a library to me. Books lined three of the walls, and the fourth wall had a large window that looked over the green treetops of Portland Square. Colorful paintings hung in the wall spaces that weren't covered by books. A thick carpet in a muted leopard-print pattern of light beiges and yellows covered the floor. It was a sophisticated room but not pretentious—and as such, I thought, it was the image of its owner.

I'd been wondering if Josh would stay with us or not, but in the end he left us to it. "You didn't say anything about me joining you, so I've made plans to meet a friend around the corner," Josh said after his grandmother disappeared for a few minutes to make a pot of tea. "But if you need anything, just call me." He took a step closer and seemed to be examining me. I could see flecks of gold flickering in his eyes. A smile slowly parted his lips. "You're different, you know, from most girls—it's as if you have some kind of secret—and I have a feeling it's a good one…"

Was Josh some kind of psychic when he wasn't writing songs? I thought.

I didn't say anything when Josh smiled again and left.

"Josh said you wanted to know about my modeling days in the sixties and seventies," Jodi said as she motioned for me to sit down. She began carefully pouring out two cups of tea. "You have me for a full hour," she announced, "so ask away. I'm all yours." As if to emphasize this, she sat directly opposite me and waited for me to start.

"That's right," I said, hesitating for a moment. I'd decided on my way here that it might be better to tell her at least part of the truth about why I'd asked to see her. After all, I only had an hour. I couldn't waste time talking in circles until I got the chance to turn the conversation to the Vanes. I took a breath and started. "I have a friend who's been hurt quite badly, and it might be because of something he discovered…something to do with Clarissa Vane."

"Clarissa Vane? But she died years ago." Jodi was silent for a moment before adding, "And you say a friend of yours was hurt? Badly?"

"Yes."

"Well, I can't imagine how anyone could be hurt on account of Clarissa—let alone after all these years—but I'll try my best to help you."

"Thank you. I guess you must have known her."

"I did," Jodi answered. "I wasn't especially close to her—she ran in lofty circles, you know—but I saw her often and I liked her very much. Clarissa was beautiful, radiant even. The fashion designers, magazines, and photographers would trip over themselves in their rush to dress and photograph her."

"Would you say she was a model or a muse?"

"Both, I suppose—although she didn't model in the way that I did. Unlike me, Clarissa didn't need to earn a living from modeling. She did it for fun—probably in much the way all these rock stars' daughters do it today. Magazines photographed her as much because she was a wealthy socialite with an exciting jet-set existence as for her face and figure. Having said that, she did have an agent and was booked for editorials and a bit of advertising. She even did a few fashion shows when she was very young, before she married. Of course, the shows in those days were very different from today's."

"And how did she become a muse?"

"Oh, that's always an unusual business. Nobody chooses to become a muse—rather they are *chosen*. Do you understand the difference? Clarissa was an obvious choice in a way that went well beyond her physical beauty—as it must with a muse."

"What does that mean?"

"Well, for instance, a muse might have such a strong and personal sense of style that a designer feels inspired just by being around her. The Marchesa Casati was one of the most enduring muses of the last hundred years. There's even a designer brand, Marchesa, named after her—and collections continue to be inspired by her. Of course, there have been many muses, from Pauline de Rothschild to Kate Moss."

I thought of the book Charlotte had lent me as Jodi reeled off more names of modern-day muses.

"May I ask what it was you liked about Clarissa Vane?"

"Oh, she was lovely. Very friendly and quite bohemian in her approach to life—despite coming from a more traditional background. She also had a lovely voice, honey-toned and delicious. She wasn't especially witty, you know, or funny or clever. She was just very lovely all round...and I think slightly naive—at least that's my impression when I look back now with a bit of hindsight."

"In what way was she naive?"

Jodi thought carefully before she answered. "I'd say in her dealings with people. Of course, that probably came from her sheltered background. But I can remember that she seemed oblivious to people who in my eyes seemed to be using her for her name and social position, for her connections, if you like. Also, many people around her were very jealous of her. I mean, let's face it, she really did have it all. And that made some people seethe with envy, although considering how much tragedy there was in her short life, their jealousy seems very misplaced now."

Jodi got up and went to her desk. She came back to me with a photo. "Here we are at a party for Halston in New York City in about 1974." The picture was black and white, and if the slick dresses, glossy lips, and dark background were anything to go by, it appeared to have been taken in a nightclub. Clarissa was the radiant middle point of the photo, the sun around which lesser planets orbited.

"There were always lots of people around her. She enjoyed being in the center of everything," Jodi continued, "but many of the people who were drawn to her were incapable, I think, of seeing past Clarissa Vane the celebrity. I'm not sure many of them gave much thought or appreciation to Clarissa Vane the young widow, which—if you could get past that face and the couture clothes—is actually what she was."

Perfect! I thought. Jodi had unwittingly given me the springboard I needed to turn the conversation around to the case. "I know," I said. "I've been reading about her recently. There was a lot of tragedy in her life, wasn't there, with the deaths of her husband and Julian, her son? And then her own life came to a tragic end, didn't it? Do you know anything about all of that?"

Jodi poured us each another cup of tea before continuing. "Her husband's death I don't know anything about. That happened just before I came on the fashion scene. I believe he died of a heart attack at his club. White's, I think it was? Anyway, it doesn't matter. However, I do remember her death and her son's because by that time I knew Clarissa quite well. I saw her regularly at shows and parties here and in Paris and New York. And we often sat next to each other on transatlantic flights.

"Boy, did she drink on those flights. I think she had a bit of a problem with alcohol in general, if I'm honest. Not that you ever saw it in her face. She was a bit ditzy sometimes too, maybe because of the drinking, though some say she might have taken drugs as well. Poor Clarissa, being widowed with three young children on top of the pressures of her position in the fashion world. I suppose it wasn't surprising."

"And how did Julian die? Do you remember hearing any of the details?"

Jodi took a sip of tea. "I know it was an accident. He drowned in the Thames. Their nanny had taken Johnny and Julian to the river, and the boys went farther along the beach than they should have. They got stranded. Julian tried to swim back to the steps against the current, but he drowned before the nanny could reach him. Clarissa was crushed, of course.

"Although—and I realize this sounds awful—some of us had the feeling that if it had been Johnny who'd died, she might never have recovered. He was her obvious favorite, and she didn't hide the fact too well. You see, even at that young age, Johnny showed a strong talent for drawing and a fascination with style—hardly surprising considering who his mother was. Clarissa was very proud of him and she liked to show him off. She saw a lot of herself in him, I think…much more than in Julian, I would say."

"Was she a good mother, do you think?"

Jodi was quiet. "I'm not sure, really. Possibly not, to be honest. She was flighty and liked parties. Some people thought she was rather shallow. And staying at home to look after the children was certainly not her sort of thing. She traveled a lot, so she had to have help in the house. And after her husband died, she was a bit lost. He was the more solid of the two.

"She partied to hide the pain, I think. But after Julian died, Clarissa made a real effort to clean up her act and tame her demons. She went into rehab and came out looking wonderfully well. I remember thinking at the time that at least Johnny and Georgie had her at home, healthy and present…until she died."

That, I thought with surprise, didn't tally with what I'd read in the newspaper reports about Clarissa being under the influence of something when she fell. I'd have to ask Jodi more about that later.

"You mentioned that Clarissa had help in the house," I continued. "Do you happen to know of a model—I think she was more of a fit model than a fashion model—named Jane Wimple? Didn't she become Clarissa's private secretary?"

"Yes, I do remember Jane Wimple, absolutely. We worked together as fit models when I was just starting out. She wasn't exactly my cup of tea though."

"In what way?"

"Well, you know I said some people were envious of Clarissa?"

I nodded.

"Jane was one of them. At least that's how it seemed to me. Not that Clarissa noticed a thing. She loved Jane—but then lots of people did. Jane was good at ingratiating herself with people. She'd start by getting you a cup of tea, then she'd pick up some little trifle she thought might interest you, and then the next thing you knew, you couldn't live without her. She always seemed very devoted to Clarissa though, and to the children—no question. But I didn't like her.

"Sometimes, when we worked together, I'd catch her looking at Clarissa and the other couture clients, and the Queen isn't English if I didn't see hatred burning in her eyes. I know it sounds dramatic, but that's what I saw when she thought no one was looking. But then one day she suddenly stopped working as a fit model and went to work full-time for Clarissa. She seemed very happy doing that. And she became very devoted to the children. Especially Johnny. He always credits Jane with nurturing his love of fashion.

"She was the nanny who was with them on the Thames the day of Julian's death. And then, after Clarissa's death, she became even closer to the children, a sort of surrogate mother. Clarissa's younger sister was their legal guardian, but she was flighty and wanted to party—like her sister, in many ways, really—so it was Jane who looked after the children."

"Do you know anything about Jane's upbringing or where she came from?"

Jodi shook her head. "Not much, I'm afraid. She was very good at hiding her past." She suddenly went quiet for a moment.

"What is it?" I asked.

"I don't want to paint a bad picture of Jane just because she wasn't my sort of person. She was very devoted to the Vanes. And lots of people liked her. I think it was just hard to really get to know her." Jodi shrugged her shoulders. "Anyway, I didn't see Jane anymore after Clarissa died."

"Really? Not at all?"

Jodi shook her head. "Not until about fifteen years later when Johnny graduated from Central Saint Martins with a big splash. Suddenly she reappeared. I was stunned because the Vane children had disappeared off the face of the earth after their mother died—and Jane did too. Apparently they'd all moved away from London. Nobody blamed them for wanting to leave a place that had so many unhappy memories. I think it was Jane who very much wanted the children to have a fresh start somewhere."

I thought of how Jane had never married or had children of her own. The Vanes were her family—had *become* her family.

"What was it like seeing Jane again after so many years?"

"Oh, she'd become quite grand, very much in charge, and inordinately proud of Johnny—as well she should be. But I can't say I sought her company…and she didn't exactly look for me either."

"And is there anything you remember about Clarissa's death? Any rumors you might have heard at the time? Or anything you read about that caught your attention?"

"Well, I knew the house on Dawson Place. I'd been there a few times for dinner and some fabulous parties. The house was beautiful then—big and grand and very alive. It was furnished with an eclectic mix of old things, bright colors, and gorgeous paintings. Clarissa was a popular subject for many painters, as I'm sure you've found out by now, and dazzling portraits of her hung throughout the house. Anyway, I wasn't surprised when I heard that she'd tripped and fallen on that staircase because I had done the same thing—but, thank goodness, I only hurt my knee.

"The staircase was made of that Italian floor material…what is it called? Terrazzo or something? Anyway, my point is that it was slippery. Somebody seemed to fall on the stairs every time I visited that house. With young children around, they should have installed a runner, but that was Clarissa for you—style over practicality. Anyway, I was furious for her and her children when I heard reports of her death in the papers. They suggested Clarissa had been drunk or under the influence of something, just to make her death more sensational. They weren't interested in the truth then, and they aren't now—not all of them anyway.

"I think you realized that this morning," she added, looking at me. "But don't worry," she said when she saw my lips purse, "it will all blow over. I've had that sort of thing happen to me in the past. It used to exasperate me! Anyway, where were we?"

"Clarissa's death. You were saying that the papers insinuated she'd been under the influence of something when she'd fallen."

"Yes, exactly, thank you. It shocked me all the more because I know for a fact that she'd finally been in really good, really healthy form—though some people were expecting her to slip back into her old habits."

"Why?"

"Well, don't forget that's always a possibility for an addict—but I truly didn't think Clarissa would for a moment. She was so determined to stay clean for the sake of her children. No, I think in this case there was some gossip going around that something was making her…well…scared. I never found out what it was."

"Scared? Not worried or anxious?"

"Perhaps. But the word I heard was 'scared.'"

"And you never found out why?"

Jodi rapidly shook her head. "I saw her just a few days before she died, at a birthday party for a friend of ours, and considering the recent loss of Julian, Clarissa was on good form—and had been for a good three months. She told us all about the holiday plans she'd made for herself and the two children. She didn't touch a drop of alcohol throughout the celebration. And during lunch she told me she wanted to stay healthy for the sake of her family—and that she felt much better."

Jodi stopped for a moment and tugged at her sleeves before continuing. "Later on, however, I met Clarissa again in the powder room. She was alone and looked agitated and nervous. Of course, I pressed her to tell me what was wrong. Clarissa was hesitant, but she did admit in a whisper that something was scaring her—her words. Then another friend walked in and Clarissa became quiet. We didn't have another moment alone. We met briefly when we were getting ready to leave, and Clarissa told me she'd call me, but a few days later she died."

A thought was forming in my mind. I took another sip from my tea as I tried to make some sense of it. Why, if Clarissa had in fact been clean and healthy at the time of her death, had the papers suggested she wasn't? Was it purely for the sake of a sensational story? But it seemed unlikely they'd have risked publishing the story unless they'd had some source to back it up. Could someone have planted the rumor? And if so, why? Why make Clarissa look bad? Who stood to gain from it? Furthermore, why was she so scared? What was worrying her?

"Jodi, I have one last question for you if you don't mind."

"Go ahead," she said.

"You mentioned Clarissa's sister. That's Caro Moretti, isn't it?"

"Ah, yes! Carolyne. She worshipped her big sister and was shattered when Clarissa died—though I think she suffered from being in Clarissa's shadow. She didn't have her sister's looks or her easy way with people. After Clarissa died, Carolyne disappeared for a few years too, until she resurfaced as a stylist at one of the big fashion magazines. She certainly worked her way up the fashion ranks. Now she's one of the most sought-after stylists in the business."

"Did she get along well with Clarissa?"

"I think so, yes, although I do remember hearing about some man trouble between the sisters. Caro accused Clarissa of stealing her fiancé, I think. There'll be something about that in the social pages of the papers, around 1976—about a year before Clarissa died."

As I put my teacup back in its saucer on the table, I noticed that my hour was up. Jodi had been generous with her time, and I thanked her for everything she'd told me.

"Any time, Axelle," she said as she led me to the kitchen where the dogs were. (Halley had consumed a fair number of biscuits, apparently.) "I hope I've been helpful, and more importantly, I hope your friend gets better soon."

"Thank you. Yes, you have been very helpful." It was difficult to sound grateful and vague at the same time, I thought, but details concerning Gavin and the case were something I did *not* want to get into right now with Jodi. "And I'll let you know how my friend gets on," I answered as I bent down and clipped Halley's leash back on.

"Well, I'm happy to have helped, and if you have any more questions, you know how to reach me," Jodi said as she smiled at me. She had a twinkle in her eye, and for a fleeting second it was as if she understood everything I was trying to do. *But how could that be possible?* I thought, dismissing the idea. *There's no way she could know.*

I was happy to get out into the fresh air. I had so many thoughts crowding my mind that the only hope I had of bringing any rapid order to them was to feel the blast of a London breeze. Plus my phone had been buzzing nonstop while I'd been talking to Jodi. A quick glance at my screen told me that the fuss about my photo with Josh had definitely not died down.

Speaking of which, I could see Josh across the street. A moment later he was by my side. "Are you going to the show at Belle's?" he asked as I checked my messages. "I'm on my way there too. I could give you a ride if you like."

I looked up from my phone and into Josh's brown eyes. I didn't know how to tell him what I felt, but I had to be honest. Taking a deep breath, I said, "Josh, it's really, really sweet of you to offer, but until the mess about the photo is cleared up, I don't… I'm not sure…" The words got stuck in my throat as I looked at him. His eyes searched mine.

It would have been easy at that point to just accept his invitation, sneak into his car, and go with him. He wasn't pushy, but I could feel he wanted to spend more time with me…and maybe in another time and place I would have given in. But for me, right now was definitely not the time. Besides, I had Sebastian.

"Axelle?"

I gave up trying to explain. There were too many conflicting thoughts running around in my head at the moment. In lieu of a verbal explanation I simply handed him my phone. "Scroll through it all," I said.

Josh took it and did just that. He carefully looked at the long list of emails and Instagram and Facebook messages featuring both our names that I'd received just since I'd been with his grandmother. He handed me back my phone. "I get it. You don't really want to be seen with me because of all of this."

I said nothing, but I felt a sort of awkward half smile freeze on my lips. "Hmm…"

"Don't worry, Axelle. Your honesty is refreshing." He laughed suddenly. "You're the first person in I don't know how long who hasn't jumped at the chance to be seen with me in public. I mean, some people will even call the press to let them know that they'll be showing up with me." He watched me for a moment. "But stop looking at me like that," he said as he teasingly pulled my beanie down over my eyes. "I totally understand. You haven't upset me at all. So relax." He suddenly went quiet and then looked at me through narrowed eyes. "You certainly are different."

I wasn't sure, but I think he meant it in a good way.

THURSDAY AFTERNOON
Halley Undercover

"Halley," I said as we jumped off our train and walked toward the exit of Bond Street Tube station, "you're about to get your first proper dose of the fashion world." She hadn't accompanied me to a show yet, but I already knew there was one thing Halley would love about today's fashion show—the fully loaded buffet table Belle was sure to provide backstage!

Ellie was waiting for me just outside the station. She was wearing aviator sunglasses, long skinny jeans, and a T-shirt under a really cool light-peach-colored jacket. A pair of strappy gladiator-style heels and an enormous, slouchy shoulder bag rounded off her outfit. Her long hair was tied loosely on top of her head.

"Axelle," she said as she bounded toward me, "your hair! What's happened?" I couldn't blame her for asking. A glance at my reflection in a shop window revealed that my hair hadn't calmed down at all since I'd left home earlier that morning. In fact, the moist London weather had worked its magic. My hair was frizzier than ever. Forget the tumbleweed effect—it looked as if a giant sponge had sprouted underneath my beanie.

"I'll admit it's not my best look…"

"At least your beanie puts it under some kind of control—although I'm surprised you can keep it on your head over that." She laughed.

"Thanks, Ellie." She had a point though.

"Well, you know what I mean… Did you leave home with wet hair again this morning or—" She stopped suddenly midstride and looked at me, eyes wide, before saying, "Wait, wait! Your hair and the beanie and glasses have nothing to do with leaving your house early this morning, have they? Or the case you're working on. I bet this is all to do with the photo of you and Josh, right? You're in disguise!"

I nodded.

"In that case, have you talked to Belle about it?" Ellie put her hand on my arm, abruptly stopping us both again.

"With Belle? Why would I talk to her about it?"

"Because it's highly probable there'll be a few paparazzi waiting for you outside the main entrance to the store. You've got to keep out of their way. So let's go in through a different entrance."

I hadn't thought about any of this! If just spending a few minutes with Josh Locke at a party was this complicated, then what was it like being his girlfriend? I said nothing as Ellie took her phone out and called Belle. I was just thankful to have Ellie thinking about all of this on my behalf. A minute later she hung up and said, "All done. Belle understood and she'll send someone over here to take us in through a mews entrance. We can go out the same way afterward. Anyway, I totally get why you want to avoid more photos, Axelle, but didn't you see Josh this morning? Or was it his grandmother?"

"Both." I brought Ellie up to date on the morning's events.

"And Josh is going to be here for the show too, right?"

I nodded. "Uh-huh…he offered to drive me here from his grandmother's."

"But?"

"But I didn't want to be seen and photographed getting out of his car with him. I've had enough attention—crudely manipulated, I might add—to last me a long, long time."

Ellie laughed. "You must be driving him bananas," she said. "I bet it's been a long, long time since anyone has refused anything Josh has asked for once, let alone twice! I think it's great!"

"Well, I'm not doing it intentionally, you know."

Ellie turned to look at me. "All I can say, Axelle, is that I think Josh Locke likes you…and I have to tell you that the more you refuse him, the more he's going to want to spend time with you. So just be careful."

"Careful of what?"

"Hurt feelings—his."

"What do you mean?"

"Does he know about Sebastian, Axelle?" Ellie asked as she turned to me.

I didn't say anything. Why hadn't I introduced Sebastian to Josh as my boyfriend when I'd had the chance last night?

"I know about the distance between you and Sebastian and all of that…but you two really fit together, and besides, I've *seen* you together. You guys click."

Ellie stopped and laughed at the confused look on my face. "Typical! You should focus a bit on your own life, Axelle, not just on those of your suspects."

Honestly, I didn't feel like looking into my own personal life too deeply right now. It was too confusing. Because although I really, really liked Sebastian, the main question circling around my brain was: how could it ever last?

Ellie's words were still reverberating in my mind while I had my hair styled fifteen minutes later. Inspired by the *Alice in Wonderland* theme of the collection, our hair was to be worn stick-straight, with the bare minimum of product, depending on the hair type. A tiny headband was the finishing touch. I'd met head hairstylist Xavier when I'd walked for the La Lune show in Paris, and he'd flown in especially to do this show. He wanted lots of movement in our hair for this show. "Think that you are zee Alice, girls," he told us backstage in his heavy French accent. "Your hair must reflect your innocence as you go down zee rabbit tunnel!"

Whatever, Xavier!

As for the headbands—Belle's weren't the classic, thin black bands of the Alice images we all know. She had teamed up with a famous Austrian crystal producer and had the most eye-catching line of delicate, bejeweled headbands specially designed. They were slim but twinkled like a million little stars as the light reflected off their hand-cut facets. Light blues and pinks, brilliant greens and purples, and more rainbow-colored hues vied with each other for attention. They were beautiful and no two were alike; each model had her own. Needless to say there was a lot of backstage "oohing" and "aahing" as we compared our respective headbands.

Our makeup, on the other hand, was all about the eyeliner. Otherwise our faces were to be left relatively bare. Foundation and powder were kept to a minimum, with only a light dusting of pastel pink blush across our cheeks and a swipe of pink gloss on our lips. It was a very pretty and fresh look, and while I was still wearing way more makeup than I ever did in "real" life, at least—I thought, as I looked at myself in the mirror—I could still recognize myself. And I could walk outside without people looking at me as if I were a slimy-skinned alien with ten legs, which was how I often felt when I left a fashion show with my hair and makeup intact!

As Shawna, the hairstylist, applied the straightening iron to lengths of my hair (it had already been straightened with a blow-dryer, but she needed the iron to get that really stick-straight finish), I leaned back in my chair and wrote a new list in my mind. I had yet to make a big breakthrough, but I did have a few new leads to follow:

> The new photo. Why was it delivered to my house this morning and who sent it? Was it meant to be a clue?
>
> Caro Moretti. She'd had some kind of boyfriend trouble with her sister, Clarissa. What had happened? And how did it end? What was their relationship really like?
>
> The newspapers. Why did reports of her death insinuate that Clarissa had been drinking or taking drugs when she fell on the staircase at Dawson Place? Jodi Lipton was certain that Clarissa's addictions had been under control three months prior to her death. So why did the papers report otherwise? What was their source? And how could this be important?
>
> Clarissa. Why was she scared? What had been frightening her just before she died?

I zoned out for a while as Shawna quietly worked on my hair and Halley snoozed under my chair. But ten minutes later I snapped to when my phone vibrated with new message alerts. My mom was on her way and couldn't wait to see me in action. Tallulah would also be at the show and was hoping to meet with me afterward. And Charlotte and Charlie from Thunder would be coming as well to watch me walk live for the first time. *Argh!* As if I didn't have enough to think about, now I had to worry about not tripping over my high heels and falling flat on my face in front of my mom and my agent!

Speaking of which, my phone vibrated again just as a stylist strapped a pair of incredibly high snakeskin stilettos onto my feet. I contorted myself like a yoga master to reach into my shoulder bag and grab my phone without moving my feet. It was a message from Sebastian:

Holmes, Jane's house is owned by Johnny Vane.

Hmm…I thought, that was interesting—and it raised a few questions:

Had Johnny bought it for her as a gift? Or for himself as an investment? It was a very expensive house on a very expensive street. How could Jane afford to pay for the upkeep? Did Johnny help her with maintenance too?

I wrote back:

Interesting, Watson.

And then we moved our meeting back half an hour to four thirty. I wanted to make sure I'd have enough time with Tallulah after the show. But before putting my phone away, I asked Sebastian for his help with one last thing:

> **If possible, could you please check up on news reports (in the social pages) of a quarrel between Caro and Clarissa over a man? Would have happened around 1976, about a year before Clarissa died.**

Sebastian:

> **No problem, Holmes. Will do. See you soon. And good luck with the show!**

The volume of the music had shot up, and we were called to get in formation. It was showtime! Like a human rainbow we stood in line, our gorgeous pastel-colored dresses shimmering under the bright lights as Belle gave us one last once-over, adjusting lapels and tightening waistbands with the deftness born of years of styling.

"You all look amazing! Remember, you're in a magical wonderland. And don't forget that you're also strong, powerful, and able to handle whatever anyone throws at you. You're Alices for the twenty-first century!" Then the first model was called, and within seconds the show was underway.

I was relieved that, even though Josh had been watching the show, I wasn't singled out for extra attention after all the publicity we'd had that morning. This might partly have had to do with the way Belle had constructed her runway—which wasn't, in fact, a real "runway," but actually more of a meandering path through the first floor of the store. This meant that space was more constrained. The photographers had only a second to catch us as we walked past them, and they were too close to the invited guests to call out names or make loud comments.

Apparently Josh had also taken to heart what I'd told him and shown him on my phone earlier. He was careful not to make any eye contact or pay me any undue attention as I walked past him. No doubt some of the photographers were looking to see if he would.

Whatever.

But while the press attention may have been dying down, my phone was still vibrating like mad. A fair number of angry and threatening messages were still coming through on my Instagram and Facebook feeds. I decided to ignore them all.

My mom came backstage and found me. "Axelle, darling, you looked absolutely amazing," she chirped loudly. "I'm so proud of you!" Mom loves the backstage ambiance and was watching the proceedings unfold around her with great curiosity. As I changed into my own clothes I could see how her eyes took in everything: the buzzing journalists, Belle being interviewed, and even Belle's backstage mood board. My mom said hi to Ellie and was delighted when I introduced her to a few of the other models I knew. Then she tried to get a few hair and makeup tips while the stylists packed up their equipment.

"Mom," I finally said, "I have to go. Tallulah is waiting for me. She's here now."

"Ooh, that's lovely, Axelle." My mom smiled. "Is she going to interview you again?"

"Hmm…yes, she is," I said, thinking that a discussion of how the case was going might almost be described as an interview.

"Good. Well, I have an appointment I have to dash off to anyway, but I absolutely loved seeing you do your stuff, darling. Listen, should I take Halley with me? She'll have to sit in the car while I have my appointment, but I'll be going home after that."

Halley looked up at the two of us, then barked at me. "I think that means she wants to stay with me, Mom," I said, laughing. "And just so you know, I'll be meeting up with Sebastian on the way home. I think we'll go out to dinner once we've dropped Halley off."

"That's fine, Axelle. I'm going to a gallery opening but I won't be back too late. All right?"

I said good-bye to my mom, and taking Halley's leash, I went to find Tallulah. Instead Josh found me.

"There you are," he said as he pushed his way across the crowded backstage frenzy. "You looked great. Listen, I have to meet my U.S. record company right now, but can I see you later? Or tomorrow?"

My eyes widened. He'd totally caught me off guard despite Ellie's warnings. *Why can't I just sink into the floor*, I thought. I couldn't think how to answer.

At that moment, however, Tallulah called me. "I'm sorry, Josh," I said. "But someone's waiting for me downstairs. I have to go." I wanted to disappear before a journalist caught sight of us together. He looked disappointed and was about to say something but then seemed to change his mind. "Fine. I understand," he finally said. I quickly waved good-bye and left.

The La Lunes had invited Tallulah to the show because of her status as a blogger with a huge following. She could sell more items for a fashion brand with a single Instagram photo or YouTube video than any expensive ad campaign in a magazine or newspaper. Come collection time, designers threw invitations and plenty of other freebies her way.

I met her on the first floor in the shoe department at the back of the store. She looked slinky and businesslike as she paced back and forth in her very high-heeled black boots, speaking into her phone. She wore a long, diaphanous black skirt underneath a denim jacket. And the most amazing ear cuff I'd ever seen was on her left ear. It looked like a small group of asymmetrical lightning bolts. I couldn't make out how the jeweler had set the tiny diamonds to look as if they were suspended.

She waved when she saw me and put her phone away. I'd made a lot of progress with the case, but until I had something more definite, I thought it better to hold my cards close to my chest. After all, I didn't have any concrete answers, and I certainly didn't want to mislead Tallulah at this stage.

At the same time, I knew that I was the only person she could talk to about what she thought had really happened to her brother. I couldn't deny *her* the opportunity to talk, so I asked her if she wanted to go somewhere quiet. But she shook her head. "I don't have the time, but where are you heading now?"

"To the Tube. Bond Street. But I'll need to use a side entrance to get out of here…" I said as I looked around for the assistant Belle had sent to help Ellie and me earlier.

"Ah!" Tallulah smiled. "I think I know why. Then why don't we walk to the Tube together? I can cover for you."

I agreed, and after a moment I found the assistant who'd shown me in. Together the three of us slipped quietly out the side entrance, leaving the chaos of the show behind us. We stepped from the La Lune store into the sunny London day and the civilized elegance of Mount Street. If the paparazzi were still around, they'd be lurking outside the main door.

"I don't have anything more to tell you, Axelle. I just wanted to quickly say that Gavin is recovering well and the doctors think they'll definitely be able to bring him out of his coma on Friday. I've continued to look through his things again, his phone, any notes I've been able to find—he's going to hate me when he comes to!—in case we missed something, but there's absolutely nothing as far as I can see."

"Have you thought any more about the name your brother gave the file of photos?"

"'Close-up,' wasn't it?" Tallulah asked.

"Yes," I said hopefully. "Can you think of anything that it might refer to? Anything at all?"

Tallulah shrugged her shoulders but kept moving at the brisk pace she'd set. "I can't, Axelle, no…"

"I've looked through the images again and again, but there is no close-up of anything anywhere on the file—at least nothing that I can see."

Tallulah stopped abruptly and smiled. "Are you sure?"

I looked at her. "Yes, I am. Why?"

"Well, you remember I said the names on his files were sometimes coded?"

I nodded.

"I just wonder whether by 'Close-up' he means there is literally something that can only be seen if you look close up."

"What? Like with a magnifying glass?"

Tallulah shrugged her shoulders. "Maybe…the more I think about it, the more I think it might just be worth a look."

"But which one? Or is it something about all of them? There are so many images on the file."

Tallulah laughed. "That's exactly the sort of thing Gavin loves! Lots of images and only he knows which one, or ones, you should really be looking at!"

She hailed a black cab, and after I'd waved her off, I tugged on Halley's leash and headed into the Tube.

Sebastian was waiting for me on the platform in Bond Street station, as planned. He was dressed in his usual outfit of leather jacket, jeans, and boots. His hair was tousled, and he smelled fresh and warm. "I'm getting the hang of your city," he said. "I'm finding my way around more easily every day, and I like it here more and more," he continued. "I never knew London was such fun."

"That's because you're from Paris," I teased. "Parisians think only Paris is fun."

Sebastian rolled his eyes at me. "Seriously though, I love all the different neighborhoods, and the Englishness of it all is…well, comforting, somehow."

He bent down to pet Halley, then took my hand (I didn't object) as a train pulled in. As the doors opened, he led me into the nearest car and we found a couple of open seats. I smiled, happy that my modeling work was finished for the day. *Being with Sebastian is so easy*, I thought, as I felt my hand in his. Half the time we didn't even need to explain things to each other—we just knew. We were on the same wavelength about so many things, and I liked that we were able to just hang out together for ages, talking about all sorts of stuff—or not. We didn't need to plan anything special to have a good time. Ellie was right. We were good in each other's company.

So why did he have to live so far away?

"A penny for your thoughts, Holmes?"

I didn't say anything.

"Are you thinking about the fact that I don't sing? And does that bother you?"

He was clearly talking about Josh. "That's not what I'm thinking about, and no it doesn't bother me. Like I told you this morning, I think it's better that you don't," I answered.

"Good." He nodded. "I'll take that as a compliment." Then he pulled some folded slips of paper out of his inside jacket pocket. "Here," he said.

They were copies of two articles he'd found about Caro's broken engagement, and both corroborated Jodi's account. Caro's fiancé had left her for Clarissa—and then Clarissa had left her sister's ex-fiancé after only a few months. Bad blood had developed between the sisters.

"Pretty dramatic, isn't it?" Sebastian asked.

I nodded. "And not exactly the picture of sisterly love either…"

An email suddenly came through on my phone. It was Jazz, double-checking that I had all of my details for tomorrow's show for Jorge Cruz. *You're going to have a blast, you lucky girl!* she wrote… *The gardens at Hampton Court Palace are in full bloom and the weather is supposed to be great tomorrow so I doubt they'll need the tent after all. Don't forget to Instagram—you've been forgetful the last few days!*

Oh and Charlotte is going, so you'll see her there. Call me if you need anything, anything at all, and anyway, we'll talk tomorrow morning. Marc Jacobs's Saturday show should confirm soon, by the way. See ya!

I finished reading the email and slipped my phone back into my shoulder bag.

Two minutes later we were walking out of Notting Hill Gate Tube station.

"I'd like to look at the copies of the news reports of Clarissa Vane's death again. And I'd like to ask Mr. Rivera a few more questions about the day Clarissa died."

Sebastian and I had stopped at a deli I liked on the way to the library to meet Mr. Rivera. We sat at an outside table, and after ordering a gelato and getting Halley a drink of water, I pulled out the photo and note I'd received that morning.

"So it's probably been sent by the same person who sent Gavin the other photo?" Sebastian said.

"That's what I think, yes. The style is so similar."

"I agree," he said as he held a copy of Gavin's old photo in one hand and the one I'd received that morning in the other. "But why would they send you a picture of the hall at the Dawson Place mansion?"

"I can only guess that it's because they're trying to tell me something about Clarissa's death. That's also what the note they sent suggests. That's why I wanted to look at the newspaper clippings again. Jodi Lipton's account of Clarissa's death didn't quite tally with what I could remember of the newspaper reports we'd read."

Sebastian set the photos on the table and pulled his notebook from the inside pocket of his jacket. He opened the flap of its leather-bound cover and took out the neatly folded copies of the newspaper reports. We unfolded them, laid them out, and carefully reread every one.

They all reported the same basic information: that Clarissa Vane fell accidentally in her home, from the landing on the second floor. She had landed on the stone floor of the entrance hall. Death was instant.

"But they don't say why or how she fell exactly," Sebastian said.

I nodded. "Jodi said that the staircase was extremely slippery. She said she'd fallen on it herself. She was absolutely convinced that Clarissa had simply slipped and fallen to her death."

"As opposed to?"

"This," I said, as I pushed one of the articles toward Sebastian and pointed to the relevant sentence.

He read it out loud. "*…she'd recently been in and out of various rehabilitation centers… Could this have contributed?* But why does this strike you as odd? From what we know, she *did* seem to do more partying than parenting."

"True, but according to Jodi, Clarissa was totally off the drink and drugs—and had been for about three months leading up to her death. In fact, Jodi was angry that the papers had hinted otherwise. And I trust her firsthand account more than I do anything in the papers..." I trailed off as I thought about what I'd just said. I believed it even more after seeing a totally fake photo of myself in the papers that morning!

I looked at Sebastian. He was suddenly very quiet, and I could see a small frown forming on his forehead. He avoided looking at me; something was clearly irritating him. I had no doubt he was thinking about this morning's photo too.

I coughed loudly and said, "The other thing that Jodi remembered about her last meeting with Clarissa was that although Clarissa was in good form, there was something that she was 'scared' of."

"According to...?"

"According to Clarissa."

"And Jodi never asked Clarissa what she was scared of?"

I shook my head. "They were interrupted. And then Clarissa promised to call Jodi to tell her more, but she never did because she died."

"And Jodi has no idea what it could have been about?"

"None. She only says that Clarissa seemed nervous when she started to talk about it."

"That doesn't tell us much though, does it?"

I shrugged my shoulders. "Not yet anyway...but she must have had a reason for being scared."

I continued to look through the clippings and learned

that Johnny and Georgie had been home at the time of their mother's death. Jane had also been present.

"But there's no mention of Caro being in the house at the time," I said.

"Although," said Sebastian as he pushed one of the clippings toward me, "it says here that she showed up shortly after Clarissa died, which they say was about two thirty p.m. But considering the bad blood between them…"

I nodded. "We should try to find out if Caro really was absent from the house at the times reported. Also, I wonder if anyone else was there. A maid or someone." I looked at the time. "Let's go, Watson. It's time to cast our net wider—and maybe Mr. Rivera can help."

THURSDAY EVENING
Time Will Tell

A few minutes later I tied Halley up by the main door of the library, and Sebastian and I walked inside. Mr. Rivera must have said something to Mrs. Sobecki because she was waiting for us. "He's in his favorite armchair," she said. "And he's expecting you. Go on. I'll keep an eye on Halley for you."

"Ah, Axelle! And Sebastian!" Mr. Rivera said when he saw us. As we shook hands he peered closely at me and said, "You're looking very smart this afternoon, Axelle."

"I've come directly from doing a fashion show. That's why," I answered.

"What? A fashion show? But what about your hair? What have they done to it? It's so, so…"

It suddenly dawned on me that Mr. Rivera had seen my hair untamed yesterday. No wonder he was having difficulty describing my fashionably styled locks today! "So straight?" I offered.

"Yes, exactly. It looks very beautiful, but I don't know that it really looks like you."

I laughed. Coming from anyone else, Mr. Rivera's

comment might not have sounded like a compliment, but I understood what he meant. "Don't worry, Mr. Rivera. It's not permanent. One wash and it'll be back to its usual self," I said as I started to comb through my hair with my fingers.

"So how can I help you today, Axelle?" Mr. Rivera asked. "And how long is this school article going to be? It must be pretty extensive by now."

As we sat down, Sebastian discreetly pulled his chair back a little from Mr. Rivera and myself. We'd decided he'd sit and listen. We didn't want to raise Mr. Rivera's suspicions with both of us questioning him. After all, we'd told him I was working on a school article, although it sounded as if he was no longer so convinced of that.

And with the questions I had to ask him today, I doubted Mr. Rivera would continue to buy my "school article" excuse at all. So maybe it was time to tell him the truth (sort of), and with a bit of luck, hopefully he'd continue to help.

"Um…actually, Mr. Rivera," I said, "I've finished the article for my school paper, but while researching it I…I seem to have come across some discrepancies in the reports concerning Clarissa's death."

Mr. Rivera nodded vigorously. "I'm not surprised—not that I ever looked into anything myself. But there was something fishy about Clarissa's death, if you ask me."

"In what way?"

Mr. Rivera shrugged. "Nothing I can put my finger on. It was just that Clarissa was so full of life at the end, despite the tragedies she'd so recently endured, and I don't know…something about the whole thing seemed odd, you know?"

"I think I do, Mr. Rivera…and that's why I'd like to look a bit more into what really happened at Dawson Place. So if you're willing to answer more questions, I'd appreciate your help."

"Of course, Axelle. Go ahead, ask away."

"You said that the stairs at the Vane house are very slippery and that Clarissa may have slipped or tripped when she fell. Can you remember anything more precisely than that about her fall? Or even just about the day in general—at the house, I mean."

Mr. Rivera started rubbing his chin. After a few moments he said, "No, not about her fall. Like I said, I wasn't actually in the house when it happened. I was in the garden. And if I had heard something specific, I would have remembered. It was so shocking, you know. It's hard to forget anything about a day like that—and I think any of the neighbors from that time would say the same.

"When it happened, for instance, it was about two thirty in the afternoon and I was working in the front yard, pruning the bushes. Otherwise it was a lovely, sunny day…and then came the terrible shock of Clarissa falling—and just a few months after Julian had drowned. All I know is that the staircase was—and still is—a very slippery one. I don't recall that anyone working in the house was surprised. It certainly wasn't the first time someone had tripped and fallen, although Clarissa was the only one who died."

"And what about Clarissa's general state of health at the time? The papers seemed to think that she'd been under the influence of something—medication for addiction or alcohol or something. They insinuate that that may have had something to do with her fall."

Mr. Rivera slowly nodded. "It's true that Clarissa had her vices—or addictions as they're called now. But after Julian died, she changed. Personally, I think that she was scared of losing Johnny too. He was her favorite, you see, and I always had the impression that she felt she had to clean up her act for his sake—and Georgie's, of course. So shortly after Julian died she went into rehab to control her addiction to whatever it was she was drinking or taking. She was really blooming again when she came out. Then, of course, she died."

So far everything Mr. Rivera was saying tallied with what Jodi had said that morning.

"I've heard that Clarissa was scared about something just before she died. Do you have you any idea what could have been frightening her?"

"Scared?"

I nodded.

Mr. Rivera frowned. "If something was frightening

her, then she hid it well because she looked radiant to me."

"And she had no worries that you knew of? Money trouble, perhaps, or something to do with her family? I've heard there was some rivalry between Clarissa and her sister, Carolyne Ryder."

"There was some quarreling between the sisters about a gentleman, I believe, but I never paid attention to the gossip. Otherwise, no, nothing comes to mind. Nothing I noticed anyway. And between Jane Wimple and Mrs. Underwood, the housekeeper, the Vane household and family was well looked after."

"Mr. Rivera, you said that on the afternoon Clarissa died you were pruning bushes in her front yard. Can you remember anything else about that day? Can you remember seeing who went in and out of the house, for instance? According to the reports written at the time, Johnny, Jane Wimple, and Georgie were present. But surely there were more people around. Like the housekeeper, or what about Carolyne?"

"You're right. Mrs. Underwood, Mary was her name, was around, but she was out shopping at the time of the accident, which is why she wasn't mentioned in the papers. She was a cold woman. I never liked her much, although she ran the household well. I'll give her that."

"You told me yesterday that she died about ten years ago."

"Yes, that's correct."

"It would help me a lot if I could talk to anyone else who worked in the house at that time, or even with anyone around here who knew Mrs. Underwood well. Can you think of anyone I could speak to?"

"Hmm…a couple of maids came and went over the years, but I'm not sure where they are now. I'll have to ask around. But I can do that for you, Axelle, if you'd like. Put a few lines in the water and see if any fish bite."

"Thank you, that would really be helpful… And I wonder if you remember seeing anyone else go in or out of the house that afternoon."

"Yes. You mentioned Carolyne, Clarissa's sister. I saw her go in and out of the house. She was there too that afternoon, yes."

"But I haven't come across her name in any of the reports…"

"That's because she left the house shortly before all the mayhem started. I remember thinking how lucky she was that she'd missed her sister's death. I don't know if anyone else saw her go and come back, because she used the side door and she was in a hurry, as if she'd forgotten something somewhere. Then again, busy young thing that she was, she was always rushing in and out of the house. It didn't exactly draw my attention—except for the fact that she used the side door."

"Hmm… And Georgie? Where was she when her mother fell?"

"Asleep, having her afternoon nap, I believe."

"Where?"

"In her bedroom on the second floor. That's where all of the bedrooms were—and still are, I suppose."

"And what about Johnny and the nanny?"

"They were upstairs on the top floor, in the playroom. They came down when they heard Clarissa scream. So I was told."

"And what about Clarissa herself? Where was she before she fell?"

"Oh, she was having her 'nap.' After she'd gone to that clinic, shortly after Julian died, her doctors ordered her to rest after lunch for a couple of hours—and it was something she took seriously. At least she went to her bedroom after lunch every day until about three or so. She relaxed, wrote her letters, that sort of thing. But she stayed in her room."

"And when did Mrs. Underwood return from her errands?"

"Just after the police arrived." Mr. Rivera was quiet for a moment before continuing. "She was a cold one, all right. Believe it or not, she didn't melt for even a second when Clarissa died. She just stood by the police like stone and said that she wasn't surprised. I know because we were all standing around close to the hall, watching and listening. Anyway, Mary—Mrs. Underwood—stopped working for the family afterward. Just like that." Mr. Rivera snapped his fingers in the air for emphasis. "From one day to the next she was gone."

"Who replaced her?"

"Some other housekeeper. One Jane Wimple found. Very unfriendly—to me anyway."

"And what happened to her?"

"When the family moved away, she found work elsewhere. She died too. Last year."

"Who looks after the house now?"

"A young woman named Agnieszka Salvador. She's the daughter-in-law of a friend of mine. She goes in and checks on it. The house got something of a reputation, you know, after those two deaths. Doesn't matter that Julian died in the Thames. People in the neighborhood started saying that the house was haunted, that going into it would bring bad luck, all that sort of nonsense.

"After the family—or what was left of it—moved away, none of the people hired to look after the house stayed for long except me. For a number of years I kept checking on the garden for them and doing basic maintenance around the house. But since I retired, Agnieszka is the first one who's stayed. It's been a year now."

"So she's not afraid?"

Mr. Rivera shook his head and smiled. "No way. She's a tough cookie, Agnieszka is. I've talked to her a lot about the house and the family's history and so on. It all happened so long ago but she actually finds it kind of interesting. Anyway, she could show you around if you like. It might help with your investigation, give you a feel for the family's past. Although you wouldn't be able to take any photos, of course—or tell people you'd been in the house. Not that anyone would notice. Apart from Georgie, no one from the family has been there for months."

Mr. Rivera looked at his watch. "Agnieszka normally checks on the house about now. She goes by every day after work—she has a day job—to ensure everything is in order. These grand empty houses are big targets for squatters, you know! Anyway, I could take you to meet her if you like."

I could see Sebastian giving me the thumbs-up from where he stood—and I had to agree. What a stroke of luck to be offered a chance to look at the house! It was exactly the opportunity I'd been hoping for—and it happened without having to invent some elaborate ruse.

"Yes, please, Mr. Rivera," I said. "I would very much like to see the house. But do you think we could both go?" I asked, looking at Sebastian.

"I don't see why not. Come on, let's go."

We waved good-bye to Mrs. Sobecki as we walked past the reception desk, and Mr. Rivera turned to me and said, "Mrs. Sobecki told me you like to solve mysteries, Axelle. Answering your questions just now, I'd say you're a natural crime buster. You might want to bear that in mind when it comes to choosing what to study."

"You know, Mr. Rivera, you have a point—and it's one I'll definitely keep in mind. Thank you!" As we collected Halley and left the library, I could see Sebastian trying hard not to burst out laughing.

✳ ✳ ✳

The key turned in the lock with one smooth, reassuringly loud click. Agnieszka pushed the heavy door open, and Sebastian and I followed her in. Mr. Rivera had headed home after introducing us outside, so it was just the three of us, plus Halley. I let Halley off her leash (Agnieszka said it wouldn't be a problem) and looked around. The hall was large, its ceiling high. Dust danced in the shafts of colored light that shone through the vast stained-glass windows.

The other day, as I had tried peering in from outside, I'd seen how the sun reflected against the brightly colored facets of the stained-glass windows, but the effect was entirely different on the inside. Dots of bright color—reds, blues, greens, yellows, and oranges—leaped around the space, their bright vivacity at odds with the faded glamour of the surroundings.

"Nice, right?" Agnieszka asked between the loud snaps she made with her chewing gum.

"It's more than nice," I said, forgetting the tragedy that had happened on the staircase for a moment. I placed my hand on the large crystal orb that decorated the newel post at the bottom of the balustrade. From this vantage point I looked up toward the ceiling and caught my breath. I heard Sebastian do the same as he came up next to me.

The ceiling above the stairs was in fact a glass cupola, so although the hall itself wasn't particularly bright because of the stained-glass windows, the stairwell was. And the higher you looked, the more light flooded the stairwell shaft. It was like a stairway to heaven—or so I thought in my present fanciful mood.

What caught my eye, however, was a large portrait of Clarissa Vane that dominated the lower part of the stairwell and hall. It hung over the staircase on a semi-landing, from where the stairs turned left and continued to the second-floor landing just above. Even in the gloomy light her incandescent beauty shone. The symmetry of her classical features gave the vast canvas a kind of serenity. A flowing turquoise gown billowed around her tall, slim frame, while on her head sat a large, black, softly shaped hat with a wide brim. The effect was unusual, bohemian, and striking.

"I can't imagine what effect she must have had in real life," Sebastian said quietly.

"That's exactly what I was thinking."

I turned to Agnieszka and asked, "Do you mind if we look around?"

"Nah, you go ahead. I'm going to take a quick look in the kitchen. It's through there, in case you need to find me," she said as she pointed across the far side of the hall to a door that was smaller than the others (which, with their size and the grand carved door frames, I assumed led into the reception rooms). "Take your time."

Sebastian and I walked through the first carved door frame into the library that I'd seen through the window the other day. I got that stuck-in-a-time-warp feeling again, but it was intensified, despite the rich furnishings, by the atmosphere of sadness and emptiness inside the house.

We walked through the dining room—faded Chinese wallpaper and a large chandelier—as well as through a rather large drawing room with faded blue decor. But the rooms I really wanted to see were on the floor above.

Sebastian and I slowly climbed the stairs. They were indeed slippery, I noted as I watched even Halley's paws slide out from under her as she scampered up ahead of us. I was thankful I was in Converse.

"So how do you want to start?" Sebastian asked as we approached the second-floor landing.

"Well, thanks to Mr. Rivera, we have an approximate idea of where Clarissa, Caro, Georgie, and Johnny—plus Jane and the housekeeper, Mrs. Underwood—were just before Clarissa fell. So I suggest working out where they were in relation to each other. According to Mr. Rivera, Mrs. Underwood was out running errands."

"Right. So Mrs. Underwood was away from the house?"

"Correct."

"And Clarissa?"

"Clarissa and Georgie were on the second floor in

their respective bedrooms. Caro was also in the house until she left in a rush shortly before her sister fell."

We stopped on the second-floor landing. From there a wide corridor ran in a straight axis through the house. Another shorter corridor crossed it further along. Doors lined both sides of the corridors. I turned the handle on the first one I came to.

I wasn't sure what to expect, but the door led into a room that, like the rest of the house, had stood still since Clarissa's tragic death. Touches of pink satin could be seen from under the corners of the white dust sheets. The furniture was painted white, the carpeting now a dull cream. The room was feminine but not a child's room. It also didn't strike me as a room Clarissa would have decorated for herself—although the only reason I thought this was because I had yet to see a portrait of her dressed in pink.

Speaking of which, there were a couple of framed photos in this room. It took me a while to see who they were of though, because the subject had changed so much. It was Caro—but as Carolyne Ryder she looked less like the cutting-edge stylist I knew and more like a Clarissa wannabe. She must have been in her late teens in the photos. Surely this was Caro's bedroom then. Was this the room she'd rushed from just before the accident?

Sebastian and I walked farther down the corridor. The second door led to a bathroom, the third to another, smaller bedroom. The last door, however, opened onto what must have been Clarissa's bedroom. It was large with an adjoining dressing room and bathroom. The light blue silk of the furnishings and bed hangings shimmered in the late afternoon sunlight that seeped in through and around the white blinds of the windows. A four-poster bed dominated the center of the room, and a generously sized dressing table stood, draped in lace, in front of the window.

A pretty portrait of Clarissa hung to the left of her bed, and under her image on a dainty night table sat an empty water carafe, a bejeweled alarm clock, and a very old telephone. Even covered up and in dim lighting, the room was elegant and impressive, yet comfortable. I didn't think many people in London had bedrooms like this one—at least not anymore. The scale of the suite was more in keeping with a country home.

"This must have been where she was resting before she fell," I said, pointing to the bed as Sebastian walked in and stood next to me. "Mr. Rivera said Clarissa's usual routine was to stay in her bedroom in the afternoon, from after lunch until three."

"I wonder what made her leave the room early," he said.

"Good point, Watson."

"I was thinking maybe one of the children had called her, but they were on this floor and the floor above, so she wouldn't have gone down the stairs to see them."

"Jane was upstairs as well, and Caro had left before it

happened...so why did Clarissa go downstairs? Was she about to go out? Actually, that makes me wonder—we don't know anything about how she was dressed. Was she dressed to go out? Was she in a dressing gown if she'd been in her bedroom? That's something else I might ask Mr. Rivera..."

"Maybe she simply needed something from downstairs. Her diary or something."

I nodded. "Could be..." I stopped in front of a small, delicate writing desk that sat in front of the window of her dressing room and opened its various drawers.

"What are you looking for?" Sebastian asked.

"Nothing special—the drawers seem to be empty anyway. It's just that some of the dust has been disturbed around a few of the drawers."

"Maybe there really is a ghost in the house."

"Maybe..."

After we'd looked at her bedroom a few moments longer, Sebastian led me along the corridor, back toward the landing, and opened the door opposite Caro's bedroom.

"This must have been Georgie's bedroom, don't you think?" he asked.

"Definitely," I said as I quickly took in the small bed and ballerina wallpaper. I put my fingers to my lips and signaled to Sebastian to be quiet. I was thinking of the note I'd received that morning. *At the time everyone asked me about what I could see, but not about what I could hear.*

Perhaps because of the cavernous dimensions of the hall and stairwell, and the hard surface of the stairs, the acoustics of the house meant that we could hear Agnieszka moving about below. We lost her if she closed a door behind her, but otherwise, sounds carried upstairs easily. Closer to us, Halley's claws clattered clearly as she ran up and down the stairs. I looked under the bedroom door. (I'd closed it from the inside.) There was a good half-inch of space between the bottom of the door and the carpet. Noise easily floated in through the gap too, I noted. Georgie could have heard all sorts of things from her bed.

We left her bedroom and I said, "Let's go up to the nursery."

The house is starting to feel claustrophobic, I thought, as we climbed up to the third floor. The sense of gloom and neglect was depressing, and I was starting to feel a need to escape. I wondered about Georgie and the occasional visits she made to the place and why she and Johnny hadn't sold it yet. They'd certainly get a fortune for it. Some mega-millionaire oligarch or banker would have a field day turning this place into a trophy house.

Like the library, the playroom was in a real time warp. It reminded me of *Downton Abbey*. An old rocking horse stood under a dormer window, and a small table and set of chairs were placed in the center of the large, low-ceilinged room. Bookshelves lined the far wall, and a large trunk was pushed into a corner.

What was interesting was that, as on the second floor, the hall and staircase acted as a sort of channel. All manner of noise from below was bounced upward on the hard surface of the stairs. Alternatively, I imagined that any noise from above would also be carried down the stairs. No matter where anyone stood in this house, the closer you were to the stairwell or landings, the more you would be able to hear—from above or below.

Sebastian and I walked to the top of the stairwell and looked down the two flights of stairs. The first sentence from the note I'd received kept playing on rewind through my mind. Quietly, I said it out loud...

At the time everyone asked me about what I could see, but not about what I could hear.

"So what had Johnny or Georgie or Jane heard?" I asked Sebastian as we leaned over the balustrade, our whispers echoing gently within the stairwell. "And was it definitely something to do with Clarissa's death? The words, 'at the time' seem to suggest it was, don't you think?"

"Yes," Sebastian answered, "and then there's the photo of the hall as well..."

"That's what my gut tells me too, Watson." Slowly we began to descend the stairs. We stopped on the second-floor landing and walked along the corridor again, making sure we'd left the bedroom doors shut—as we'd found them.

"And what about Caro?" I continued. "Had she

heard something that made her leave the house in haste? I find it odd that she was absent at precisely the time her sister fell to her death. Or am I reading more into these details than I should? After all, it didn't take the police long to decide that it was accidental."

"That's because everything points to an accidental death," Sebastian countered. "It's only you who doesn't think so," he added with a smile. "But then you think everything is suspicious."

"Thanks, Watson. So what do you think then?"

"Well, actually I think you might be on to something," Sebastian said with a laugh.

"Ha, Watson! Good answer."

"By the way, what about Mrs. Underwood, the housekeeper?" I asked after a moment.

"Holmes, she's dead! If you think she sent you the photo this morning, then your levels of suspicion are way too high—even by your standards!"

"Very funny, Watson. And thanks. I know she's dead, but Mr. Rivera's words keep running through my mind—the bit about how the housekeeper said she wasn't surprised that Clarissa had died. What did she know, I wonder?"

I stopped directly beneath Clarissa's portrait and we both looked up at it. She smiled down serenely, her beauty and style still very much alive in the painting. "Or," I asked as I looked up at her, "had the beautiful model and muse herself said something that had predicted her own death?" I took a deep breath and turned to Sebastian. "This case keeps going around in circles in my head... It's so frustrating!"

"You know what I think?" Sebastian asked as we walked down the last few stairs.

"No, Watson, enlighten me."

"There's only one course of action to take at a time like this."

"Okay, and what is that?"

"I think we need a cheeseburger and a good side of hot fries."

I laughed. "Sometimes, Watson, your state-of-the-art sleuthing techniques amaze me."

"I'm glad something does, Holmes."

Before leaving Dawson Place I had to ask Agnieszka one last question:

"How many phones does the house have?"

"Two," she answered. "One in the corridor between the hall and the kitchen and one upstairs in Clarissa's bedroom."

Hmm...I stored that useful bit of information away, thanked her for her help, and we exchanged numbers. She agreed that I could call her if there was anything else I wanted to check out.

I attached Halley's leash and we headed home. Halley had been on the go with me all day (her second day as an undercover model dog!), and I knew she was hungry. So we stopped by my house long enough to leave her there and feed her. While Halley ate, I quickly ran up to my bedroom and took my laptop from my desk and something else I thought might be useful. I put them both in my shoulder bag, and then leaving Halley behind, Sebastian and I walked around the corner to the Lucky Seven Diner.

The diner was busy—it was a Thursday evening, after all, and London is an especially buzzing place on that night of the week. After a short wait, a small booth was ours. We slid in and wasted no time in ordering—and continuing with our work.

I took out the list I'd made during the La Lune show, as well as my laptop and the other item I'd taken from my desk.

"What's that?" Sebastian asked.

I laughed as I passed it to him. "You're not the only one with state-of-the-art sleuthing techniques, you know."

"Yeah, but a magnifying glass? I mean, that's like straight out of a Hercule Poirot mystery," he said.

I rolled my eyes. "When I spoke to Tallulah earlier, she said there might be a clue in the file name Gavin used for the photographs on the stick. She thought 'Close-up' could be taken literally. And while we can, of course, zoom in and out of the images with my laptop, it might be easier with the magnifying glass."

"You have a point. But looking through every image in microscopic detail could take days!"

I smiled. "Think of it as a game, Watson. I bet it

won't take us as long as you think, and besides, I have to do it. Time is ticking." And as long as the case remained unsolved, Gavin remained at risk of another attack.

"Right, Holmes," Sebastian said. "Then I'll hang on to your state-of-the-art detective aid, and if you open Gavin's file on your laptop, I'll take a closer look at the photos while you get cracking with your notes."

"Now you're talking, Watson."

A while later, Sebastian took a long sip of his milk shake. "So far, I can't find a thing." He sighed.

"How far have you gotten?"

"About halfway through."

"How about we switch for a while?" I suggested. "I'll look at the images, and you can take another look at Gavin's photo and mine from this morning. Maybe something will jump out at you."

I handed Sebastian the two photos, and he pushed my laptop and magnifying glass across the table.

After some time, Sebastian said, "If there is a clue in these photos, it's buried deeper than Atlantis."

I stretched my back—I'd been slumped over my laptop, magnifying glass in hand, for way too long—and finished my milk shake before answering Sebastian. "Well, keep the faith, Watson. There has to be one in there somewhere. I mean, Gavin's attack didn't just happen for no reason."

"You're right. But apart from Tallulah's belief that there is a connection between the images on this stick and his attack, we don't really have anything concrete to go on, do we?"

"We have my gut instinct."

Sebastian rolled his eyes.

"What? That counts for something! And by the way, if there's no connection, then why was I sent a photo?"

"You have a point." He ran his fingers through his hair and then leaned back in the banquette, his head cradled in his hands. He looked gorgeous, I thought, and for a moment the case melted away. I loved his broad shoulders and the way his smile teased me when he gave me that certain look. He was good at watching and observing, and he didn't feel the need to fill silence with words. I liked that about him. I pulled my eyes away from him and forced myself back to the task at hand.

"So, nothing?" I asked as I pointed at the two photos Sebastian still held.

"No. Not unless you want to hear that they remind me of my father." He laughed. Sebastian's father was the Chief Inspector of Paris Police and wore a trench coat and scarf with more flair than anyone in the Burberry ads ever did. What he and these photos could possibly have in common intrigued me.

"Tell me, then."

"My father always writes and doodles on the left-hand side of papers first. Just like someone has on these."

I'd definitely noticed that the word *Hall* was written in the upper left-hand corner of the photo I'd been sent.

And I'd also noted that the photo that Gavin had been sent had a notation or doodle—it was illegible—in the left-hand border of the photo that he had been sent. But I hadn't given these observations more thought than that.

"So why does he do that?" I took a pen and my notebook from my shoulder bag and noted how, instinctively, I would aim for the upper right-hand corner of a photo. Okay, but so what? And yet something clicked in my mind as I practiced this simple exercise. Something so obvious that I kicked myself for not having realized it sooner!

It dawned on me just as Sebastian said: "Because he is left-handed."

Suddenly I was buzzing. Sebastian's face faded from sight and the noises around me became an indistinguishable hum. Something was finally coming together. I thought back to every meeting I'd had with Johnny, Jane, Georgie, and Caro. I'd seen it, but I certainly hadn't given it any thought. Again I kicked myself for my lax observation. But I was going to make up for lost time. Starting now.

"Axelle? Have I missed something?" Sebastian was waving his hand in front of my face.

"Sorry." I smiled. "But, Watson, I owe you one."

"Thanks. I'm thrilled to know you owe me one—and don't worry, I'll collect—but are you saying you think the person who sent these photos is left-handed?"

I nodded.

"And do you know for a fact that one of our suspects is?"

"I do."

"But you're not going to tell me which one, are you?"

I smiled and shook my head.

"In that case, Holmes, I think you owe me two."

Sebastian walked me home, just like he had on Tuesday night. It was only Thursday but the last couple of days had gone by in such a blur of following clues, chasing leads, and modeling work that Tuesday could have been two weeks ago.

We stood outside in the warm air for a few minutes, holding hands. Gradually he drew me to him, until I was close enough to feel his breath on my skin. As our eyes locked, he gently ran his finger over my lips and leaned in to slowly kiss me good night. He was in London until Sunday, but already I was missing him, dreading his absence.

Finally we parted, but I felt him watching me as I walked up our front path and into my house. I turned and waved before I stepped inside. Sebastian smiled and waved back before he disappeared into the night.

Halley was waiting for me when I walked in. My mom still wasn't home, so after sending her a quick message to say that I was back and was going to bed, I let Halley out for a last tour of the garden before we both climbed upstairs. Just as I reached my bedroom, a text message came through. It was from Agnieszka.

What does she want? I thought, as I unlocked my phone and started to read her message.

> **Mr. Rivera says he's found someone who can tell you about Mrs. Underwood. He asks if you can meet him at the library at 9 a.m.**

I texted back:

> **That's great! I'll be there, thanks, Agnieszka. And please thank Mr. R for me!**

After washing off my makeup and brushing my still-straight hair, I padded back to my bedroom. My mind was still whirring with what seemed like a gazillion thoughts about the case. I was hoping they would all suddenly fall into place. Before I slipped into bed I sat at my desk and picked up the paper copy of the old photo Gavin had been sent. I turned on my bright desk lamp and aimed it at the photo. Then, with the magnifying glass, I took a very slow and very careful look at it.

Both Sebastian and I had studied it while we were at the diner, but the light hadn't been as good there. I went carefully over it again, from left to right and top to bottom. After a minute something did in fact catch my eye. I turned my laptop back on and opened Gavin's file. I found the photo in the file and looked closely at it under the light and with the magnifying glass. Hmm…

the tiny fleck seemed to be there too, but on-screen it wasn't as sharply defined.

The tiny spot I was looking at seemed to be part of the original—and not just a surface scratch on the photo itself.

I knew my father had a better magnifying glass in his study, so I quickly ran down to fetch it. Back in my bedroom I looked again at the spot in question until a chill ran through me and the hairs on the back of my neck stood on end. I bent over the photo for a long time, paralyzed by what I saw. Mudlarking, indeed. This minuscule spot looked like nothing, and yet it was everything. If my suspicions were correct, then I finally knew why Gavin had nearly been killed.

So had he discovered this long covered-up detail as I had, just by studying the photo? Had there been a note attached to the original hand-delivered photo? Assuming there was, that note must have helped Gavin uncover this clue much faster than I had. But how had he proved he was right about it? Because I'd have to find a way of proving it too. Furthermore, had Gavin had any idea what he was getting into by following up on the photo?

And yet his photo—his clue—was only a small part of this mystery. The photo I had been sent was related to a different long-buried secret, and yet both secrets were connected.

I felt sick to my stomach and had to sit down on my bed. I took some deep breaths and thought about everything I'd have to do in the morning.

I was seeing Mr. Rivera again first thing, and I needed him to verify something that he'd said. I also needed to meet Georgie as soon as possible. And I'd need Agnieszka's help later in the day—not to mention Sebastian's and Ellie's—that is, if I was going to get Johnny, Georgie, Caro, and Jane together the next evening. It was time to confront them all with the truth. What was it my grandfather used to say? *The truth always comes out in the end. You may have to wait a long time, but a secret doesn't remain secret forever.*

I was about to prove my grandfather right.

FRIDAY MORNING
More Pieces of the Puzzle

I woke up in a panic as the water pulled me down. Cold and clammy, it pressed against my throat, choking all the breath out of me. With all the force I could muster, I pushed myself up and out of it. It took me a minute to realize that I was sitting up in my bed, in such a cold sweat that my pajamas were clinging to me. Halley snuggled closer and slowly the nightmare receded. It was light outside, and according to my alarm clock, it was five o'clock. *Just as well*, I thought as I got out of bed. *I've got a long day ahead of me. I could use the early start.*

I picked up my phone and was relieved to see that Josh's obsessed fans finally seemed to have stopped messaging me. I then wrote to Tallulah, saying I hoped to have good news for her later that night. If I didn't, then I strongly suggested we should update the police on what I'd pieced together. But one thing at a time, I told myself.

I also asked her to keep me updated on Gavin. He was, after all, supposed to come out of his induced coma today.

Next I sat at my desk and went through all my notes, starting with the ones I'd taken on Tuesday morning when I'd met Tallulah for the first time. There was one more niggling point that kept playing on rewind in my mind. It was a question Sebastian had also raised. Why had Clarissa gone down the stairs at that moment on that afternoon? Mr. Rivera had said that everyone in the household knew Clarissa rested for a couple of hours after lunch every day. So something must have caused her to get out of bed…

I sat at my desk, thinking about this as the dawn light burned through the morning mist. The songbirds were busy in the garden, trilling and chirping, filling the air with music. I got up and gazed out of the window for a while, thinking and thinking, until finally, after putting myself in Clarissa's place, I came to an answer that I thought made sense.

I took my phone and called Sebastian, hoping he'd be awake. He answered right away.

"Yes, I'm awake, Holmes. And if you're calling this early, it can only mean one thing. Case solved?"

"I think so, yes."

"But you need help to tie up the loose ends?"

I laughed. "How'd you guess?"

"That, dear Holmes, is because I know you. And I'm ready whenever you are."

After looking at my schedule we decided that the best idea would be to meet at the Johnny Vane offices, right after I'd (hopefully) seen Georgie.

"So eleven a.m. at Holborn Tube station it is," I said. "Fine. See you there."

"Wait! Hold on, not so fast! In the meantime, can you do a couple of things for me?"

"No problem, I'm all yours. What do you need?"

"This might sound odd—"

"I'm used to that from you by now, Holmes."

"Ha-ha. As I was saying, this may sound odd, but just trust me, will you? I'd like a list of the locations of the pay phones closest to the Dawson Place mansion at the time of Clarissa's death. Do you think you can help with that?"

"Absolutely. I'll try to have it by the time we meet. What else?"

"Can you buy a small can of paint? A sample size in a bright color. Brick red would be good—but not too dark. And could you get a sort of painter's uniform? Cap, splattered shirt, that sort of thing?"

"Are we still working on the same case?" I could practically feel Sebastian smile from across town. "Or are you just two steps ahead of me?"

"I'm many more than that, Watson!" As I said goodbye and put down the phone, I thanked the detective gods for Sebastian's help. It was crucial that I found out the locations of the pay phones. I knew that wouldn't take Sebastian long, but it's the sort of thing I'm not very good at. As for the paint and painter's outfit, well, he didn't know it yet, but that was also something I thought he'd be good at.

I went back to my desk and quickly riffled through my notes again, and then I wrote a new list:

Mr. Rivera
Georgie
Sebastian: pay phones, paint
Jorge Cruz: show at Hampton Court (with Sebastian)
Dawson Place tonight: Johnny, Georgie, Caro, and Jane.
 (Plus Agnieszka (?), Ellie (?), and Sebastian)

Yes, that was better, I thought as I turned and walked to my bathroom. Hopefully everything would go according to plan.

Halley was on my bed and barked as I shut my laptop. "What is it, Halley?"

She answered with a few whimpers.

"Are you ready to help me again today?" I asked as I pulled my outfit together.

She barked.

"Good. Then let me finish getting dressed and we'll go."

Dark-blue jeans, another T-shirt (this one from Jorge Cruz, and appropriate, I thought, considering I'd be doing his show later that day), and a really cool jacket I'd found at H&M. It was black and had the most amazing razor-sharp shoulders. I topped the outfit off with my glasses. Then I went in to say good-bye to my mom and to tell her that I'd be gone—with Halley—for the day.

"She seems to like doing your fashion rounds with you, doesn't she?" my mom asked as she tickled Halley's belly.

"Yes, she does," I answered. Needless to say I didn't mention how much Halley was enjoying the extra walks and adventures my sleuthing took us on.

"Well, enjoy your day, Axelle darling. It sounds like it's going to be exciting. Jorge Cruz should be fun."

If only she knew, I thought. Then, without going into detail, I mentioned that I had plans for that evening with Ellie (hopefully—I still had to ask her) and Sebastian. "I'm not sure when I'll be back."

"Well, it is Friday, so as long as you stay with Ellie and Sebastian and one of them brings you home, then I don't see why you shouldn't stay out till midnight. I'll be waiting for you though."

"Thanks, Mom." I had a feeling my night would go on much later than that, but I'd cross that bridge when I got to it, I told myself.

"And what about Josh? And the photo situation?" my mom asked. "I don't see any photographers outside this morning," she said as she walked to my dad's study and looked out along the street.

"Well, it does seem to have calmed down," I answered as I checked my phone again. There were no new messages since I'd checked earlier. That was a good sign! "Plus I'm going to see Josh later—he'll be at the Jorge Cruz show. He sent me an email late last night about the 'photo situation.'" I had a missed call from Josh too, but I didn't tell my mom that part. "His lawyers have managed to get the papers to admit that they were in the wrong. An apology will be forthcoming, which is great, isn't it?"

"Thank goodness for that!" my mom said as she planted a kiss that landed half on my forehead. "Darling, really, it's hard to kiss you with those glasses covering half your face."

I pushed them back up my nose. Honestly, would my mom *ever* get over my glasses?

"Anyway, I'll see you tonight."

"Absolutely, Mom." I put Halley on her leash and left.

Mrs. Sobecki was just going up the library steps when Halley and I arrived. Mr. Rivera was waiting for me at the bottom.

"Good morning, Axelle, and good morning, Halley. We don't need to go in the library this morning. We should get to Dawson Place as soon as possible. Follow me," he said with a wave of his hand. "By the way," he continued as I walked beside him, "how did it go with Agnieszka yesterday? Did she show you everything you wanted to see?"

"Yes, she did, thank you. And it's given me a clearer picture of how Clarissa fell."

"Good, good. Isn't the house wonderful on the inside? It's a shame no one lives there anymore." Then, as we turned onto Dawson Place, he said, "I'm taking you to meet Nancy Bell. She actually worked at the house as a maid at the time of Clarissa's accident. She started shortly after Mr. Vane died, so she saw plenty of the drama. And, by the way, she's another one who didn't get on well with Mrs. Underwood. Like me, she's lived around here since she was a child, so she knows all the neighborhood gossip. If she can't answer your questions, nobody can." He smiled.

Nancy was waiting for us at the gates in front of the house. She was petite and quite old—about Mr. Rivera's age—but her memory was still sharp, especially when it came to the Vanes. "They were our very own reality show! Not that that sort of television program existed back then," she said. "But if it had, they could have made one called *Dawson Place*. Drama, beautiful people, addictions, money, affairs—you name it, we had it right here," she said as she pointed to the house. "Clarissa was lovely though. The day she fell was a sad, sad day."

I got to work right away. "One of the former housekeepers, Mrs. Underwood, said that she 'wasn't surprised' when Clarissa fell. Do you know what she could have meant by that?"

Nancy nodded her head rapidly. "I didn't like her, and I thought it was incredibly rude of her to talk like that with poor Clarissa not even cold in the ground. Anyway, let's hope justice has been done up there by now," Nancy added with an upward glance at the sky.

"To be honest, everyone in the neighborhood knew that Clarissa liked to drink and sometimes took pills to make her happy. After losing her husband and a son within a few years of each other, is it any surprise? That old trout Mrs. Underwood had no sympathy for Clarissa. She passed her silent judgment on all of us, in fact." I saw Mr. Rivera nod in agreement with Nancy's last sentence. "And she always said something would happen to Clarissa—"

I interrupted Nancy. "Specifically because of her addictions or for any other reason?"

Nancy was surprised by my question. "I never heard of any other reason but that one," she said. "Her unhappiness and addictions, I mean."

"Mrs. Underwood never explained herself?"

"Not that I know of."

"So she could have been referring to something else?"

Nancy shrugged her shoulders. "If she was, I didn't know about it."

"Mrs. Underwood was out when Clarissa fell, wasn't she? Did she normally run her errands at that time in the afternoon?"

Mr. Rivera and Nancy both said, "Yes," before Nancy explained further. "Once the family and Jane had had lunch and things were cleared up, then Mary—Mrs. Underwood—would leave. She was normally gone for an hour and a half or so. Back then we didn't have these large delis and enormous supermarkets like we have now. She'd go from one small grocer to another. Markets too. Even to Fortnum & Mason to get tea. She'd take the Tube."

"And were you still in the house when Clarissa fell?"

Nancy slowly shook her head. "No. I always left as soon as Clarissa disappeared upstairs for her nap. That lunchtime was the last time I saw her."

This line of questioning had taken me about as far as it could, I felt. I decided to change tack while I still had both Mr. Rivera's and Nancy's attention.

"Mr. Rivera, yesterday you told me that Caro dashed out of the house shortly before her sister's accident but came back again not long after."

Mr. Rivera nodded. "That's correct."

"Can either of you remember any more details about that?"

Mr. Rivera shook his head. "No. It was as I told you—she was in a hurry, as if she'd forgotten something."

"But in a hurry to leave or in a hurry to come back?" I pressed.

He shrugged his shoulders and stood thinking for a moment. "I've never thought of it that way, but I guess I'd have to say both. She rushed out, using the side door, but then hurried back in too—again using the side door."

"Which was unusual?"

"For Caro and Clarissa, yes. They always used the front door. And like I said, she was dressed more casually to go out than usual. It was as if she'd left something somewhere and was dashing out to get it, if you know what I mean."

I did know what he meant, but if Caro had rushed out to get something, then why did she rush back in? Unless she'd had a reason to return. An appointment perhaps? And then all her plans changed, of course, when she returned home and saw what had happened. But then why had she used the side door? I had an idea why, but I wasn't able to confirm it just yet.

"Hmm…thank you."

Nancy hadn't seen Caro leave, but she had plenty to say about the argument between the sisters. "Caro was engaged to be married, though for the life of me, I can't remember the name of her fiancé. Anyway, when the fiancé met Clarissa he really fell for her. Needless to say this all happened long after Mr. Vane had died. Caro's fiancé was her first love, and goodness she was furious when he left her for Clarissa. Then again, who wouldn't be? And when Clarissa turned around and left the man, well, Caro was fuming. She couldn't get over it."

"Hmm…" This echoed what Jodi had said about the sisters and what Sebastian had found in the newspapers. But now I needed answers to two more specific questions, questions that were important to my theory about the day she died.

"So Clarissa was definitely in her bedroom before she went down the stairs?"

Nancy nodded. "Yes, I believe so," she said. "After she'd been through rehab, Clarissa always rested in her bedroom after lunch. Doctor's orders. I saw her go up before I left."

"And how was she normally dressed when she was resting?"

"She always changed into a robe," Nancy said. "She had some lovely ones. She liked to be comfortable because she'd either lie on her bed or write letters, and sometimes she'd sleep. I'd lay the robes out for her and then she would dress again before she went out in the evening—and she went out nearly every night, by the way."

"And how was she dressed when she fell?" I asked.

"She was dressed to go out, actually," Mr. Rivera answered. "I remember that because at the time I thought it was proper that the police saw her fully dressed."

"But she would normally have been in a robe at that time?" I said, wanting to be completely clear.

"Yes," Nancy answered. "Absolutely."

I was buzzing. The answers to my last questions were just as I'd expected. I thanked Mr. Rivera and Nancy for their help, and then I left. Time was ticking on.

As Halley and I caught the Central line from Notting Hill Gate, I quickly messaged Ellie, asking her to help me that evening. She wrote back with a laughing emoji:

> **I had a feeling this might happen, so I've kept tonight free for you—and the weekend too!**

I thanked her and said I'd explain more at the Jorge Cruz show that afternoon. Fifteen minutes later my train stopped at Holborn. Sebastian was waiting for Halley and me when we stepped out of the station and into the light. Without a word he handed me an envelope. I opened it and pulled out a folded map.

"The dots represent the neighborhood phone boxes at the time of Clarissa's death," he said.

"Watson, you're amazing! Thank you," I said. We stood to the side of the pavement, and I laid the map out on a stack of boxes next to a magazine vendor's stand. A quick glance told me that some of the phone boxes were still there, while others were long gone. But the one that seemed most relevant stood on the same corner today as it had in the 1970s.

"Axelle, can I ask what this is about? Why the phone boxes? What have they got to do with anything?"

I smiled. "That, Watson, you'll find out this evening."

"You never let the cat out of the bag, do you?"

"No, Watson, I don't. It was one of my grandfather's cardinal rules: don't reveal your hunches until you know they're right."

"Fine. I'll be patient."

"Good things come to those who wait, Watson."

"They'd better." He smiled.

"And what about the paint? And the clothes?"

Sebastian held up a plastic bag. "I found a one-stop paint shop and voilà! I got everything you wanted, but it would be good to know what it's for. Or, let me guess, you can't tell me."

"Actually, this time I have to tell you—because you have a crucial role to play."

"I thought my role was always crucial to you."

"Steady, Watson. Let's concentrate, please."

"I am concentrating."

His gray-blue eyes seemed darker than usual this morning, and frankly, he smelled amazing. *Let's face it, Axelle*, I told myself. *If anyone around here is having a hard time concentrating, it's you.*

"I'm glad." I smiled as I folded the map and put it in my shoulder bag. As we walked toward the Johnny Vane headquarters (I was on my way to see Georgie), I explained.

"I'm pretty sure Johnny Vane will be at the Jorge Cruz fashion show later this afternoon. Apparently he was Jorge's mentor, so he's bound to be a VIP guest."

"And?"

"And I need him to remove his gloves—something that he apparently never does."

Sebastian stopped and looked at me, alarm wrinkling his brow. "However," I continued, "I figure that given the right circumstances, he will take them off."

Sebastian's alarmed expression turned to one of outright surprise. He lifted the plastic bag he was carrying. "Are you thinking what I think you're thinking?" he asked.

"Probably." I laughed. "I'd like you to come to the show with me, but dressed as a painter and decorator. Then I just need you to accidentally spill some paint on Johnny's gloves. If that doesn't make him take them off, then nothing will. And it shouldn't be as complicated as it sounds, because you know how chaotic things get after a show. That chaos will work to your advantage."

"And why do *I* have to do this?"

"Well, *I* would—but he knows I'm delving into his family's past, so he'll be careful to avoid me and he certainly won't remove his gloves around me. At least if my theory is correct, I'd be very surprised if he did."

"And I guess there's no point in asking you to share this theory with me, is there?"

"Correct, Watson," I said, smiling. "Anyway, he won't know you from Adam, so I bet you can get the gloves off."

"Fine. I'm game. But what do I do once they're off?"

"Observe."

"Observe?"

I nodded. "Yes, his hands. The *tops* of his hands. And concentrate on looking at them carefully. Check the skin tone and look for any marks, scars, whatever."

"Are you serious?"

"Very. Now we just have to think of a way of getting you in…although perhaps Charlotte can help us." I pulled out my phone and called her. Once I got through, I briefly explained that I needed to get Sebastian into that afternoon's show (without telling her about the paint spilling bit).

"And this has to do with Gavin?"

"Yes, it does. It would help me help him, if that makes sense."

"All right. I might be able to get Sebastian in, but it'll be standing room and at the back. Is that okay? Shall I say he's a journalist or something?"

"The back is fine, and yes, he is studying journalism, so say he's covering the show for a fashion story."

"Good. I'll make my calls now, and if I have any problems, I'll call you back. If you don't hear from me pretty much right away, consider it done. I'll text you about where to meet once we're there. It'll probably be best if Sebastian comes in with me."

I thanked Charlotte and stopped just around the corner from the Johnny Vane offices. Sebastian agreed to wait outside with Halley. I took my beanie off and quickly combed through my hair. Then I removed my glasses. I stood more chance of getting in to see Georgie if I looked like a model. I walked the short distance to the entrance, pushed the heavy glass door open, and marched up to the reception desk with my fingers crossed. I really needed to see her.

Fortunately the receptionist on duty recognized me, and after a quick call to Georgie, I was shown to her office without any delay. However, after agreeing to see me so readily, Georgie was now as quiet as a clam. Apart from hello, she didn't say another word. Then again, I knew she was scared. She would probably wait for me to make the first move.

I took a deep breath and decided to get straight to the point—even if it meant going out on a limb. "Georgie, I know it was you who sent Gavin the photograph," I said. "And you sent one to me too, didn't you?"

Immediately, I saw her pull back from her desk. It was the tiniest of shifts, but when her cheeks flushed with color and she made a sharp intake of breath, I knew I was right.

"But I'm here to help," I added quickly as Georgie stood up and padded over to the large window of her office. She gazed out with her back to me. "I know you're scared. But you have to tell me what it was you heard all those years ago. I think I know what it might have been, but you have to give me a couple more pieces of the puzzle so that I can figure it all out.

"The piece you gave Gavin is not enough. Time is ticking by, and he's still in the hospital because of the trail you sent him on. Will you help me?" I waited a moment, but still she said nothing. "If you're uncomfortable telling me any more, then write it down. Or would you rather we met somewhere else, away from here?"

She chewed her lip and sat back down at her desk.

"If it helps, please write whatever you want to say down for me."

She nodded and grabbed a sheet of paper and a pen.

She seemed to have come to a decision. Quickly she wrote a note and pushed it back across the table. "Take it and leave now," she whispered. "I'll meet you there in fifteen minutes. It's a private square. Wait by the main gate."

I left her office and looked at the directions she'd given me. I followed them to a small square ten-minute walk from the Vane offices. I called Sebastian on my way there and told him to follow me. Georgie arrived two minutes later. She was fishing the key to the gate out of her handbag as she walked up to me. "I live on this square, which is why I have the key." She was shaking so much she could barely open the gate.

"This is the only place I know that is really safe. You need a key to get in, and you have to live on the square to have one. Sorry about all this…" We sat on the first bench we came to.

She was petrified. Not that she looked it—years of living with the burden of a guilty secret had taught her to develop an inscrutable mask—but the energy of fear was coming off her in waves. I knew that she'd taken a huge risk in sending the photographs to Gavin and me, and she was taking another huge risk in seeing me now. But just seeing me wasn't enough. She'd have to talk too.

She sat with her legs uncrossed and her hands fidgeting in her lap. After a few moments I realized that if I wanted her to talk, I'd have to find a way to make her.

"I knew it was you who sent us the photos. It was the

coffee stain on the photo you sent Gavin and the notes you wrote in the upper left-hand corner of the one you sent me. You're left-handed, Georgie, aren't you?"

She nodded silently, her hands continuing to fidget.

I plowed on. "In the note you sent me, you said you'd heard things. I've been in your old house, Georgie."

Her eyes darted rapidly to mine as I said that.

"And I know how the sound travels up and down the staircase. And although I know that you were very young—about three or four—when your mother died—"

Georgie nodded again.

"—I think you heard a lot of things. And I can guess some of it. Shall I tell you what I think?"

I told Georgie as gently as I could what I believed had happened at the Dawson Place mansion all those years ago. Tears welled in her eyes, and soon huge sobs racked her body. I waited quietly until she calmed down. Then finally she started to talk—and everything was as I'd thought.

By the time I left, we'd made plans for that evening. Now, after taking the first desperate steps to seek help—by sending Gavin and me the photos—Georgie was willing to help me reveal the truth to everyone. I just had to hope that she wouldn't back down when the time came.

FRIDAY AFTERNOON
Backstage Drama

Georgie and I got up from the bench and walked back toward the garden gate in silence. We parted with no more than a brief good-bye. Georgie still looked terrified, and I couldn't help wondering whether she was already regretting our meeting. If she could just hold fast to my plans, she would soon be able to begin a new life—without a guilty secret.

I stood and watched Georgie disappear down the road. A moment later Halley and Sebastian came around the corner, and together we walked back to Holborn station. From there we caught a train to Waterloo and then another to Hampton Court Palace. As the trains whizzed along the tracks I told Sebastian about my meeting with Georgie. We also discussed, as best we could, Sebastian's role at the show. But there were a few other models on the train out of Waterloo—we were all walking for Jorge—so for the sake of discretion, I had to drop the case for a while and listen to the snippets of modeling conversation that wafted toward me.

"I'm thinking of going to Japan to model for the

summer... Do you think it could be fun? Or would I just feel really homesick?"

"I can't believe I fly all the way into London and the model flat I'm staying in doesn't have enough bedsheets for me! I told my agency to buy some as soon as possible!"

"I'm so excited! My mom is coming to visit me! It's her first trip to London so I'm going to take a couple of days off to sightsee with her... What should we see?"

"I'd really like to start college in the fall and study English lit. Do you think I'll be able to model and study at the same time?"

Although I was becoming familiar with the kinds of topics the girls were discussing, they still sounded as if they were coming from some kind of parallel universe—or "Planet Fashion," as Ellie called it. In any case, having a life-or-death mystery to solve, I had other priorities to think about.

The half-hour train ride to Hampton Court passed quickly, and before we knew it, we all got off the train and followed the signs to the hair and makeup area. It had been set up under a small tent near the garden we were going to walk through when we showed the clothes. The weather was beautiful—not a hint of rain in the blue, cloudless sky. Jorge Cruz's "Bloomsbury" theme couldn't have had more cooperation from our famous weather if he'd planned it. Who says it always rains in England?

Sebastian and I parted at the entrance to the hair and

makeup area. He wasn't allowed in without a security pass so he'd be on his own from now until we met at the end of the event. He texted Charlotte to let her know he was here. She'd promised to make sure he got into the show area of the garden. Then, during the event, he'd slip off to the washroom and change into his painter's outfit. As soon as the show was over, he'd head to the backstage tent.

Johnny would inevitably head there too—right after Jorge had taken his bow on the garden runway—so he could congratulate his former protégé. During this after-show chaos, Sebastian would "bump" into Johnny and spill the paint on his gloves. Sebastian had seen Johnny Vane at Belle's party so he knew what Johnny looked like.

If I could manage it, I'd try to be nearby, but the backstage frenzy was difficult to predict, and for all I knew, a blogger or journalist could suddenly corner me for a few minutes' question time. Of course, I could get out of it, but I would need an excuse that didn't draw unnecessary attention. I had the feeling that our paint-spilling plans might just cause a scene.

The clothes were beautiful, now they were fully finished. I'd wondered how successfully Jorge would adapt his typically American clothes—sporty, minimal, and sleek—with an English Bloomsbury aesthetic, but he'd done it well (in my opinion anyway!). He'd taken classic English flower prints, for instance, and had them digitally enlarged to give an abstract impression of an English garden. They looked modern and fresh. The synthetic fabrics he used, combined with the way he had digitally manipulated the colors and patterns, gave the clothes a sharp edge.

Each girl went out only once, because we were made to walk a long, meandering path through the palace's famous Knot Garden. There would be no time for a change of outfits. Carpet had been laid out on the garden's gravel paths—thankfully! That made walking in our heels much easier. Meanwhile, the front-row editors, celebrities, pop stars, and assorted fashion personalities would sit on dainty gilded chairs placed along the sides of the paths.

The show went without a hitch. I caught Charlotte's eye, and she smiled at me as I walked past. I saw Johnny later. Like everyone else at the show, he had his sunglasses on (for once it was actually justified—the sun was shining!), so I wasn't sure if he'd recognized me. Josh was impossible to miss. He was surrounded by an A-list of gorgeous pop stars and hot Hollywood actors. For the sake of discretion, he didn't seem to react to me at all, but I knew from the tiniest of nods and from the way he smiled ever so gently that he had. I also saw Sebastian way at the back in a corner of the garden that had been reserved for standing-room-only invitations. He gave me a thumbs-up as I walked past him on my way to the backstage tent.

Shortly afterward we were all called out to walk a final turn around the runway, then Jorge came out to take his bow. As soon as I could, I dashed back to where I'd left Halley and all of my personal belongings in a corner of the changing area. The backstage chaos was about to begin!

I pulled my clothes on as quickly as possible and brushed my hair. Fortunately, the Bloomsbury look—at least as Jorge saw it—translated into loose, natural hairstyles with a bit of texture. It was easy to brush out and, I thought, looked nice—certainly better than my usual tumbleweed.

As for my makeup, I left my eyes on but wiped away the lipstick and some of the foundation. Then I grabbed my shoulder bag, took hold of Halley's leash, and headed toward the hubbub in the middle of the backstage tent. Right away I felt someone take my arm and whisper in my ear. It was Josh.

"Here you are," he said. I shouldn't have been surprised. If anyone could navigate their way around the fashion landscape—backstage or front row—it was Josh.

And although I was pleased to see him, this was really not the moment.

"Yes, here I am," I said as my eyes scanned the scene over his shoulder. I was looking for Johnny and Sebastian—not that it was easy to spot them. Fashion journalists and photographers buzzed all over the place trying to get a quote from any of the models—and Jorge, of course. The hairstylists and makeup artists weren't exempt from questions either. Everyone wanted to know what and who had been the inspiration behind the hair and makeup.

"I know this isn't the best place to speak, Axelle, but I want to know when I can see you."

At that moment, I finally caught sight of Sebastian again. He was, I thought with a smile, nearly unrecognizable. His painter's cap was pulled low over his brow, and his usual leather jacket and jeans had been replaced with a paint-splattered shirt and trousers. He was even wearing rubber gloves. (*Good thinking, Sebastian*, I thought.)

In one hand he carried a paintbrush, and in the other the small can of paint. The only thing I didn't see was the bag where he must have stashed his own clothes... Where was it? I had the feeling we'd have to make a quick getaway, and if Sebastian had to go back for his bag, it would slow us down.

If I took it with me, he'd be free to escape quickly. "Josh, I'm really, really sorry, but I have to get going—now."

"You're driving me crazy, Axelle," he said as he deftly stepped in front of me, blocking my way. "How can I get to know you better if we never get a moment alone outside a studio or away from a runway? I've got to see you, and I won't let you go until you tell me something—anything."

"Then how about we talk tomorrow morning?" Sebastian caught sight of me, and I could see him rolling his eyes as he watched me.

"Fine. I'll call you. Now off you go to wherever it is you're rushing to." He smiled and let me past.

I hurried over to Sebastian. I brushed close to him but we didn't make eye contact. In fact I took my phone out and pretended to check my messages. Meanwhile he whispered under his breath, "Don't tell me, Mr. Pop Star had something important to say about the case?"

"Funny, Watson. Now where is your bag with your clothes? I have a feeling we'll have to make a quick getaway."

"With or without the pop star joining us?"

"Are you jealous, Watson?"

"Not at all, Holmes. I just want to be clear about our plan."

"I bet. Now will you tell me where your bag is, please?"

"Under the far table near the exit. I've covered it with my leather jacket."

"Good. I'll get your bag while you do what you have to do. We're about to cause a scene. Are there any other exits here?" I asked as I looked at the one I'd used to come in. It was reserved for the models, and as far as I'd seen, it only led to the hair and makeup area. We'd get cornered for sure if we took that way out.

Sebastian nodded toward the far corner opposite us. "Only that one, the one I used to get in here. It leads out to the gardens where you walked. You look good in heels, by the way."

Before I could stop myself, I blushed bright pink. *Grrr!* Why did he have to have this effect on me? I took a quick breath, ignored his comment, and answered as calmly as I could, "Good, then that's the one we'll use. You do what you have to do, and I'll cover for you as you escape."

"How are you going to do that?"

I nodded toward the fire extinguisher I'd spotted at the side of the tent, just a few feet away from us.

Sebastian raised his eyebrows. "If that's your idea of cover, then we are definitely going to cause a scene." He smiled.

"Hmm. And here," I said, as I took a small can of hair spray out of a basket of free samples one of the hair-product sponsors had placed on the tables backstage. "If anyone tries to follow you, use this on them. Hair spray is horrible when it's sprayed in your face." I took one for myself too. "Run to the exit and then toward the river. Get rid of the painter shirt as soon as you can and head for the Thames. They'll probably expect us to avoid the boats they've lined up to take the guests back to London."

"Which is why we'll take one?"

"Exactly."

At that moment Ellie showed up. "Here I am. Can I help?" she whispered. "In a way that doesn't put an end to my modeling career?"

I nodded. "We're about to cause a scene. I'm going to distract everyone with the fire extinguisher so Sebastian can get away, but it would be great if you could do something as well."

"Just tell me what you need."

"Do you think you could run out of here once the chaos starts? Wait until Sebastian starts to run, then chase after him. As soon as you both have some cover, take off in a different direction from him. Try to keep as many of the security guards as far away from us as possible."

Ellie nodded. She was excited, and more importantly, she was actually wearing sneakers. "I told you I thought something like this might happen today." She smiled as she wiggled her feet. "So I decided to throw my heels to the wind this morning, Axelle, just for you."

"Thank you," I said. And I meant it.

I found Sebastian's bag while Ellie got into position. Then I watched from a distance as Sebastian, his back turned to the chaos of the tent, opened the small can of paint. He turned and walked up to Johnny, holding the open can of paint. As he drew nearer he pretended to stumble, and then I saw him bump into Johnny from the side. He'd taken careful aim, and I watched with relief as the contents of the can landed on Johnny's gloves. Mind you, I didn't see it as much as hear it.

Angry expletives exploded from Johnny's lips. In a stroke of quick thinking, I saw Sebastian smear the paint all over Johnny's hands with the paintbrush—presumably pretending to brush it off? Now Johnny was really agitated, and at this point Sebastian dropped his brush and paint can to help remove the gloves.

I noticed Sebastian taking a good look at the tops

of Johnny's hands—and then the questions started: "Who are you?" "What are you doing here?" and so on. Two burly security guards made their way toward Johnny, Sebastian, and the small crowd that had formed around them.

"Time to move, and you'd better keep up," I told Halley as I snapped her leash off her. (I knew she'd stick by my side without it—and besides, I needed to have my hands free). I grabbed the fire extinguisher (which was much heavier than I'd expected) and broke the safety fastening. "Sorry, Jorge," I muttered to myself as I aimed the nozzle at the curling iron I'd noticed on a hairdressing table behind me. At least, I told myself, I could make it look as if I was really trying to put a fire out.

The water surged out with force. "*Fire!*" I yelled. "*Fire!*" It took a few shouts but then chaos really broke out. People started to scatter and head toward the exit in a panic. I watched as Ellie and Sebastian began to maneuver their way through the backstage mayhem.

Meanwhile I continued to hold the fire extinguisher. I was now aiming the nozzle in all directions, pivoting on my foot as I twirled. I needed to create as much confusion as possible. Once I knew I'd given Ellie and Sebastian enough of a lead, I thrust the fire extinguisher into the hands of a confused-looking fashion blogger.

"You've ruined my clothes!" she screamed at me.

All I could think to do was to yank some of Jorge's dresses from the clothing racks next to me. "Here!" I said.

"Try these on for size!" Then, before her look of surprise wore off, I yelled *"Fire!"* again and pushed myself into the panicking crowd. Slowly I forced my way out of the backstage tent and into the gardens, Halley at my heels. I fell in with a group of models leaving the show, and still carrying both my bag and Sebastian's, I chatted with them about all the commotion going on in the tent and how nice it was to get out of there.

I really did feel sorry about unleashing so much chaos at Jorge's show, but what else could I do?

I was passing a large, clipped box bush when I heard a loud hiss. I turned and saw Sebastian. I bent down and pretended to tie my shoelaces while I pushed his bag toward him. Then I got up and fell back in with the models. A few seconds later, Sebastian joined me and we kept walking with the models all the way down to the dock. There we got on one of the departing boats and sailed off into the sparkling afternoon light.

Sebastian and I stood at the railing and caught our breath before I asked him what I was desperate to know.

"Did you see any distinguishing marks on the top of Johnny's right hand?" I said as I looked at him and brushed the hair out of my eyes.

Sebastian shook his head. "Nothing—not a single blemish or scar. Absolutely nothing."

I let out a loud breath of air.

"Is that what you expected to hear?"

"Yes—at least, it's what I'd hoped to hear."

"So what's next, Holmes?"

I looked at my watch. It was four o'clock. We'd have just enough time to eat something before meeting Georgie and Agnieszka at Dawson Place.

"It's time to uncover the Vane family's long-buried secrets."

Ellie called me to say that, after I'd given her the signal to run, the security guards had indeed followed her out of the backstage tent. She'd led them past the Knot Garden and through a few palace courtyards before slowing down. Once they'd caught up with her, she'd delayed them further by accusing them of harassment. She let them placate her for a while before explaining that she'd actually been running away from the fire. By then, Sebastian and I were long gone.

Ellie had just gotten on a train to Waterloo. We agreed that Sebastian and I would hop off the boat at Surbiton meet Ellie on the Surbiton station platform. We'd all travel to Waterloo together. From there we'd all take the Tube to Notting Hill.

Georgie's message came through just as we pulled in to Waterloo:

> **Axelle, everything is in place. Everyone will be there at 7:30 p.m. But I'll meet you at 6:30. Is that early enough?**

We'd planned to meet at Dawson Place. That morning, in the private garden where we'd spoken, I'd told Georgie about my plans to confront Johnny, Caro, and Jane at the family home. When I'd told her she'd have to be present too, she'd been nervous and hesitant. But I'd insisted that she needed to be there to help start the dialogue—after all, why would they open up to me? She'd finally agreed, and a short while after we'd parted, she'd messaged me to say she'd notified Caro, Jane, and Johnny as per my instructions. She'd told them that someone had been in touch with her about a family secret that concerned Clarissa Vane and Julian and that they were planning to go to the press with their story the following morning.

Apparently the ruse had worked.

I wrote back to Georgie to confirm our meeting time.

Before I walked with Ellie and Sebastian to the Jubilee line platform, I quickly called Agnieszka to confirm the meeting with her too. I needed her to let us into the house before the others showed up. Otherwise, if Georgie was late or backed out at the last second, my plan could fail before it had even started.

Our brief conversation proved what Mr. Rivera had claimed—that Agnieszka was a tough cookie. She hardly knew me, but as soon as I'd so much as hinted about my plans for the evening, she'd insisted on helping out. And after I'd shared a few more details, she became determined to station herself in the shadows of the second-floor landing, phone in hand, ready to call in support if necessary (and it was highly likely, considering the people I was expecting).

When I asked again whether she was really sure that she wanted to help me, she'd answered without any hesitation. "Absolutely. I'll help you, no problem. And don't worry, I can handle myself." An image I had of her from our last meeting sprang to mind. She'd been standing in the hall, backlit, her wiry frame and short, spiky hair starkly outlined in the light, the silence of the house punctuated by her gum snapping and knuckle cracking. I believed her when she said she could take care of herself.

"So what are we going to do once we're at the house?" Ellie asked as she, Sebastian, Halley, and I walked out of Notting Hill Gate Tube station and headed in the direction of the library. A pizzeria I liked was open just across from the station—and, importantly, they had a few tables set up on the pavement just outside their large shop window so that Halley could join us. They even offered a vegetarian, gluten-free pizza option for Ellie.

"Well," I answered, "I don't mean to sound so theatrical…but I think it's time the Vane family secrets saw the light of day."

"And I don't suppose you're ready to share them yet?" Sebastian asked as we sat down.

"No, not quite, Watson." I smiled. Ellie and Sebastian rolled their eyes at me as our order was called. As we ate, I outlined my plans for that evening's meeting at the house. Ellie got up to make a call to the agency, and Sebastian looked at me for a moment before saying, "There's only one part of your plan that has to change, Holmes."

"And what's that?"

"My part in the proceedings." He leaned in to me across the table and said, "There's no way I'm going to stand outside—away from you. I'm not leaving you on your own in that house."

"But Agnieszka will be with me."

"Yeah—upstairs."

"I'll be okay, Sebastian. Honestly—"

"Forget it, Axelle. Nothing you say will change my mind. I'm not leaving you on your own, so you'd better just find me a good place to hide—inside and near you."

He looked totally kissable, sitting there in his leather jacket (the paint-splattered duds long gone), insisting he knew what was best.

"I like it when you play tough, Watson," I said as I reached for a last small piece of the pizza.

He grabbed my wrist, his warm hand encircling it tightly. "I'm not playing, Holmes. I don't want you to get hurt. And if you keep looking at me the way you are now, it's not just tonight that I won't want to leave you on your own. It'll be always."

Sebastian still hadn't let go of my wrist when Ellie came back to the table.

"Am I interrupting something?" she asked, a small smile turning up the corners of her lips.

"No," I answered. "We're just discussing the positions

we'll be taking up at Dawson Place. Sebastian thinks he should be inside."

"Me too," Ellie said. "In fact, I think I should be upstairs somewhere—not that I've seen the house. But if you two plan on being downstairs, why don't I stay at some kind of vantage point upstairs with Agnieszka? I can act as a lookout."

I was outnumbered and I didn't like it.

"You know, since meeting you, Axelle, I've changed my gym routine to include some martial arts," Ellie continued, "and I really like it. So, okay, maybe I'm way smoother on the runway than I'll ever be at landing a karate chop, but still…I can actually do a bit of martial-arts-movie stuff. So, don't worry about me. I'll be watching, and if you need help, I'll be downstairs in a flash." She took a mask out of her shoulder bag, the kind that has holes for the mouth and eyes. "I'll have to use this of course. And I'll have to hide my hair under this," she added as she pulled out a black beanie. "I'm happy to help, but I can't risk being recognized! If word gets out that I'm helping to put fashion designers in jail, my modeling career will be finished faster than new trends are made. Anyway, so upstairs, right?"

I bit into my piece.

Sebastian laughed. "Give in, Axelle. Sometimes your friends do know what's best for you."

Grrr!

Just as we got up to leave my phone pinged. It was a message from Tallulah:

> I'm at the hospital—they're going to try bringing Gavin round in the next few hours. Good luck with the plan!

I texted back:

> Thanks—I'll need it!

FRIDAY EVENING
The Past Finally Speaks

The house was so silent. Even though I'd been inside just the other day, the silence still hit me like a wall as I stepped into the hall. Even the grandfather clock standing in the corner didn't tick anymore. Time had stood still at the Dawson Place mansion for a very, very long time.

If all went according to plan, however, that was about to change.

Georgie was just inside the hall, setting her handbag down when we walked in. She was nervous. I could see that just from the way she stood. Her shoulders were hunched, and her hair was pushed absentmindedly behind her ears. She looked preoccupied—which, considering the task ahead of her, was hardly surprising.

I gently shut the door behind us and then quickly introduced her to Sebastian and Ellie, and Halley too. (I registered Georgie's slight look of surprise at seeing Halley—but I knew my dog would be able to stick to whatever plans I asked of her.) Of course, Georgie already knew Agnieszka from her visits to the house, and though Georgie was surprised to see her arrive with us, Agnieszka simply waved and said, "Never mind me. I'll be quiet as a mouse." Then she disappeared upstairs before Georgie collected herself enough to start asking questions.

"Are you ready, Georgie?" I asked as I faced her. The early evening sun on the stained-glass windows in the stairwell threw patches of candy-colored light across the hall. Circles of red, orange, blues, and greens danced around the room. It was like standing in a kaleidoscope. With a discreet wave of my hand I motioned to Sebastian and Ellie. Sebastian understood what I meant: start searching for places to hide. Behind me I heard them both move quietly off.

"I hope so. I think so…but I am nervous," Georgie continued. "What if I'm wrong?"

"You're not. Don't forget that I'd uncovered enough clues to unlock the past before you spoke to me this morning. I can prove what I know, and I'll do whatever it takes to bring the truth to light. I promise. The events of the past will be cleared up, and your family history will be rewritten—correctly this time. And you'll finally be able to move forward with a clear conscience. Life will begin again for you."

"But why does it have to be like this? Someone here is going to suffer tonight, and it's my fault."

"No, it's not your fault, Georgie—not at all. But sometimes the past needs to have its say too. Besides, if the truth isn't revealed now, it'll come out eventually—next week, next month, or whenever. You can't bury the past forever, you know."

Georgie nodded.

"All I need you to do is to start the conversation, just like I explained earlier. And I'll take over as soon as I can. Remember, Caro, Jane, and Johnny would never have come here tonight if I'd tried inviting them on their own. They'd have thought I was completely mad. So I need you, Georgie. If I'm to clear this up and put an end to your nightmares, I need your help. Okay?"

"Yes," she said finally.

"Thank you," I said. "We don't have much time, so let me show you where I'd like this to happen." I led her to the library. From the far end of the large room, an elegant mahogany writing desk faced the arched doorway into the hall. Behind me was a curtained window that I knew looked onto the garden at the back of the house, and opposite, across the room, was a huge fireplace. Apart from another large window to the left of the desk, the rest of the wall space was covered with bookshelves. On an easel in the left-hand corner behind me was a portrait of Clarissa.

The portrait showed her face. Her blond hair was lit like a halo, her elegant head turned three-quarters toward us. Even in this musty, faded room the portrait was radiant, the many tones of orange and red glowing in the dim light.

"We'll wait for them in here," I said as I stood with Georgie in the middle of the room. "We'll leave the front door unlocked and you can call them in. If you can get everyone to sit on the sofas here, that would be good. I'll be hiding—here, perhaps," I said as I drew open the curtains of the large window behind the desk and watched the room come alive. With the soft evening sunlight that suddenly filled the library, the musty yellow walls and fabrics began to shimmer.

Sebastian quietly walked in and told me that he was going to hide in the folds of the faded, green velvet brocade curtains that hung in the doorway between the library and the hall. Then he drew open the curtains of the other large window in the room and helped me to arrange the heavy folds. "Is this where you'll hide?" he asked as I slipped behind the golden-yellow damask fabric. Once I was well concealed, I leaned my head out a bit, hoping the shadows of the heavy fabric would hide my face.

"I think so. Do you see me?"

He stepped back a few paces. "No, not at all."

"Perfect." I nodded as I slipped back out and asked Halley to sit behind the curtains. (She promptly rolled into a ball and rested her head on her front paws.) "Then that'll be my spot. I should be able to hear everything and see enough from there, and they'll all see me when I step out. Are Ellie and Agnieszka in position?"

Sebastian smiled and nodded. "All set for action, Holmes."

"Good, because I think we'll get some."

Before either one of us could say anything else, a loud creaking sound made us both jump. But it was only Ellie, stepping into the room. "Get to your places—they're coming! Johnny's black Range Rover is at the top of the street." Then she ran back upstairs.

Sebastian slipped into position while I quickly reassured Georgie one last time before I also took up my position.

Everything was set to go.

They walked into the house more or less all at the same time. Georgie called out to them, and I watched as Johnny, Caro, and Jane filed into the library, Jane leaning on a cane. Georgie stood in the middle of the room. She looked pale and fearful as they settled themselves on the sofas. I hoped she'd be able to go through with our plan.

"So what's going on, Georgie?" Johnny asked. I couldn't help but notice that he'd changed his outfit since I'd last seen him backstage a few hours ago—his gloves were now splatter free.

"And how long is this going to last?" Caro asked. "My flight to New York leaves tonight."

"Anyway, why would you possibly want to discuss Clarissa and Julian now? Tonight?" Jane said. "Simply because some random person has told you they know something about us?"

Get going, Georgie, I thought. Jane had just given her the perfect lead-in. Fortunately, she took it.

"The random person, as you put it, Jane, actually

knows quite a bit about us and our family history… and…and…"

Great, I thought, *she's faltering already.*

But Georgie took a breath and managed to continue. "And what they've told me rings true with what I remember about when Julian and my mother died."

"Georgie, darling," Jane said, "you were so young when all that happened. What memories could you possibly have?"

"Not many, I admit," Georgie said quietly, "but I can't deny the little I do remember anymore. We have to talk about my mother and brother—"

"They're mine too, you know," Johnny said.

"I know, I know, Johnny. My point is that I need to talk about them and it can't wait—especially now that someone is threatening to go to the press with what they know."

"So what do they know?" Caro asked.

"A lot, actually."

Caro rolled her eyes while Georgie pulled the originals of the two photos she'd sent Gavin and me from her bag. She laid them on the low table between the two sofas, and the others peered at them.

"Is this some kind of joke?" Johnny asked.

"No. And you especially, Johnny, should take a close look at the photo of you and Julian."

"I already know that photo," he said. "I've seen it my whole life."

"Yes, but have you ever noticed this?" she said as she held the photo up and pointed to a small spot on Johnny's right hand.

"What are you talking about, Georgie? What are you saying?" he said as he took the photo. "That spot? I can barely see it. And so what?"

"Take your gloves off and I'll show you."

"Georgie," Jane said, "someone has clearly filled your head with nonsense. There are people, you know—specially trained people—who can help you resolve any issues you have with your past. In the meantime, I'm not sure telling your brother to take his gloves off is the place to start."

"Thank you, Jane, for your vote of confidence in my ability to think for myself—" Georgie stopped to collect herself. I watched as she struggled to regain her courage. After a moment she said again, "Take your gloves off, Johnny."

Caro looked at Jane, and Jane looked at Johnny. "Just do it, Johnny," Caro said. "Humor her."

Johnny did.

"Don't you see, Johnny? You don't have a mark on your right hand, do you? And yet in the photo you do!"

"What are you talking about, Georgie?" Johnny was getting angry and exasperated.

"In the photo—as a child—you had a red birthmark on your right hand. And now you don't."

Johnny snatched the photo from the table and stared at it.

"Johnny, calm down," Caro said.

"So what do you mean exactly?" Johnny yelled as he threw the photo back on the table, ignoring Caro. "What are you getting at?" I could see his fists clenching now.

Georgie stood, shaking. She looked pale. "There were two twin brothers. Johnny was born with a mark on his right hand. But Julian wasn't…"

"And?" Johnny said in a low growl.

"I'm trying to tell you that you are not Johnny—you are Julian. It's the truth, and someone has been hiding it!" A loud sob escaped Georgie as she spoke. I watched as she picked up the photo. "This copy is our mother's. I found it here, in her desk upstairs. She had it in an envelope in a secret compartment of her desk." Georgie's voice trembled. "And on the back of this photo it is clearly marked which twin is which—and in our mother's own hand."

"This is absurd, Georgie," Jane said as she stood up. "You really do need help—and I'm willing to find you the right doctor."

"And I can tell you that Johnny is Johnny," Caro said. "I'm old enough to remember." She was angry now and glared at Georgie as she continued. "Stop being so stupid, Georgie. You can't possibly have any idea what you're talking about."

But Georgie was adamant. "No, no. Someone's been

lying. Jane, you have a copy of this photo at your house, but you've always told us that it was Julian with the mark on his hand!"

"And?"

"And you were wrong!"

"Georgie," Jane said softly as she walked toward her. But Johnny also took a step toward Georgie, blocking Jane. He looked threatening, his face angry, his body poised as if for a fight. I could see fear rising in Georgie, and I knew that if I didn't step in soon, my chance—and Georgie's and Gavin's—to put the facts straight would be lost.

"I know what I'm saying sounds crazy, Johnny—but you are Julian!" Georgie said.

"*Shut up!*" Johnny yelled at her. He was nearly frothing at the mouth. Then he spun toward Jane. "Do you know anything about this, Jane?" he asked.

"Nothing. She doesn't know what she's saying, Johnny," Jane said. I couldn't tell if it was the light, but Jane was beginning to look feverish. Her eyes appeared slightly glassy, and perspiration was breaking out on her brow. "Like I told you, she needs a doctor."

Georgie was sobbing now, nervous and scared. She seemed to have gone as far as she could on her own. With a quick signal to Halley to stay put, I stepped out from behind the curtain. "I'm afraid to tell you that Georgie knows exactly what she's saying," I said.

"What are you doing here?" Johnny asked with a

short laugh of disbelief. "This is getting more melodramatic by the moment. Who invited you? Or are you the mystery person who has threatened to go to the police?"

I ignored his questions and looked at his right hand. There was no mark there. I quickly picked up the photo off the table.

Johnny pulled out his phone, but before he was able to place a call, I quickly said, "I wouldn't if I were you."

"Really?" Jane said. "Go ahead, Johnny. Call the police. She should be locked up for trespassing." Out of the corner of my eye I saw Jane grip her cane more firmly.

"I wouldn't, Johnny," I said as I moved behind the desk, putting myself out of Jane's reach, "because I think you'll all be interested to hear what I've got to tell you about Julian and Clarissa. But if you'd prefer me to tell the police first, then by all means, call them."

"You didn't even know Clarissa, you nosy brat. How could you possibly have anything of interest to tell us?" Caro asked. "Is this why you were trying to talk to me the other day about your bizarre interest in my sister?"

Ignoring Caro, I picked up the photo of Johnny and Julian and handed it to Johnny. "Look at it, Johnny," I said. "And flip it over. Look at your mother's writing and if that doesn't convince you, maybe this will..." I nodded to Georgie. She walked to her handbag and pulled out a large, white envelope that had yellowed with age. She pulled out a folder and handed it to Johnny.

"Those are medical records. Your mother had been so worried about your identity that she'd gotten hold of these. You'll find that the twin with the birthmark on his hand—the twin who drowned—was indeed Johnny. I'm sorry to have to tell you this, Julian."

"This is preposterous," Jane said. "And if you insist on pursuing this lie then I—we—will have to stop you."

"Jane, how much of this is true?" Johnny said as he perused his old medical files.

"None of it."

"But that's a lie, isn't it, Jane?" I said. "Furthermore, I believe you to be the person responsible for switching Julian for Johnny that day by the Thames, and I also think you know exactly what happened to Clarissa when she fell down the stairs, because you were there, weren't you? You pushed her!"

Georgie started to sob quite uncontrollably. Meanwhile, Johnny turned his rage on Jane. "What is she talking about? What happened to Mother?"

Caro turned white as a sheet, but she was watching Jane carefully.

Johnny studied the photo again. "It is my mother's writing," he said, his teeth clenched.

"And don't you think she'd know which of her sons was which?" I asked.

He continued to look at the photo.

"This is preposterous," Jane said. "Clarissa barely recognized herself on some days. Her imagination often ran away with her. You didn't know her, but she was a stupid, flighty, irresponsible wretch of a woman! God, how I hated her!" she screamed as she turned to Johnny. "Clarissa didn't deserve you!"

Watching Jane, I was glad to have as much backup in the house as I did—the woman was clearly unstable. I tried to remain as cool as possible. "That may be," I said, as I took the medical records in hand, "but these have nothing to do with her imagination." I turned to the four of them. "Let's start at the beginning…

"Once upon a time there were twin boys. Born to fashionable parents, they were also born into style. Their father was a well-known socialite and their mother a famous fashion model and muse. Both boys expressed strong and distinct interests in style from the moment they were old enough to hold a pencil.

"Tragically, the father died an early death, leaving the young mother, Clarissa Vane, alone with three young children to raise. Fortunately, however, Clarissa had a good friend in the talented and ambitious fit model named Jane Wimple."

Caro suddenly got up and said she had to use the bathroom. I watched as she left the library, but I couldn't stop at this point—not now that I finally had their attention. I quickly glanced toward Sebastian's hiding place and watched as he slipped out to follow Caro as she crossed the hall.

"Jane, you formed a strong attachment to the Vane

family. Soon you were running the household and acting as a surrogate mother to the three children."

"Clarissa was never there," Jane said.

"So I've heard," I said.

"Who else was going to look after them? She wasn't fit to care for anyone other than herself. She was selfish and incapable of doing a thing on her own—let alone keeping her family in order. All she wanted to do was party and travel, model, and sit for artists. Clarissa was a terrible mother and a pathetic wretch."

"So you stepped in. Fine... I'm only wondering at what point your strong attachment to the children—or more specifically to the quieter twin, Julian—became a pathological obsession? You became inordinately attached to Julian and began to feel like he was your own, didn't you?"

Jane opened her mouth to speak. Her eyes were wide and she didn't blink, and her voice had dropped in pitch. She spoke as if she were in a trance. "Clarissa ignored him too much. Julian was the more intense twin. He was talented but you needed to give him time before you would see it—and that was something Clarissa never had. At least not for Julian."

I nodded and quietly said, "And then one day, when you and the children had gone to the Thames for a bit of treasure hunting, an accident happened, didn't it, Jane?"

Jane looked at me, her eyes still wide, but said nothing.

"You were with Georgie, watching from up on the

footpath. The boys, meanwhile, were still out on the beach when the tide started to come in, and somehow, on this day, they'd wandered off further than usual and perhaps in separate directions. They didn't know how fast that water can rise, and distracted by Georgie, you didn't notice either until they were already stranded, in danger of being swept away completely by the current.

"You ran to help Julian first—he was your special favorite, after all. You pulled him out just in time. Maybe he was coughing, spitting up some water, but he was okay—or at least, he would be after some rest and a warm bath. But Johnny, he was not all right—not at all. The current had knocked him off his feet and carried him away, and by the time you caught up with him, he was no longer breathing. And when you pulled him onto the shore it was clear he was dead. Wasn't he, Jane? Johnny was dead?"

Jane was looking at me and starting to shake. Whether with rage or fear, I wasn't sure. Georgie and Johnny were silent.

"Johnny had died, but Julian was alive. And while I think you must have been in shock, a part of you was also thinking about Julian, the twin you saw as 'yours.' You loved Julian, didn't you, Jane?"

"I loved Julian—yes. And was that so wrong of me? He was like the child I never had. It was Clarissa's fault anyway. She always neglected him. She gave more—so much more—of her attention to Johnny. She thought he was the clever one, the one who was more like her, you see. Clarissa believed he was the one who had a real future." Suddenly Jane got up and started to pace the room.

"Not Julian though. No, never, never Julian. And yet Julian was so special. He had talent—real talent!" Jane turned to look at "Johnny" now and continued to speak to herself as if the rest of us were no longer in the room. I had the feeling she was reliving the past, watching it unwind before her eyes as we spoke. "But I knew, I knew you were destined for great things. And look how right I was! I knew—and Clarissa, as usual, did not. She was never right about anything!"

"So as you stood beside the Thames that day, with Johnny dead and Julian alive, you thought about what Johnny's accidental death could mean to Julian—more attention from his mother, more nurturing of his talent. But you also thought of what Johnny's death would mean to you, didn't you? You were frightened you'd lose your job, weren't you?" Axelle asked.

"I knew that Clarissa would fire me on the spot if I said her beloved Johnny had died, while if Johnny was the one who lived, there was a chance she'd let me stay. She was cruel that way. Everyone thought Clarissa was so nice"—Jane stopped as her glance, rotten yet cunning, swept over us—"but she wasn't always nice, and certainly not when it came to Julian."

"And you couldn't bear to be parted from him, could you, Jane?"

She shook her head and looked at him. "No, I couldn't bear to be parted from Julian. He was mine." Jane softened her voice, speaking to "Johnny" directly now. "Already at that age you trusted me more than you did your own mother. When we were on the beach that day, before the police came, I told you a story. Do you remember? I told you that from that moment on, you would be known as Johnny, and that all your dreams would come true—just like in a fairy tale. Do you remember? And you didn't question me. Oh, you were such a clever child! It was as if you understood everything I wanted for you!"

"So you switched the boys, didn't you? You said that Julian had died and Johnny was alive?"

Jane's eyes seemed lit from within as if by red-hot embers. "Yes!" she spat out. "Yes, I switched them! And I have been vindicated! If I hadn't switched the boys' identities, Clarissa would never have let me nurture Julian's talent as I did. It would have been lost to the world!"

I began to wonder where Caro was. Surely she should have been back by now. But I pushed the thought away and continued.

"You took a gamble on the birthmark, didn't you? You figured that with Clarissa being gone so often—"

"She was neglectful, often drunk and sometimes worse! There were days she could barely remember who she was."

Still no sign of Caro. And what about Sebastian? Where was he?

I turned my focus back to Jane. "Yes, you figured you could fool her, didn't you? And it worked for a while—until she decided to clean up her act."

"She was stupid and cruel," Jane continued.

Caro, I thought, as I continued to listen to Jane, had gone in the direction of the kitchen. Maybe she was still in the bathroom there but somehow I doubted it... so where else could she be? Had she gone out through the side door? And if she had, wouldn't Sebastian have stopped her? Did she have the keys? I had a bad feeling about it.

"I never understood why everyone loved Clarissa," Jane went on. "She could do no wrong. But people didn't know her like I did. They didn't see her hurtful, neglectful side, and I was right. She never noticed the mark was missing, you know. I was careful to put gloves on Julian, and if need be, I drew a small mark on his hand with a bit of makeup. With my training as a model, I was good with an eye pencil and concealer. Clarissa never noticed!"

"But what about the birthmark on the real Johnny?" I asked. "Didn't anyone find it odd that dead little 'Julian' suddenly had a birthmark on his hand? Or did you cover your tracks there too, Jane?"

"Oh yes! I had such a brilliant idea! It was quite simple really—I took care of it when no one was watching with a sharp piece of glass I found on the shore. I scratched his hands as if he'd scraped them while he was drowning, just enough to hide the birthmark. And, again, that stupid woman never realized!"

"But once Clarissa was clean she discovered what you'd done, didn't she? Is that why she began to feel scared? She probably confronted you, didn't she, Jane? Maybe even told you to leave? Or threatened to call the police?"

Think, Axelle, think! Where else could Caro have gone?

Jane nodded. "But she was so silly. It took her ages to work out what had happened, and by then it was too late! Julian had become Johnny, and I wasn't going to let anything get in between us—certainly not Clarissa. I'd taken care of her family for too long. I'd set things right and Julian had already begun to blossom now that he didn't have to constantly compete with his brother for attention. And then, suddenly, just because Clarissa went to a fancy clinic she wanted her family back and me gone? Ha! No way! Not after I'd taken care of those children for so long!"

I reminded myself that this was a large, old house. There was a strong chance there'd be a service staircase near the kitchen. Had Caro gone up those stairs? And had Sebastian followed her? Or had he lost her?

And what about Ellie and Agnieszka? They were both stationed upstairs somewhere. I'd told them to keep their eyes and ears focused on the main stairwell…

but what if Caro had gone up a back staircase? Could she have snuck up on them unnoticed?

"And so you threatened her, didn't you? Maybe you even threatened her life."

Were Ellie and Agnieszka still in position? Or had something happened to them? I didn't hear anything... Was their silence good or bad news?

"I did, yes. Because she had gone too far. She had threatened me! Threatened to fire me for negligence! Ha, the irony of it! Fire me for negligence—after she'd neglected her own children and I'd taken care of everything!"

"So you decided to get rid of Clarissa..."

At this moment we all heard a muffled shout followed by a loud thud upstairs. Johnny and Georgie ran to the hall, but I stayed and watched Jane. I couldn't risk taking my eyes off her.

"Who's there?" Johnny yelled before disappearing up the stairs. Then I heard Georgie scream and saw her fall to the floor.

In that same moment Jane sprang up and tried to run. Without thinking I ran after her and grabbed at her jacket, bringing her down. But she was stronger than she looked, and she threw me off. I fell backward and hit my head on the low table, landing with a thud. Pain seared through my skull. I was dizzy, but I forced myself to sit up. As I tried to see through the pain, I could just make out Jane as she picked up Johnny's medical files and the photos Georgie had brought. She took them to the fireplace, drew a lighter from her pocket, and held the flame to the papers until they caught.

I tried to steady my breathing for a few seconds, and then, grabbing hold of the low table, I pulled myself up.

Satisfied that the files were burning, Jane now walked to the desk and picked something up before turning back to me. The sharp, crazed glint in her eye and her small, cruel smile didn't exactly reassure me. And then I noticed what she was holding in her hand. It looked like a heavy ball of some sort. She raised her arm high over her head, and I watched as it caught the light. That's when I realized it wasn't a ball—it was a glass paperweight.

I dropped to the ground and rolled out of her way just as her arm came down, smashing the paperweight into the corner of the low table. Glass scattered around me in a rain of tiny splinters as Jane screamed in anger. In that second, out of the corner of my eye, I saw a blur of white fly over me. A loud growl was followed by another of Jane's screams. When I rolled back toward the sofa and pulled myself up, I saw Halley, her paws off the ground and her teeth clenched firmly to Jane's sleeve.

Suddenly Sebastian came running into the library and threw himself on top of Jane, although Halley was doing a good job of holding her still. I sprang to Sebastian's side, helping him as he twisted Jane's arms behind her back. A few seconds later the library and hall were flooded with light as Mr. Rivera entered the house with the police.

It turned out that Georgie had fainted in the stairwell. (She'd seen Ellie in her black ninja outfit—face mask included.) She needed to lie down once she'd woken, so rather than take everyone to the station right away, the police questioned us all at the house.

They started by hearing the account of my movements for the entire week, beginning with Tallulah's visit about Gavin. Sebastian and Ellie were questioned too, after which Ellie busied herself with enthralling half the policemen in the house with a display of her martial arts moves.

From where Halley and I quietly sat in the hall afterward, I was able to hear the Vanes being questioned. There would be more cross-examinations in the coming days, of course, but thanks to Jane's fresh confession, the police were eager to immediately press forward with their most pertinent questions. I concentrated on hearing all that I could, and the full picture became apparent.

Caro had indeed gone up the old service staircase. Sebastian had lost her for a moment, and by the time he'd discovered the staircase and followed her up, she'd hit Agnieszka on the back of her head and was ready to do the same to Ellie.

But how had she known that Ellie and Agnieszka were upstairs? Pure chance, it seemed. As I'd deduced from my investigations, Jane was not the only guilty party involved in Clarissa's death. Caro had had a role to play too. And so, spooked by my threat to bring in the police, she had gone up to look in her sister's desk and remove any evidence that could have pointed to her own part in the murder. She must have feared that, along with the photos and medical files, Clarissa might have kept news clippings about the broken engagement, evidence of the bad blood between them. Jealousy, after all, is a strong motive, and it had certainly motivated Caro to help Jane with her sinister plan. But as she was heading to Clarissa's room, Caro had instead spotted my friends.

In any case, she wouldn't have found anything in the desk. She didn't know that Georgie had been through it thoroughly in the last few weeks (and I certainly hadn't seen anything in it when I'd quickly looked on Thursday evening).

We all watched as Jane and Caro were taken from the house in handcuffs. "Johnny" accompanied the police too. He would have to help with the formalities of the arrests. And he'd have his hands full preparing for the press once the story leaked out.

Georgie and Agnieszka were taken to the hospital to be checked out. Although Georgie had only fainted, she'd hit her head hard on the hall floor.

Luckily Sebastian had been able to warn Ellie before she got a knock to the head too, catching up just as Caro was moving toward her, a heavy vase in hand. As soon as she heard Sebastian shout, Ellie had unleashed her new martial arts moves. The loud thud we'd heard was Caro hitting the floor. And while Sebastian secured

Caro upstairs (with, of all things, a curtain tie-back that he'd taken from one of the bedroom windows while holding Caro with her arms twisted behind her back), Ellie had run downstairs to find me—which was when she'd frightened Georgie into fainting.

As we all left the house, I couldn't help asking Mr. Rivera how he'd known to come to the rescue with the police. He laughed. "Simple. I looked through the windows and saw trouble was brewing. I doubt anyone else on the street would have noticed. You know, nowadays neighbors don't have the time to look out for one another or be nosy like we used to. But I saw some lights on, I saw Jane's face, and I watched as Caro got up and left the library. It didn't look good."

Ellie, Sebastian, Halley, and I watched as the police cars and ambulance drove off. I thanked Mr. Rivera, and after a while, he walked home. Then we turned and looked back at the house.

"It's hard to imagine that so much was going on in there just a short while ago, isn't it?" Ellie asked.

Sebastian and I nodded. The house stood quiet and dark, and the four large rooftop eagles watched us in stony silence as we turned and left.

"So how exactly did Clarissa die?" Sebastian asked.

I'd dropped Halley off at home and quickly fed her

before Ellie, Sebastian, and I headed to the Lucky Seven Diner around the corner.

I bit into a hot fry and said, "Well, she was pushed by Jane—although she'd had Caro's help. What Jane didn't know was that Georgie had heard her threatening Clarissa before she pushed her. Georgie may not have been able to understand precisely what Jane was saying, but she certainly understood the tone of her voice."

"How awful!" Ellie said.

I nodded. "Jane obviously never expected four-year-old Georgie to hear her—she was supposed to have been asleep—or to have remembered."

"And how did Caro help?" Sebastian asked.

"Remember how you asked what could have gotten Clarissa out of bed when everyone knew she would usually be resting?"

Sebastian nodded.

"Well, that got me thinking, because you actually had a good point, Watson."

"Thank you, Holmes. Can I have that in writing?"

"No."

"Why am I not surprised?"

"Anyway…why did Clarissa, who was at that point dressed in her robe and in the middle of her downtime, suddenly dress up and head downstairs? Perhaps if there was an emergency or, more specifically, an emergency call of some sort? And that jibed with what Mr. Rivera told me about Caro's movements just before and just after her sister's death. Plus I'd noticed the phone next to Clarissa's bed—one of two in the house. She'd have answered if it had rung."

"And that's why you asked Agnieszka how many phones were in the house and where—and why you had me check on the neighborhood phone boxes."

I nodded. "Once I had the idea of a phone call, the next logical step was to see if there was a pay phone an easy five-minute walk from the Vane house—and there was."

"But why not just knock on Clarissa's door or call her downstairs?"

"Because that would have been too risky. Jane wanted to scare Clarissa without anyone else being in the house—and in such a manner that it would look like an accident. Pushing her down some stairs that were known to be slippery and dangerous was an obvious choice, and with Clarissa dressed to go out, it could look as if she'd been in a rush to get somewhere. And Jane's timing was perfect, because the housekeeper was shopping at two thirty p.m., the maid had left for the day, and Mr. Rivera was busy outside. But how could Jane persuade Clarissa to leave her bedroom at precisely that time? She needed to give Clarissa a reason that couldn't be ignored."

"So Caro called with a fake emergency?" Ellie asked.

I nodded. "Yes. And Clarissa answered, believed whatever lie she was fed, dressed, and ran down the stairs. Georgie said Jane was waiting for her mother on the landing. She heard Jane go down just before she heard her mother—only Jane didn't go down all the way."

"And…?" Sebastian asked.

"And as she pushed Clarissa, Jane must have said something horrible or threatening, or both. Like I said, Georgie didn't understand the actual words, but she was certain whose voice it was—and the tone of that voice—right before she heard her mother scream."

Ellie shook herself. "That's so nasty. Wow. What an evil woman."

I nodded. "You should have looked into her eyes. She looked psychotic by the time the police arrived. Of course, Jane didn't kill Johnny. The Thames did. But then afterward she chose to deceive everyone."

"I wonder if Clarissa would really have fired her if she'd thought Johnny had died rather than Julian."

"We'll never know. But in any case, what's important is that Jane clearly believed Clarissa would have fired her. And that was a risk she absolutely refused to take."

"But what about Caro in all of this? Why didn't she do more to protect the kids? How come she didn't notice anything when Jane switched the boys? I mean, didn't she know her nephews better than that?"

"Better than what? Their mother? I doubt it. Caro was too busy riding on Clarissa's coattails to notice the kids. She was partying, traveling, and trying to make a name for herself in the fashion world. And don't forget that at the time the real Johnny died, she was heartbroken over Clarissa stealing her fiancé from her."

"You don't think Clarissa purposefully intended to hurt her sister by having the affair, do you?" Ellie asked as she bit into her lentil-melt veggie burger.

"Probably not as much as she did. Of course, she had the affair before she cleaned herself up, so to be fair, perhaps her judgment wasn't at its best. Then again, what matters isn't what Clarissa thought, but what Caro thought. She was already jealous of her sister, so losing her fiancé and first great love to the sister she was already envious of must have eaten at her insides, day and night. From what I gathered when the police were questioning her, she fell in pretty quickly with Jane's scheme to scare Clarissa, although for Caro, it was more about revenge. Neither of them really expected her to die—or at least that's what they're saying now."

"So Caro must have been surprised when she returned to the house and discovered her sister was dead," Ellie said.

I nodded. "Of course, by then it was too late for her to say anything. She'd done the deed and made the call. She was a vital accomplice to Jane's crime."

"And the police didn't think to ask her where she'd been or what she'd been doing?" Sebastian asked.

"Not really. Like Mr. Rivera said, she was often dashing in and out of the house, although perhaps not from the side door, but that didn't seem particularly strange. And the fact that Mr. Rivera saw her leave and return—so she was clearly not in the house when Clarissa fell—was all the police were really interested in at that time."

"And when did Georgie notice her mother's belongings? The secret drawer in the desk, the medical records, all that stuff?" Ellie asked.

"Mr. Rivera told us from the beginning that the family rarely visited the house. However, he'd seen Georgie go in twice in the last month. I started wondering why. Why her? And what did she do when she was there? Taking the little of what I knew about her character into account—she's quiet and secretive—I thought she was probably looking for something. And once I saw what a time warp the house was in, I felt even more certain that was the case."

"So that's why you looked at Clarissa's desk when we were in her bedroom. But you didn't find anything in there, did you?"

"It was exactly because I found nothing in it—well, that and the fact that the thin layer of dust had been wiped clean around the drawer—that made me think my theory was right. Georgie had been searching for something, and the empty drawer made me believe she'd found it. She admitted as much when we spoke in the garden this morning. She said she just couldn't take the nightmares anymore, that she had to find out if what she thought she remembered was real."

"I wonder what will happen to Johnny Vane's company," Ellie said. "Will he keep the name Johnny, do you think?"

I shrugged my shoulders. "I suppose. After all, it's been his name for most of his life now. Don't forget how young he was when the accident in the Thames happened. The shock of what happened that day must have left him immensely vulnerable to Jane's manipulation. I overheard him crying at the end of the police interview earlier, you know, saying that Jane had always been the mother he felt he'd never really had.

"He would have done—and did do—whatever Jane asked him to do. So when she asked him to wear gloves, and when she told him to answer to the name of Johnny from then on and said that it would be better for the two of them, he didn't ask any questions. He just buried the memories and went along with her. He was as dependent on her love as she was on his.

"Although he might feel differently now. But I think it will take him some time to get over this betrayal and deception. Georgie has been untangling it over a long period of time, but for Johnny, it's all quite fresh—even if the knowledge has been buried inside him all this time."

"So the gloves he always wears," Ellie asked, "that was Jane's idea?"

"Originally, yes. But perhaps after a while they just made him feel safe. In his head he probably couldn't let go of the fact that Jane had made him wear the gloves. And then, of course, they became part of his 'look.'"

Sebastian and I filled Ellie in on what we'd been doing the last few days, until after a while the three of us were too tired to go on. The buzz of the evening's excitement had worn off, leaving us barely able to speak.

Ellie and Sebastian walked me home and then continued on their way in a taxi. I'd be seeing Ellie at the Marc Jacobs show the next day, and I had plans to meet up with Sebastian afterward.

I was so tired and relieved to be safely back home that even my mom's sudden appearance on the landing outside my bedroom didn't scare me. She was not happy about the phone call she'd received from the police concerning my activities, and she let me know in no uncertain terms that she and my dad would have some strong words to say to me about foolishly putting myself in such a dangerous position.

"You should have told me everything from the start, Axelle," Mom said.

I remained silent—after all, what could I say?

After my mom left, I washed my face, brushed my teeth, and slipped into bed. I fell asleep before you could say Mulberry, with my arm around Halley's snoring warmth.

SATURDAY
Picnics and Plans

"Axelle?"

Someone was calling my name. And it sounded as if they were calling from the end of a tunnel somewhere underground, deep, deep in the earth's core. Who was it? And how did they get there?

"Axelle?" I heard it again—only this time it was not coming from the deep, deep center of the earth. The voice was, in fact, only inches from my face, and it was coming from someone who should have known better: my mom.

She'd peeled my duvet away from my face and was peering at me.

"Mom, honestly, if you'd like you can use the magnifying glass on my desk. You might be able to see me better."

"Good morning to you too, Axelle. And there's no reason to get mouthy with me."

"Mom, do you think we could just backtrack a bit and pretend this isn't happening? Don't you have a client to see or something?" Now she was pulling up the blinds on my windows. I flipped onto my stomach and buried my face in my pillow as the sun streamed into my room.

"Actually, Axelle, you're the one with an appointment. Tallulah is here to see you. She's downstairs."

I sat up. Tallulah? *Argh!* I'd completely forgotten that I'd agreed to see her this morning! We'd made the appointment late last night on the phone. I'd been eager to find out how Gavin was doing. But by the time I'd finished with the police it had been too late to meet her, and I'd been too tired to do anything beyond eating a burger and rehashing the case with Ellie and Sebastian. Tallulah and I had set the time for ten this morning—and I'd completely forgotten.

I sprang out of bed and watched with amusement as Halley buried herself deeper into my duvet.

"And don't forget you have the Marc Jacobs show at noon!" Mom called as she went down the stairs.

I rushed to my bathroom and showered as quickly as I could. *No time to dry my hair*, I thought. Another day, another tumbleweed. Well, if models all had perfect hair, there'd be no work for hairstylists, now would there?

In fact, I thought, as I watched my hair start to frizz, *the hairstylists of the fashion world owe me!*

I dressed quickly. Today's outfit consisted of a short, striped top, boyish gray pants that looked really cute (I thought so anyway) tucked into my black Doc Martins, and—I think it was the Johnny Vane influence—a black leather biker jacket my mom had bought me after

I'd finished my exams. It was actually really cool, and perfect for the sunny yet breezy (judging from the treetops) early summer weather. I rounded it all off with my brightly colored camouflage Mulberry backpack. I put my glasses on and went downstairs to meet Tallulah.

My mom left the house just after I came down. She had some shopping to do—my dad was coming back tonight—so after a quick good-bye I was on my own with Tallulah. I showed her into our living room and we started to talk.

"How's Gavin?"

Tallulah smiled the first big smile I'd seen from her! "Thank you for asking. I'm happy to give you a glowing report, finally! Gavin's well. He's out of the coma and they're running tests, but it looks like he's sustained no long-term damage. I need hardly tell you what a relief that is to my parents—and me. He hasn't been able to say much yet but we're positive he'll soon be as good as new. Axelle, will you please fill me in on what has happened though? The police have been in touch and I'll be going to the station straight from here, but I want to hear it from you first."

Without missing any details, I told her about the previous night's confrontation and everything that had led up to it.

"I had no idea it would all be so complicated," she said.

"Neither did I," I said. And I meant it.

"It's hard to believe it was Jane who attacked Gavin,"

Tallulah said. "But of course who would ever suspect a 'blind woman'?"

"I know. It's obviously a role she likes to play to throw people off their guard. She tried it on me when I surprised her at her house on Wednesday night, pretending she couldn't see the photo. But if you hadn't mentioned there'd been a blind woman on the Embankment the morning Gavin was attacked, I'm not sure my alarm bells would have gone off. When I was at her house I saw the cane she used for her disguise in a vase in her hallway. And when I started putting two and two together, I wondered if she'd had a role in hurting your brother…but it took me a while to figure out why."

"And she was the one who ransacked our flat?"

"I think so, yes. The police will confirm everything—and press charges, I presume. But it seems she did it on her own, which may explain why it was done so neatly. You should see her house."

"It's tidy, is it?"

"Very. I can easily imagine her making those clean cuts you described in your mattresses. I guess she was also the person who followed your brother that day when he ducked into the pub up the road from you, convinced someone was tailing him."

"And did Jane make an arrangement to meet with him on the Embankment Sunday morning?"

"I'm not sure. It sounds like Gavin will soon be up to confirming what his plans were that morning and I'd love to ask him. All Jane wanted to talk about last night was what a monster Clarissa was. I did hear, however, that Jane was desperate to get her hands on the copy of the photo that Georgie had sent to Gavin—not that she knew it was Georgie who'd sent it."

"Then how did Jane even know that Gavin had the photo?"

"The police asked the same question last night. And according to what Johnny said, after your brother received the photo he asked Johnny about it. Johnny laughed the whole thing off, but he did mention it to Jane…thinking she'd laugh it off too. Only she didn't. In fact, she became consumed with the idea that Gavin was on to her.

"She was sure he'd discovered the correlation between the birthmark and what happened all those years ago—and I have a feeling she might have been right. Gavin had spent quite a bit of time photographing Johnny and must have seen him without his gloves on at some point."

"I knew it," Tallulah said as we wound our meeting down. "I knew everything was connected somehow. Thank you, Axelle, for believing me, and thank you for getting to the bottom of it all."

We eventually left the house. I did have a show to do, and Jazz had already called twice to make sure I wasn't going to be late. Tallulah accompanied Halley and me to Notting Hill Gate, and we talked all the way. We made a quick detour via the Dawson Place mansion though. Tallulah was very curious to see it.

"It looks creepy," she said as she looked up at the four large, stone eagles keeping watch from the corners of the roof. "They should sell it. Why hang on to it when it's got such a creepy history?"

"Well, I think they will sell it now. I'm sure Jane and Caro would have liked to have seen the house sold years ago. In fact, Georgie told me Caro and Jane had often talked to her about selling the house, but Georgie had refused to sell her half of it. She and Johnny—or do I call him Julian, it's so confusing!—had inherited it. She wanted to hang on to it to have somewhere where she could 'visit' her mother and feel close to her.

"In fact, by hanging on to it, she made it possible for me to uncover the truth. If the house had been sold and subdivided or who knows what, it would have been impossible to piece together the events of that sunny afternoon all those years ago. But I think now that she's had closure, Georgie will want to sell."

Tallulah and I parted ways at Notting Hill Gate. She looked forward to telling Gavin everything but nonetheless asked me if I would visit them both as soon as he was back home in their flat so that I could talk to him myself.

"Absolutely," I said. "I would really like to meet him. I'm curious to know how much he'd already figured out."

Halley and I hopped on the Tube and caught a

southbound Circle line train. Five minutes later we got off at South Kensington station. From there I walked the short distance to the Natural History Museum, where the Marc Jacobs show was taking place.

To be honest, my mind wasn't really on the show. I knew it was kind of a "big deal" as the agency put it—Marc Jacobs always is—but after the week I'd had, complete with the extremely close-up (no pun intended!) view I'd had of fashion's less attractive side—jealousy, deceit, lies, and a sick suppression of the truth—walking down the runway wasn't really what I wanted to focus on at that moment.

"Your mind is totally elsewhere, today, Axelle," Ellie said as we sat backstage having our hair done. "You're still thinking about the case, aren't you?"

I nodded.

"And? What else?"

"And nothing else."

Ellie laughed. "I know you too well for that to work with me, Axelle."

"All right, Nancy Drew, then what else do I have on my mind?"

"Sebastian, I bet. You're meeting him afterward, aren't you?"

I nodded as I fed Halley one of the organic doggy treats I'd brought from home.

"Well, just so you know—although it doesn't take a detective to guess what I'm going to say—Josh is here too. He's already been asking about you. I have no doubt he's planning on coming backstage just to see you."

In fact, Ellie was right. Josh did come to see me, but he wasn't alone. I'd changed into my own clothes, brushed my hair out, and was just removing my makeup when I heard him come up behind me. I turned, and there he was dressed like a pop star—with his grandmother.

I thanked her again for everything and told her that my friend was out of danger. "I'm so glad I could be of help," she said. She winked as she said it, an easy smile on her lips, as if she understood everything I wasn't telling her. I wondered if the story of Jane's arrest had already made it into the media.

"I hope we meet again, Axelle," she said, then before I could shake her hand, a microphone came between us and she turned to answer some questions for a news channel.

A moment later, Josh discreetly motioned for me to follow him. I did, but I made sure to stay a little bit behind him. Once we reached some large screens that were acting as room dividers, Josh and I slipped around them unnoticed.

"So when will I see you again, Axelle?" he asked. "Or do I have to arrange for another surprise meeting in a revolving door?"

Josh was nice, sweet, good-looking, and charming—not that I ever thought I'd say all that when I'd first bumped into him. And although it was actually fun to connect with someone like him on the fashion side of my life, there was another person in my life who I connected with more.

"Josh, I really like you...but there is someone else. It's a bit complicated right now, but I'm happy."

"Why did I have the feeling you were going to tell me something like this?" Josh said lightly as he took one of my hands.

He wasn't making this any easier but I knew I had to be honest. "Josh, you and I have totally different lives. I'd constantly want to run away from the realities you have to deal with—paparazzi, fans, and all the rest... I mean, I hate that stuff! And I don't think I'd ever be at ease with it."

"Yeah, but that's precisely one of the reasons you're so special—that and your spiky stubbornness." He smiled. "Seriously though, you're the first person I've met in I don't know how long who isn't obsessed with my fame—although for a while there you did seem to have a thing about my grandmother. I've never had that happen before," he said, laughing.

"Listen, Axelle." His voice dropped to a near whisper as he looked at me, his eyes flickering softly in the light, and ran his hands gently through my hair. "I hear what you're saying, and I can wait. It's not like you and I don't live in the same city, and it's not like we won't see each other at another show. I'm going on tour on Monday and I'll be gone for a few months...but how about I give you a call when I get back?"

He laughed when he saw my lips move into that sort of frozen half smile I have when I'm not sure what to say. "You're incredible," he said. "And by the way, don't change while I'm gone. I'll be very disappointed if I come back and you actually agree to a date with me." He was smiling, but then he suddenly leaned in and gently kissed my cheek. "Take care. I'll call you when I'm back. Now, why don't you step out first and I'll follow in a couple of minutes."

I nodded slowly as I looked at him for a moment, unsure of what to think about everything he'd just said. All kinds of conflicting feelings and thoughts raced through my mind. A part of me couldn't help but be flattered by his desire to get to know me better, and yet the way he was so sure that I'd come around to him seemed almost...arrogant. *Argh!* Where was my Clue-like ending? I'd had one for my case, but not for my heart.

"Take care, Josh, and have a blast on your tour," I finally said—and I meant it. Then I turned and quietly returned to the backstage frenzy beyond the screen.

It was a stunning Saturday afternoon: blue skies, high clouds, and a light breeze. It was a short distance to Hyde Park. From the museum, Halley and I walked along Exhibition Road, into the park, and across to the Serpentine Gallery. Sebastian was waiting for us there, and he even had a picnic lunch—blanket included.

"You're a genius," I said.

"That's high praise indeed, Holmes, especially for just a couple of sandwiches."

"You're right. I'd better taste them first."

"Ouch. Still spiky, even after the day we had yesterday?"

I punched him on the arm.

We walked until we found a quiet spot (we were hardly the only ones picnicking in the park that afternoon) under a lovely old oak tree. From where we sat we had the most gorgeous view toward the Italian garden end of the Serpentine. Swans glided serenely across the water and birds chirped overhead. It was the most tranquil ending to an otherwise action-packed week.

"You know," Sebastian said after a while, "I've been thinking about a way I could spend more time here."

"Really? How?"

"Well, before I tell you about my plans, there's one thing I want to do first."

And before I could say anything, Sebastian pulled me to him and kissed me hard. Before long his kisses became slow and sweet. We kissed for a long, long time. And let me just say, there's definitely something about being outside on a warm, sunny afternoon on the grass under a lovely old tree, kissing a gorgeous guy, that's quite special. I'd always wondered what the big deal was with picnics and stuff, but that afternoon Sebastian showed me exactly why the cliché worked.

I don't know how long we would have remained lip-locked, but suddenly my phone rang.

And rang.

"Answer it," Sebastian said as he pulled away from me. "Maybe it's your mom or Tallulah."

In fact, it was Jazz.

"Axelle," she said excitedly, "I know it's a bit late to be calling now, and on a Saturday, but what I've got to ask you absolutely, totally cannot wait until Monday."

I practically had to hold the phone away from my ear. Jazz was actually squeaking with excitement.

"Italian *Vogue* is doing a shoot on Monday in Milan, and they'd like to book you for it. It would mean leaving tomorrow. I know it's last minute—even for fashion—but they couldn't decide on the girls. Anyway, now they've chosen you, and you'll be doing the booking with Ellie. I don't have to tell you that doing Italian *Vogue* is as good as it gets in modeling. It will give your career a huge push, Axelle, huge."

Jazz had to take a moment to catch her breath after her words had tumbled out so rapidly. "And then Charlotte thought you could stay there for a week and do some castings, go-sees, and so forth. You already have another option—for Miu Miu—so you could very well end up with more bookings. Can I tell *Vogue* we'll confirm?"

I didn't know what to say. Sebastian was leaving tomorrow evening, and so far we hadn't had a chance to do any sightseeing at all—thanks to me. If I accepted the booking, we wouldn't even have tomorrow. After all the fuss I'd made about us being so far apart all the time, I couldn't decide this on my own. I turned to look at him.

Sebastian had heard the whole conversation. He shrugged his shoulders and nodded at me.

"Are you sure?" I mouthed.

Again he nodded and gave me a thumbs-up.

Well, why not then? I thought. I'd studied like mad for my exams and still had some time to kill before the results came in and school started again. I was sure my mom would be all over the idea. In fact, she'd probably want to come and visit. And Ellie and I hadn't done a booking together since Paris. Working with her again would be fun. Besides, I'd never been to Italy. And I loved pasta. And pizza. And gelato.

I told Jazz I had to ask my mom but that I'd call her back ASAP.

My mom sounded even more excited than Jazz, if that was possible, so I called Jazz back and told her to confirm.

"That's great, Axelle! I'll get you the flight times later today."

"So what about your plan? The one you wanted to tell me about?" I asked Sebastian afterward, as we lay side by side on our backs and watched the clouds drift past overhead.

"Well, I'm thinking that there may be a Part I to my plans now…"

"How so?"
"Well, I've never seen the Duomo."
"The Duomo? Like, the cathedral? Which one?"
"The one in Milan."

HOW TO SPEAK SUPERMODEL

Axelle's guide to surviving in the world of fashion

If you want to blend in with the fashion set, it's worth learning the lingo. Here's a handy guide.

*BOOK: This is another word for the all-important portfolio models have. A book or portfolio is used to show clients and designers both how a model looks in photos, and what kind of work they've done.

*BOOKER: A staff member at an agency whose job is to handle requests from clients and to represent and set up appointments for models.

*CASTING DIRECTOR: Hired by a designer to organize fashion-show castings. They meet hundreds of models, watch them walk, and look at their portfolios before narrowing the choice to those models that best fit the designer's vision.

*FASHION MUSE: A person, often a model, who inspires a fashion designer with their sense of style, personality, and beauty. Think Audrey Hepburn and Hubert de Givenchy, or Kate Moss and John Galliano.

*FITTING: A session that may take place before a fashion show or photo shoot where the clothes to be modeled are fit onto the model.

*GO-SEE: An appointment for a model to see a photographer or a client. Unlike a casting, there is no specific brief.

*LOOKBOOK: A set of photos used by fashion designers to show their newest collections to clients. Usually bound like a small book.

*MODEL FLAT: A flat that a modeling agency owns and rents out to models who are either too young to rent an apartment on their own, or who are just starting out and have moved from another town or another country.

*MOOD BOARD: A collage of inspirational images, texts, and even samples (like fabric) that fashion designers, editors, and photographers use to spur their creativity.

*NEW FACES: Models who are new to the business.

*OPTIONS: An option is put to a model by a client to see if he or she would be available for a shoot. Options are then either confirmed as a booking, or released.

*RESORT COLLECTION: A collection that is shown in between or preseason to the regular spring-summer and autumn-winter ready-to-wear collections.

*TEAR SHEETS: These are photos that are literally torn from magazines, and that a model can use in her book. Tear sheets from magazines like *Vogue* and *Elle* are what every model hopes to have in her book.

*ZED CARD: This is basically a business card for models. A5 in size, zed cards normally show at least two photos, as well as basic info such as a model's hair color, eye color, height, and agency contact details.

And if anyone's still suspicious that you don't belong, just throw in one of these handy phrases:

*"OMG, I love the **seventies vibe** you've got going!"*

*"Five years does **so** not qualify as vintage!"*

*"Keep **working** that ear cuff!"*

*"I'm so into **a tiny handbag** right now, aren't you?"*

"I know—it's **so perfect**. And it's my judo belt!"

"This season it's **all about** a low ponytail!"

"Stripes aren't just for sailors, you know!"

"**Right now** it's all about nude—makeup, duh!"

"**Check out** the heels on my clogs!"

"Look at how these **colors clash**! Perfect, right?"

"Going out tonight? Just wear your pajama bottoms and a **vintage T**!"

<u>Now don't forget the air kisses, darling! Mwah, mwah!</u>

THE LONDON LIST

<u>Carina's favorite places to visit in Britain's very own fashion capital</u>

"Visiting London is one of my favorite things to do! This sprawling city oozes history and fabulous street style. And what atmosphere! Cozy corners for tea and scones, secret gardens, and world-class culture—not to mention the strong Sherlock Holmes vibe you can't help but feel on a foggy night down along the River Thames. I'm often asked for my favorite things to see and do in London—so here they are."

<u>HYDE PARK:</u> One word: marvelous. This park is a romantic dream in the heart of London. Bridges, swans, centuries-old oak trees, Italian gardens, vast lawns, and a picturesque lake you can row a boat on—it's all here. Don't forget to pack a picnic!

V & A: For me, a trip to London isn't complete without a visit to the Victoria & Albert Museum in Knightsbridge. This enormous treasure trove has something for everyone—including the largest fashion collection in the world. Meander past the Roman sculptures, glittering gemstones, and exquisite children's book illustrations before stopping at their cafe. I can spend all day in this place.

SKETCH: It is said that this tea salon on Conduit Street in Mayfair is the most Instagrammed restaurant in London—and one look at its stunning pink interior will show you why! So if you feel like treating your inner fashionista to an Instagram-worthy English tea, then this is your place. Just be sure to bring your bejeweled powder compact with you to check your lips, dahling! Scones or no scones—you'd better look fab!

WATERSTONES PICCADILLY: I'm a huge fan of the Waterstones bookstores, and this one is fabulous! It's the biggest bookstore in Europe, covering eight floors, and has a cozy cafe with large windows overlooking buzzing London. You can have your tea with a view! What's not to love? Bookworm heaven!

OFFICE ON KING'S ROAD: Like my detective, Axelle, I love a pair of sneakers, and this small shop on King's Road, just a stone's throw away from lovely Sloane Square, is where I go to treat my tootsies. The last pair of Converse I bought here are covered in pink sequins. Fab!

ROYAL OPERA HOUSE: I love the ballet, and the Royal Opera House in Covent Garden is where I like to get my fix. I go as often as I can, sit smack in the middle of the auditorium, kick back, and enjoy! And don't forget to check out the dazzling view of lovely London from the rooftop terrace. If the ballet doesn't make you swoon, this will!

BURBERRY: I confess that I don't have one of Burberry's iconic trench coats—but I wish I did! They make the most beautiful ones, all lined in their famous house check. And their classic designs are just as detective- and fashionista-worthy today as they were when Burberry first introduced them at the turn of the last century. One day…but in the meantime, I'll admire from afar—and buy a cute version from the High Street!

WAHACA: Whenever I'm in London I indulge my craving for Mexican food at this colorful and lively restaurant near Covent Garden. It's only a five-minute walk from the National Gallery, so it's perfect for lunching after an exhibition. I always order the taquitos and fresh guacamole!

MUNGO & MAUD: Dogs need fashionable accessories too! So if you're a dog lover like Axelle (and me!), you'll definitely want to check out this tiny emporium devoted to upscale doggy necessities. Whether it's a chic and colorful collar and leash set, or a packet of doggie biscuits, you'll be sure to find something special for your four-legged best friend here!

SOUTH BANK: Want to see the quintessential London view and people-watch at the same time? Then this is the place for you! Lined up for your viewing pleasure you'll find the striking Palace of Westminster, iconic Big Ben, the London Eye, and the glorious Thames. Don't forget to buy an ice cream!

HAVE FUN

Acknowledgments

THANK YOU:

To my wonderful publishers on both sides of the Atlantic...

Usborne Publishing and Anne Finnis, Sarah Stewart, Anna Howorth, Amy Dobson, and Hannah Reardon for your time and talent. I am ever grateful for the chance I've been given to work with you all. And Martin Stone, thank you for always being so friendly!

Sourcebooks for your time and talent! Special gold star thanks go to Dominique Raccah, Steve Geck, Katherine Prosswimmer, Elizabeth Boyer, and Kathryn Lynch.

Jenny Savill and Andrew Nurnberg at Andrew Nurnberg Associates—because you're fab!

Sarah Doukas, Simon Chambers, and the exemplary team at Storm Model Management for your enthusiasm, helpfulness, and professionalism! Special super-sparkly thanks to Lucy Baxter, Lou Grima, and Daniel Kershaw for your expertise and time. You took my research to a whole new level!

Christophe Robin, for being you.

Kelly, Marina, and Victoria, for so much.

To my brother and sister: Axelle has no siblings—but this is no reflection on us!

Gustav, for everything.

CARINA'S FASHION CREDENTIALS

Get the inside story on the creator of Model Undercover

Carina Axelsson is a former fashion model whose jet-setting career saw her starring in advertising campaigns and fashion magazines across the globe, including shoots for *Vogue* and *Elle*.

After growing up in California, Carina moved to New York and then later to Paris, where she studied art and rounded off her days in fashion with a short stint working as a PA to international fashion designer John Galliano. Her experiences—along with a love of Scooby-Doo and Agatha Christie—inspired her to write the Model Undercover series.

And as for her character's unusual name…

"Sometime before I wrote the first notes about this girl detective there had been posters up all over Paris with a cut, spunky-looking, long-haired singer named Axelle. I think they were advertising her concerts or her new album. It was the first time I'd seen the name Axel—which I only knew as a man's name—feminized and in French. I loved it right away. And obviously the name became lodged in the corner in my brain because as soon as this girl detective came into my mind, the name attached itself to her. She never had another. And just so you know, it's pronounced with the accent on the second syllable, like the verb 'excel'—not like the car part!"

Carina now lives in Western Germany with her partner and four dogs. She writes and illustrates full-time. You can find out more about Carina at carinaaxelsson.com.